I0735073

Tough

HIDDEN HEARTS BOOK 5

COPYRIGHT

Published on January 28, 2017, by Diversity Ink Press and Mary Crawford. Author may be reached at MaryCrawfordAuthor.com.

ISBN: 978-1-945637-32-2

Cover by Covers Unbound

HIDDEN BEAUTY SERIES

Until the Stars Fall from the Sky
So the Heart Can Dance
Joy and Tiers
Love Naturally
Love Seasoned
Love Claimed
If You Knew Me (and other silent musings) (novella)
Jude's Song
The Price of Freedom (novella)
Paths Not Taken
Dreams Change (novella)
Heart Wish (100% charity release)
Tempting Fate
The Letter
The Power of Will

Hidden Hearts Series

Identity of the Heart
Sheltered Hearts
Hearts of Jade
Port in the Storm (novella)
Love is More Than Skin Deep
Tough
Rectify
Pieces (a crossover novel)
Hearts Set Free
Freedom (a crossover novel)
The Long Road to Love (novella)
Love and Injustice (Protection Unit)
Out of Thin Air (Protection Unit)
Soul Scars (Protection Unit)

OTHER WORKS:
The Power of Dictation
Vision of the Heart
#AmWriting: A Collection of Letters to Benefit The
Wayne Foundation

Dedication

To those who have
survived the unthinkable
and come out
the other side —

You have my
never-ending
admiration.

CHAPTER ONE

SAVANNAH

WHEN I SET UP my little shop, Paint Your Art Out, I thought I'd left my days of aimless drifting behind. I hate starting over with a passion. If I never see crumpled up newspaper and recycled moving boxes again, it'll be too soon.

Still, when some strangers track you down and tell you that your little sister, who you haven't seen in sixteen years, is dying, you drop everything and pull up every root you've ever planted — no matter the cost.

I sway a little on my feet as I stand up to grab a box cutter. *Crap! When was the last time I took a break from this chaos?*

I stick the blade in the pocket of my jeans and wipe the dust off my hands. Locking the door behind me, I head to the little coffee shop next door. I finally closed up shop for good in Georgia when I found this place. For a while, I was trying to be in two places at once, but it was simply too hard. Shelby and Mark helped me find this place. It's been a little bit of a mixed blessing. I don't know who the last tenants were, but they completely destroyed the place before they left. I've been working for over two weeks just removing garbage and broken fixtures.

Sweat forms on my upper lip and I wipe it away with my sleeve. I know I probably should've waited until later tonight to try to remove those stupid baseboards and rearrange my shipment of clay. At the rate I'm going, I might be open before Christmas — if I'm lucky. This place is such a mess that I'm weeks behind. I'm sure Gainesville is a nice place to live, but this is the first time I've had a chance to even peek my head outside and come up for air.

I stop in front of Tough Breaks and just take it all in for a few moments before gathering my strength to step inside. The first thing to hit me is the smell. It's rich, earthy, spicy and warm all at once. The bouquet of strong odors sparks long-ago memories of a time when my life was normal and seemingly sane.

Before I can get too lost in my sea of memories, a tall guy with an easy smile and laugh lines at the corners of his eyes opens the door for me.

"Seems to me it's a tad too warm to be standing out on the sidewalk. What can I get for you today?"

I feel the urge to back away. He is just too much … well … too much … *everything*. His voice is deep and husky, with a raspy edge. It makes my skin feel flushed and chilled all at once.

He smells like all of my favorite things — coffee, chocolate, and almonds with a dash of cinnamon. The man makes me want to drool. It's too bad I decided to be perpetually single about half a lifetime ago.

When he lifts his arm up over my head to hold the screen door open, his shirtsleeve slides up his forearm to reveal an intricate tattoo. Some guys go overboard getting 'statement pieces' to impress people, but his seems organic. I'm so busy studying him that I almost miss his inquisitive glance as I duck under his arm.

I step over the threshold into the little shop and find it hard to absorb. It seems to be part restaurant and part sidewalk museum. There are antique toys, cameras, and magic paraphernalia on nearly every surface. I stand in the middle of his shop and turn in a slow circle as I try to take it all in. I could spend days in here just looking around, or I could sit in one of the oversize chairs and sketch people as they come and go.

There seems to be a kaleidoscope of customers here. A sea of blue and orange as college students in all states of alertness and dress congregate, some of them are clearly studying, while others are simply shooting the breeze. A young kid is drinking what must be hot chocolate with an older gentleman. I smile as he licks a ring of whipped cream off his lips, but misses a spot on his nose. An older teenager is glued to her computer; she reminds me of my niece, Ketki. A couple is talking quietly in a private corner in the room as a party is having some sort of business meeting in the middle of the restaurant.

My people-watching is cut short when I hear a sharp bang as a wooden gate closes. The guy has stepped behind the counter. I look up in surprise.

"Oh, you work here? I didn't realize it was casual Friday." I raise an eyebrow.

He glances down at his stained white tank top and torn cotton over-shirt.

"Yeah, about that …" He grimaces. "Totally not my idea. My supplier managed to dump an ungodly amount of chocolate syrup on me. Unfortunately, these were the only clothes I had with me. For the record, the one-hour cleaner downtown takes more like three."

For the first time in a while, mirth bubbles up from deep inside of me and erupts in the form of a strangled laugh.

"Hey, pick on a guy when he's down, why don't you?" The man sticks his bottom lip out in a toddler-like pout.

Clearly, I am out of practice interacting with people.

"I didn't mean it like that." I wince as I try to explain. "I've had a bunch of bad luck recently. I thought I was the only one."

He has his back toward me as he fiddles with machinery remarkably similar to my sister Shelby's ridiculously fancy coffee machine. I always say she could open a coffee shop in her own kitchen.

When he turns around, he places a drink in front of me which looks more like artwork than a beverage. It resembles dessert, yet it smells like deep, rich mocha.

"I think you made a mistake. I haven't ordered anything." Even as I protest, my eyes are drawn to the hand-rolled wafer cookies embellishing the fancy drink.

The man sees my internal battle and encourages me, "Go ahead, I made this for you."

I pull away from the counter. "How could you even know what I like? You don't even know my name."

"Why is that, by the way?" He wipes down the counter in front of me. "I know you've been here a couple of weeks."

"It's not as if anyone's rolled out the welcome mat for me in this city. I couldn't even find a company to come out and fix my air conditioner. The guy they finally sent must've thought I had stupid written across my forehead. He was trying to up-charge me for a bunch of work."

"I hate companies like that. Do they think small business owners don't talk to each other?" He shakes his head in disgust. "I feel bad — I didn't introduce myself. I'm Casey. Casey Moore. Things have been crazy around here. One of my bar-backs was in a car wreck, and one of my suppliers declared bankruptcy and took a bunch of my money with them."

"I swear it must be something in the air," I mumble to myself. Speaking louder, I respond, "Nice to meet you, Casey; I'm Savannah."

"Got a last name, Savannah?" Casey asks.

I stare him down. "Not one I share with guys I meet in strange cities I just moved to."

His brown eyes take on a copper hue as he smiles warmly. "Smart move. I approve."

When I bristle, he clarifies his statement. "Seriously, you wouldn't believe what I overhear in this place. People practically give each other their whole tax history and every piece of identifying information they own. It's scary."

"That's just weird." I relax a bit. I suppose he's merely making conversation.

He wipes down the rest of the long antique bar top and straightens the napkin holders and straws. "Your drink is melting. Do you have something against iced coffee and ice cream? I made that ice cream yesterday, so I happen to know it's tasty stuff. It's got real vanilla beans in it."

I swallow a groan as I eye the delicious-looking drink. "So, you made this drink up for me on the fly? You don't know anything about me, but you just guessed that espresso, chocolate, and homemade ice cream are my favorite things in the whole world?"

Casey shrugs. "I'm in the business of feeding people's cravings."

I look at the drink skeptically. "This is a little more than guessing whether I take my coffee black or with sugar and cream. My tastes are a little eccentric."

"I make a version of these cookies with almond filling in the middle. I happen to be out of them today. I suspect you might like those even better."

Before I can answer him, I hear the waitress at a nearby table practically growl, "Sir, I'm here to serve you coffee and *only* coffee. Don't touch me!"

I spin around on the little bar stool and locate the table. In horrifying slow-motion, I watch as an immaculately dressed businessman grabs the waitress by her wrist and uses his other hand to capture her jaw in a vice grip. She shrieks in pain.

"Listen, wench; you'll do what I tell you because I'm paying your boss good money. There's no coffee on the planet worth eight dollars a cup. I figure there must be fringe benefits and Sugar, you could put your mouth to better use."

In an instant, my past and present collide with such force I'm overcome with a white-hot rage. It starts at my feet and rushes over my entire body. Without conscious thought, I vault out of my chair. The world around me falls away as my focus becomes riveted on the scene in front of me.

The creep wrenches the waitress's neck so violently she screams out in pain. Before I can say a word, he grabs her by the wrist and hisses, "What use are you?"

With one violent move, he smashes her wrist over the heavy wooden armrest of the chair. An older gentleman struggles to his feet to confront the jerk as the barista shrieks and almost collapses to the ground.

I toss a chair out of my way as I pull the box cutter from my pocket and hide it up my sleeve. The noise distracts him enough that he lets go of the waitress and whirls around to face me. Out of the corner of my eye, I see another customer help the victim escape toward the safety of the bar area.

The scumbag immediately draws my attention back as he taunts me with a leering smile. "Oh, look-y here. I prefer blondes over dark meat anyway."

An almost eerie calm washes over me as I settle into a character I've been running from for as long as I can remember. I take a deep breath and purposefully make my voice breathy, high, and cotton-candy-sweet. "Oh, I just bet you do! Strong, powerful men like you generally do."

I try to tamp down my nausea as the man preens. "Now there is a woman who knows what a real man likes."

It's a good thing that I didn't get a chance to drink much coffee because if I had, it would've all come back up the moment the guy whipped out different kinds of breath mints and lip balm. He takes off his Armani jacket and flexes his muscles like some high school kid.

The older man warns, "For Pete's sake, Donelson, this isn't the place for —"

I'm trying to edge my way toward the front door without attracting his attention. When he notices my furtive movements, I try to distract him with some provocative conversation. "This'll be extra exciting. Most guys don't like to be adventurous. I can do things which would blow your mind."

These are apparently the magic words — because the deranged businessman lunges toward me in an effort to grab me. The guy may think he has the upper-hand because he's bigger than me, but he just made a massive strategic error. I manage to duck under his arm and quickly move behind him. I grab the back of his T-shirt and pull it over his head. My odd strategy does three things. It temporarily blinds him, immobilizes his arms, and makes him madder than a snapping turtle.

Even though he can't see me, he is lashing out and punching me. He lands a pretty good blow near my left eye as I'm trying to hold the shirt over his head. Finally, I've had enough. I retrieve the blade from my sleeve and hold it against the tender area underneath his jaw.

"Stop. *Just freakin' stop.* I've got enough going on in my life without letting you treat me or any other woman like that."

The dumbass struggles some more until the blade nicks him. "Casey, did you call the police? This creep doesn't seem overly bright."

"I'm working on it. Dispatch says they should be here any minute. It seems like you've got everything under control, Rambo." Casey is trying to be lighthearted, but I hear the stress in his voice.

I take a shaky breath and readjust my grip on the guy's shirt. "Funny, but I can't help but notice you're the one whose muscles have muscles. Yet, I'm still the one who's taking care of business while you're busy hiding behind the bar."

"Now, if I didn't know better, I'd say you didn't mean it as a compliment."

The guy I'm holding down starts to squirm again. He hasn't stopped running his mouth since the moment he saw me. It isn't anything I haven't heard before, but he is close to being able to get his feet back under him and leverage himself up off the floor.

I drill a knee into his kidneys as I shout across the coffee shop, "Casey, I'm not playing. I could seriously use some backup. For a desk jockey, this guy is pretty strong."

Groaning with frustration, Casey breaks the bad news. "I'd love to, but I'm jammed up here. That pervert broke Natalie's wrist in a couple of places. The bone is sticking out. I'm holding her arm still until the ambulance can get here."

I don't have to see all the grisly details to envision the scenario in my mind. I shudder as my mind translates his words. *Crap!*

"Where are they coming from, Alaska?"

A woman in a hard hat comes over holding out some strips of plastic. "You look like you could use a little help. You need some zip ties?"

"That's a fabulous idea in theory, but I don't have the extra hands I need to put them on." I look up at the random woman offering help.

"No sweat. I could hogtie this guy in my sleep." She shrugs as she assesses the situation.

"Knock yourself out." I breathe heavily. "Watch

yourself. This guy has a mean left hook." I wince against the pain I've been trying to ignore.

"Not a lot scares me, especially guys who pick on women." The woman steps in front of me. "You can let go of him now. I've got this."

Reluctantly, I let go. After having been in a battle with him for who knows how long, my fingers don't want to obey my brain. Finally, I lean back on my heels and scoot away. Before I can catch my breath, the woman has his arm bent behind his back and is zip tying it to his belt.

This causes a new round of profane verbal vomit. Without the shirt anchored over his head, the guy looks positively deranged. I'm worried for this woman's safety.

Surprisingly, she doesn't seem to be. She ducks when he throws a punch in her direction.

"See, now that was just plain stupid," she chastises with a smirk. "The difference between me and your last victim is you won't take me by surprise and I can break your wrist right back. Not only that, see the power pole out there — you know, the one out there by that super busy street? I could string you about halfway up there in your skivvies and leave you there so you would know what it's like to be humiliated in front of everybody."

The woman grabs his other wrist and pulls it high on his back until he yelps with pain. She purses her lips in disgust, but quietly zip ties his left wrist to his right one and then attaches both to his belt loop.

Enraged, he turns and spits in her face. "You and what army?"

An older gentleman comes over and hands the woman a napkin. "We could've used some like you in my Ranger unit when I was in the service."

I look down at the pervert trussed up like a Thanksgiving bird. "I'm sorry to burst your bubble buddy, but it seems to me that it didn't take an army to take you down. It took two women on their coffee break."

To my surprise, the people in the coffee shop begin to applaud and the barista who was attacked starts to cry softly. "Thank you for helping. I don't know what he would've done to me if you hadn't stepped in."

"You stupid witch, if you would've done what I told you to do, none of this would've happened."

The woman straightens her hard hat and picks up the safety glasses which fell out of her pocket. She blows out a deep breath and shakes her head. "I can't say I'm surprised, but some people never learn. I'm Haley Normandy, by the way. I'm glad I was here at the right time. I'm a little disappointed I don't get to string him up on the line, though. It would've been a good lesson."

"You weren't kidding about that?" Casey asks.

Haley chuckles. "No sir. I'm one of the top linemen in the state. There aren't very many people who can beat me up a pole. I have one of the best safety records around too."

"Cool — but what I really want to know is where all of your kick butt self-defense moves came from?" I size her up with even more respect.

"I had three older brothers. One was on the wrestling team, and the other was huge into karate. A girl has to learn to defend herself one way or the other." Haley gives a small shrug.

"I tend to be unnaturally curious, but I have to know what your other brother was into?" Casey asks, presumably to provide a distraction to the barista who is whimpering in pain.

Haley laughs out loud. "Chess."

"Which brother taught you to be the better street grappler?"

"Would you believe that it was Austin, the chess player?" she answers with a smile. "There is nothing better in a fight than to be able to think strategically."

The front door of Tough Break's slams open and two police officers come around the corner with their guns drawn.

Natalie is sitting on a barstool behind the counter with her arm over a dishpan and Casey is standing behind her holding her arm in place, trying to limit the damage from the protruding bone.

"You guys are a little late. If those good Samaritans hadn't stepped up, I'd probably be dead or abducted or something," she says hotly, as she tilts her head in my direction.

The officer lowers his gun. "Ma'am, I'm going to need you to get down."

Natalie trembles with rage or fear — I can't really tell from here. "I don't think you understand: I can't move. My boss is the only thing keeping my arm in one piece and you guys took forever to get here."

"I'm sorry ma'am. The perpetrator might still be present and we need to clear the building," the officer says looking around the area where Natalie is sitting.

Casey lets out a loud burst of frustration. "The perpetrator *is* here. He's right over there where my customers — yes, I said customers — took care of him because there wasn't anyone else in blue or any other color here to do the job."

The other officer pokes his partner on the shoulder. "He's over there, and it looks like they conveniently packaged him to go."

They walk over to where Haley and I are standing next to the creep. After they scrutinize the situation, the first officer looks back at Casey and states, "Impressive work."

Casey shakes his head. "You must've misunderstood me. I was back here helping my barista. This was the handiwork of the women."

"Darn right it was. I want those bimbos arrested. They assaulted me for no good reason. I was simply having coffee with a few business associates and these crazies went all hormonal on me. It's like they have some sort of bondage fetish or something."

"It's funny how he neglected to mention he broke a woman's wrist because she objected to being groped on the job," Haley says. "All she was doing was filling his coffee cup,"

The second officer takes in the scene at the guy's table and questions an older gentleman standing by the table resting on his cane. "Did you see what happened? Is that a reasonable summary?"

The older gentleman looks at the officer and nods tightly. "Well, just put it this way: if John acted that way toward my granddaughter, he'd find buckshot in his private parts — if he had any left, that is."

"I see. You will be asked to give a complete statement later, but I appreciate your input. We will be in touch."

The man takes a business card from the officer, looks

down at the guy on the floor and says, "Donelson, you can consider any business between our companies concluded. I'll support nothing you are involved in. I don't do business with criminals."

After the man makes his way out of the coffee shop, the guy on the ground screams at me and Haley again. "Look what you whores did to me! I've been working on the contract for months. If I wanted to have a little fun with the waitress, you all should've minded your own business. I know you women read those porno books all the time and have weird, sick fantasies—who's to say the waitress chick is not one of those? I was just making her little fantasies come true."

"Now I'm sorry I didn't string you up on a pole like I threatened to," Haley rolls her eyes in disgust.

"Aren't you going to arrest her? That witch just made terroristic threats against me!"

"I would imagine you probably have bigger problems to deal with at this particular moment, sir." The officer rolls the guy to his feet and escorts him toward the door.

On the way out, the guy lurches toward Natalie and hisses, "Oh good, I broke your wrist. I hope you never work as a waitress again. You suck at it."

The other officer grabs the guy from the other side and hustles him out the door, and it seems like everyone in the whole coffee shop breathes a collective sigh of relief.

I grab a cocktail napkin off the bar, write down my phone number, and hand it to Casey. "Please tell me you have a decent surveillance system. Natalie will need it in court. If the police department needs to talk to me, they can reach me here. I need to get back to my shop."

Natalie glances up at me with a world of pain and fear in her eyes. "I don't know how to say thanks. You saved my life."

CHAPTER TWO

CASEY

IT TOOK FOREVER TO get Natalie settled into the hospital. The doctors aren't taking any chances with her wrist because the break is severe. When I finally left her with her family, she was already in surgery.

I wish my life could be fixed as easily as Natalie's wrist, but I know it's not that easy. She was not the only victim today. My stomach turns when I think of the kids who were there and had to watch the whole horror show unfold. I know at least one of the kids comes to my coffee shop with his aunt because his dad is in prison for killing his mom. Unfortunately, my caramel hot chocolate fan also had a front-row seat to today's train wreck.

Speaking of front row seats, I am wondering if the phone number Savannah gave the cops is legit. I have been trying to text her for hours and haven't gotten a response. My gut clenches in fear when I think of the danger she put herself into to help Natalie. It was like watching my worst nightmare in slow motion. I wanted to stop her, but she was already tangling with the guy before I could move a muscle.

As I pull up in front of my shop, I realize the lights

to Savannah's place are still on. She rarely stays this late. Even though we hadn't met in person before today, I've been paying close attention to my newest neighbor. Her natural, unadorned beauty is eye-catching and her intrinsic shyness is intriguing. I don't want to violate her privacy — but my gut tells me something's not right. I walk up to the big picture window and peek in, shielding my eyes against the glare of the streetlight.

At first, nothing seems out of the ordinary in the chaos of her moving boxes. I look more closely, and I notice she's lying on the ground with her legs sticking out from behind a pile of boxes. I pound on the glass to get her attention; when nothing happens, I dash over to the front door and try the handle. *Crap!* It's locked.

I run over to my shop and grab a set of spare keys from my cashier's till. I sprint back to her front door, praying that the landlord was too lazy to change the locks after the last tenants moved out. Yelling her name, I rush toward Savannah's side. My heart is beating a million miles an hour. This is like history repeating itself. What if I'm too late like I was before? What if that Donelson jerk got out of jail and decided to exact his revenge?

I flip on a light, and as I approach, I can see Savannah is breathing — though her breaths are quite shallow. She is so pale! As I gently brush her long blonde hair out of her eyes, I can see a light sprinkling of freckles across the bridge of her nose. The swelling around her eye is quite noticeable. She'll have an epic shiner tomorrow.

I slide the back of my hand across her forehead and she doesn't even flinch. There is a light sheen of sweat on her face and neck, although it's cool in her shop. I shrug out of my jacket and place it over her shoulders. It is large enough that it practically covers her whole body.

I'm trying to remember back to my last first-aid lesson. I think music by N'Sync was still riding high on the charts when I last took a class. Still, I'd be willing to bet she's going into shock.

I pull over a stack of deconstructed boxes and sit down on them while I decide what to do. Something tells me Savannah would not be thrilled if I called emergency personnel for the second time today. Clearly, I can't leave her like this. I don't know how hard that degenerate hit her. Maybe she's got a skull fracture or something.

Just as I'm about to hit send on my 911 call, Savannah rouses a bit. Instead of treating me like a knight in shining armor, she scrambles away from me and trembles.

"Savannah? It's me, Casey, from next door. We met this morning."

It's as if a gear catches in her brain. She takes a deep shuddering breath. "What are you doing here? I'm sure I locked the door. I always lock the door — I'm very careful about that kind of stuff."

"Don't worry. You had everything locked up tight. The landlord gave me a key before you were the tenant so I could keep an eye on things." Leaning closer, I tilt her face into the light so I can examine her swollen eye. "I found you on the floor. I think you should go to the hospital. That jerk hit you pretty hard. You could have a concussion or something."

"I don't think it has anything to do with this," she says pointing to her face. "This is nothing. I've had worse."

"Well, people don't simply pass out for no reason. There might be something serious going on."

Her stomach growls loudly. She points to it. "Or, it

could be that I haven't eaten anything in hours."

"You do know I run a restaurant, right? I never turn a hungry person away."

Savannah's spine straightens and she clenches her jaw. "I don't remember asking for your charity. In fact, I didn't ask for anybody's help."

Savannah sways on her feet again. Alarmed, I slide my arm around her waist. I hook my jacket with my toe and flip it up so I can catch it and put it back around her shoulders.

Savannah stares at me blankly. She seems to be having trouble focusing her eyes.

"Sugar, when was the last time you had anything to eat?" I ask as I shepherd her to the front door.

She focuses for a moment and mumbles, "I don't know. I was planning to make myself a sandwich last night, but the bread was all moldy. I thought I'd make myself some scrambled eggs — but there were no eggs in the fridge. The only cereal I could find in the house was shredded wheat and I was out of milk. I was so tired that I went to bed."

"You mean you haven't had anything to eat in a day and a half?" I ask incredulously, biting my tongue to prevent myself from saying much, much more.

Savannah rolls her shoulder indifferently. "When you say it like that, it sounds much worse than it actually was. It's not the first time I've skipped a meal or two and it probably won't be the last. It just caught up with me this time."

"You have to take care of yourself." I turn off her lights and lock the door behind us.

"No kidding, Sherlock!" she answers abruptly. "I've been a grown-up for a while. I think I can handle this. I'm going to go home and wash off that perv's stink then I'm going to sleep for about three weeks. I can't remember the last time I was this exhausted."

Although I know she has a point, I can't help but argue. "You're missing a couple of things on your agenda. You forgot to feed yourself again. How will you get home?"

"I'm not too proud to eat peanut butter out of a jar and the state of Florida says I'm legal to drive."

"That may be true, but my mom would kick my butt if I let you. I haven't eaten yet either. I've been at the hospital with Natalie and her family. I'll make us some dinner and some coffee. I'll even make yours decaf if you prefer."

"I should probably make a stand for my independence here and all that jazz — but, to be honest, I'm too tired. This has been a heck of a day, so if you want to feed me real food and hot coffee, who am I to complain?"

"Exactly. Sometimes, you have to pick your battles. I always say, if someone is being nice to me, I won't say no."

Savannah comes to a complete stop in the middle of the sidewalk; she tilts her head as she studies me. "You don't get out much, do you? Most people who offer to do nice things for you are up to no good."

Wow, there are so many misconceptions in that one little statement — I'm not even sure how to respond. Now is probably not the best time to tell Savannah just how much I've been out in the world during my life.

Honestly, I owe the fact that I'm even here today to the kindness of one person who went out of her way to be nice to me when she had nothing to gain.

I shrug as I open the door to my shop. "Sometimes, you get tough breaks and sometimes not. Tonight, I'm giving you a break with no strings attached. Think of it as a small repayment for what you did for Natalie today. If you hadn't been here, things could have gone much worse."

Savannah steps across the threshold into the coffee shop. Gone is the expression of pure wonderment and joy she had this morning when she saw my eclectic collection of antiques. She holds her hand over her mouth and her shoulders begin to shake.

"Savannah … I'm an asshole. I shouldn't have brought you back here so soon. Let me grab some stuff from the refrigerator. We can go somewhere else … anywhere else. You name the place."

With purpose and deliberation, Savannah walks over to the bar and picks up a cocktail napkin to wipe her nose. I have to hand it to her. The woman has guts. Even I find this place a little spooky after hours. Our building was renovated as part of a downtown revitalization effort, but it's still old and it creaks at night. When you superimpose the natural environment over the events of today, it's an intimidating place to be.

Savannah shakes her head and gives me a grim smile. "I'm one of those people who have to face my fears. I guess there is no better time than the present. I was just hoping that somehow I had dreamed this up in my head. When I was little, I taught my sister how to read and write by writing stories. Some of our stories got pretty scary, but nothing could ever match what I saw here. It will be awhile before I stop seeing Natalie's mangled arm when I close my eyes."

"You and me both," I admit as I work on prepping food for dinner. "I about had a stroke when I saw you rushing into the situation instead of running to safety; not that I'm not grateful, but what were you thinking?"

"The girl was simply doing her job. She said, 'No'. I heard her loud and clear. When he didn't listen, I had to make him stop." She presses her lips together in a firm line.

"So, it was just that simple for you?" I turn to slide sandwiches under the salamander and stir the soup.

Savannah arranges the coffee stirrers and sweetener packets on the bar and fidgets in her seat. "I wouldn't exactly call it simple. It was just the right thing to do."

"I can't argue with you there." I pour us both a fresh, steaming cup of coffee. I raise my cup in salute. "Here's to women who stand up and do the right thing — even when it's tough."

"It's too bad I couldn't get to the guy before he did any damage. I feel so awful about what happened to Natalie."

I open my freezer and pull out a scoop of ice and throw it in a plastic bag. I tie a knot at the top, wrap it in a clean bar towel, and hand it to Savannah. "What he did to you wasn't very nice either."

"I don't know which hurts worse: my black eye or my pride that he snuck one by. Usually, I'm a little quicker."

"I think it's clear you came out the winner — you're plenty tough."

"I'm flattered you think so, but I feel anything but

tough right now. I think I'll stick a little closer to home from now on."

Her simple declaration takes me off guard. I know we technically just met, but somehow, this feels different. I can't even describe how or why. I own a busy coffee shop, I see dozens of gorgeous women every day and a lot of them aren't shy about letting me know they are single. There is just something about this tough, spunky, wary woman which fascinates me. I realize I would be incredibly disappointed if I didn't get to see her again.

The timer on the salamander buzzes. I pull the sandwiches out and pour the soup into oversized mugs. I stick everything on a serving tray and carry it over to my favorite table.

Savannah cautiously follows me, giving a wide berth around the table where the incident happened. When my ice machine starts to cycle and makes a loud grinding noise, Savannah startles. "Well, I guess I'm awake now."

"Happens to me all the time when I'm here by myself." I gesture to the booth. "Have a seat. Dinner is served — several hours too late, but I hope it hits the spot."

Savannah's eyes widen as I set a mug of soup and an overstuffed grilled cheese sandwich in front of her.

"Casey, you are totally creeping me out. First, it was the coffee. Now, you totally nailed my favorite comfort food. How in the world did you do that?"

"I wish I could claim some special skill, but in this case, it's sheer luck. Tomato soup and grilled cheese sandwiches are a go-to meal for a lot of people. It's exceptionally tasty and easy to put together on the spur of the moment."

"Whatever you say. I just know that if I were one of those girls who believed in happily-ever-after, I'd marry you for meals like this. That's all I'm sayin'." Savannah takes a big bite of her sandwich and moans in appreciation.

"Is this the right place? Sometimes, my phone app can get turned around." I glance around the exclusive gated community trying to hide my surprise.

"I didn't expect to fall asleep. I'm so sorry," Savannah says as she yawns and stretches. "Yeah, this is it. It's a little over-the-top for me — okay, let's face it, it's *way* over the top for me. But, a good friend of my sister's fiancé runs this swanky security business here in town and Tristan says this is one of the safest complexes in town."

"Tristan Macklin? Small world! Identity Bank did my security system at the shop."

Savannah sits straight up in the seat and grins widely. "Oh my gosh! Do you know what this means?"

I shake my head, a little stunned at her change in demeanor.

"It means your Pervert-Of-The-Day is as good as convicted. Tristan's cameras are so good that the jury can count the guy's blackheads if they want to. There won't be any question about what happened to Natalie. It'll all be there in living color from multiple angles."

"You know, you're probably right. I didn't even think about all of that because Tristan hid the cameras so well I forget they're there. I think they're backed up off-site somewhere, so I don't even have to mess with them. I hope that guy gets lots and lots of jail time."

"I don't know how much faith I have in the justice system, but what he did to Natalie was horrendous. I hope it counts for something."

"With all the witnesses we had today, I have to believe something will be different this time. I mean, the guy practically spilled the whole story on the spot with the police officers watching."

Savannah sighs. "It's good that Tristan has it all on video, but I've seen some weird stuff happen once the lawyers get a hold of it, so I'm not holding my breath. Thank you for taking care of me tonight — dinner was delicious."

Savannah draws in a shaky breath as she climbs out of my car and punches in the code to her gate.

I watch her walk up her driveway and wipe away tears. Not for the first time in my life, I wish I had a magic wand to rewind time. It would've been interesting to meet Savannah under less dramatic circumstances.

CHAPTER THREE

SAVANNAH

MY DOOR BELL HAS to be the most annoying sound in the world. Whoever lived here before me had a thing for Broadway musicals, and the chime is currently belting out some number from *Oklahoma!* Why in the heck is my doorbell ringing anyway? There goes my plan to hide away from the world …

I throw on some sloppy sweats and peek at the special monitor Tristan set up for me. What in the world? Why are Shelby and Mark here? It's not like my sister to stop by unannounced.

Oh no! Maybe her cancer is back.

Maybe something has happened to Ketki, my niece.

I rush to answer the door. "Shelby, what's going on? Is there something wrong?"

"Funny you should ask. We came over to ask you the same thing." Mark examines me intently, pausing briefly at my right eye.

"Why would you think anything is wrong?" I studiously ignoring the fact I look like Holyfield's sparring partner.

My sister grabs my hand and leads me over to an overstuffed love seat where she sits down. She pulls me down beside her as she explains.

"Ketki is doing a school project on cyber-bullying, and she set up an alert to notify her if anyone in the family was mentioned. Some guy is making some pretty wild claims about you. He's threatening to sue you."

I look up at Mark, the attorney in the family. "What is she talking about?"

"John Donelson wants you charged with assault and battery. He says you caused him great emotional distress and committed slander."

I lean my head against the back of the love seat and growl in frustration as I rub my eyes with my palms. I shake my head.

"I'm not sure he has any blood flow to his brain."

"What do you mean?" Shelby asks

"Well, for starters, did he happen to mention exactly what was happening before all this so-called abuse took place?"

Mark grimaces. "Shelby couldn't bring herself to watch the whole interview. She was way too pissed off after the first fifteen-seconds. Unfortunately, I did watch the whole thing. He made it sound like you flew off your rocker and randomly attacked him because you hadn't had enough coffee."

"That is an outright lie! I might like my coffee, but I don't attack people for it. He left out a few facts — you know, like the one where he broke the waitress's wrist so severely she had to have surgery."

"How did you get mixed up in the middle of all

that?" Mark asks.

"If I know my sister, she put herself in the middle of it. Am I right?" Shelby looks to me for confirmation as she pulls my hair away from my bruised face.

"I couldn't stand around and do nothing. Natalie said, 'no'. In my book, that means 'no'— regardless of how rich someone is or what your job is."

"Where was the staff of this Starbucks or whatever?" Mark asks, skeptically.

"Casey was working behind the bar when it all happened. He couldn't really do anything because I sprang into action before anyone else. I didn't even have time to think it through completely. I just reacted on a gut level. Then Casey had the job of holding Natalie's arm together until medical personnel got there."

"Why couldn't the EMTs do their job?" Mark asks.

"I'm sure they could have if they'd actually been there — but they took forever to arrive. Later, they told Casey they weren't there because they had encountered a motor vehicle accident on the way to the scene. Apparently, it involved a near fatality of a child, so they had to stop and help another unit. Even though I understand all that, it felt like it lasted for an hour and a day."

Shelby reaches her arms out to give me a hug and I freeze.

I allow myself to be hugged, but I don't know if things will ever be the same between Shelby and me. All the years we spent separated seems to have fundamentally changed our relationship as sisters. Our brother's death impacted us both in ways we'll probably never understand. Even though it's been a couple of years since we've been reunited, I feel like we are still out of sync. I don't know how to fix it; we've lived a lifetime apart, which is far longer than we ever lived together.

Shelby gives me one last squeeze as she pats my shoulder. "It must've been terrifying."

I consider this for a moment and then dismiss it. "I wasn't actually scared for me; I was frightened for Natalie because I could tell her arm was badly hurt. Mostly, I was just angry. I was furious. This woman was trying to do her job — probably for minimum wage — and this smug piece of work thought she owed him a blow job because she was a woman. How dare he decide to smear my name all over social media because I hurt his pride? Did I mention he broke her arm in two places? All because she wouldn't let him feel up her private parts and give him sexual favors with his non-dairy creamer."

Mark nods. "I can tell this guy isn't a quick learner or he would've cut his losses and run from you the first time. You are not someone to be taken lightly."

"All I did was pull the guy's shirt over his head. You should've seen Haley. She zip-tied him and threatened to string him up on a power-line."

"I hope she meant by his private parts," my sister quips.

"I'm not so sure she wouldn't have, but unfortunately we didn't get to try out that theory because the police arrived."

"Can I meet this Haley?" my sister asks.

Before I can answer her, the alarm to my complex buzzes. Since almost everyone I know in Gainesville is sitting in my living room at the moment, I don't have any idea who it might be. I flip on the little surveillance camera so I can see who is at the gate. Much to my shock, I see it's Casey.

I push the intercom button. "Casey? What are you doing here?"

"I figured you probably didn't have anything to eat in the house, so I brought you some breakfast."

"You didn't have to. I have been fending for myself for years." I protest.

"I understand. Just consider it a random act of kindness."

"A random act of kindness is paying for someone's postage stamp or an extra order of fries at McDonald's; it's not bringing someone food. I'm not a stray dog."

"Last I checked, I get to decide how I allocate my random acts of kindness. Now, are you going to let me in?"

I roll my eyes in frustration as I glance down at my baggy sweats and 'artists do it with flair' tank top. I am so not ready for company — especially overwhelmingly sexy company like Casey's.

I look at Shelby with panic in my eyes and mouth, "Help!"

Shelby turns to Mark. "Go meet this guy at the gate and talk guy-talk for a bit."

I push the intercom button. "I'll send my sister's fiancé down to let you in."

"See you in a bit," Casey responds through the static.

As soon as he signs off, I bolt to the shower as Shelby starts to clean up the living room and kitchen. It's not a terrible mess — she just knows I'm weird when it comes to having company over. I guess that comes from our days of having no place to call our own.

Now that I have a home, when other people come to see it, I want it to be spotless. That was always a sticking point for me growing up. People always assumed, because my sister and I were essentially homeless, we were stupid, dirty and lazy. We were none of those things, but we also had no control over the choices our parents made. They intentionally kept my siblings and me out of school. Eventually, my brother—he was born with some sort of illness—died and Shelby and I were split up.

I've never forgotten the way we were treated.

Even if I become rich and famous by some weird fluke, I'll never forget what it's like to sit on a street corner and not know where our next meal would come from or to have to pretend like we were playing in a water fountain when it was forty degrees outside because we had nowhere else to bathe.

I barely have enough time to slide into my favorite denim dress and boots and throw my hair up into a sloppy bun before I hear the guys congregating in my kitchen. As I go around the corner, I see Casey lifting up his shirt and showing his abdomen to my sister.

A surge of jealousy hits me as Shelby laughs and says, "That is totally awesome."

What am I doing? Casey is *not* my man. I *don't* do relationships. Whatever goes on between Mark and Shelby, is it really my business? I don't know what to do with these feelings of possessiveness because it's kind of a first for me. I take a deep breath and try to act casual.

"Hey," I inject with a little too much cheerfulness in my voice. "I hope you saved some for me."

Casey pulls out a chair. "We haven't started yet — we

were just talking about what a small world it is. See this tattoo on my side? Rogue did it for me. Your sister was telling me about the role Rogue and Ink'd Deep played in helping her detect her skin cancer. It just goes to show how few degrees of separation there are in the world."

I take a half a second to mentally slap myself. I hadn't even considered there may be an innocent explanation for what I saw. I instinctively went to the worst case scenario even though I know my sister is a great person and I haven't seen Casey be anything but upfront. The only jerk in this equation is me.

I drag my focus back to the conversation and remark to Casey, "Did she also tell you how the tattoo shop brought everyone together? She met Mark at Ink'd Deep and, because of her cancer diagnosis, Mark went looking for me. Tristan helped him find me, and Tristan provides security for your business. The whole thing is crazy."

"So, you could argue it's fate that I'm standing in your kitchen serving breakfast this morning?" says Casey.

"I suppose you could argue that, but I'm not sure it would be very successful. I think it was just a fluke that I decided to turn left instead of right yesterday when I went in search of coffee."

"Ouch! You really know how to wound a guy," Casey says as he places a water bottle in front of me. "You're supposed to tell me the smells from my restaurant were so amazing that you couldn't resist their lure."

"Okay, I'll concede. The smells from your shop are pretty amazing."

"Besides, I bought you a present," Casey says as he holds out a bright yellow bottle.

"You brought me a fancy water bottle?"

"This is no ordinary water bottle. It's a carafe made for holding hot liquid too. I made a special coffee blend just for you. I hope it will inspire another marriage proposal."

"What?" screeches my sister as she snatches away my coffee. "I'm not giving this to you until you spill the beans. What are you talking about?"

I grab for my coffee. "*It was a joke*, okay?" I snap. "I was tired and said something I shouldn't have. Anybody who knows me knows I don't do marriage. Heck, I don't even do relationships."

Casey shrugs and looks at Mark. "I don't know, man. You're the attorney, you tell me. She told me if I kept cooking for her and making her things she liked, she'd marry me. I watch those court shows on TV. I know that verbal contracts are enforceable."

Mark squirms a bit in his chair. "Usually, courts are quite reticent to enforce verbal contracts of such a personal nature."

Shelby wads up a napkin and throws it at her fiancé. "Whatever happened to family loyalty?"

Mark shrugs as he responds diplomatically, "Sorry Shel. As much as I love you, you know I can't pick sides; I have to give the right answer."

"There shouldn't even be sides. I simply let my mouth run away from me when I was exhausted. It was a stupid brain fart. Nothing personal guys, but the events of the last couple of days should tell you why I don't trust men."

Casey squats down beside me and holds my gaze until I've calmed down enough to look at him. "Don't worry Savannah; I'm not that guy. I'll never be that guy.

When I said, 'no strings attached', I meant it."

I breathe a sigh of relief as I flash Casey a small grin.

"Thanks, Casey. Everything looks delicious. Thank you for bringing me breakfast. I know it doesn't seem like I'm grateful, but I am."

Chapter Four

Casey

Who knew a few breakfast croissants and a little coffee would create so many more questions than it would answer? It was fun getting to know Savannah's family and realizing we share the same group of friends, but Savannah remains as big a mystery as ever. She isn't disclosing much about herself, and her family isn't spilling any beans either.

Shelby was more than happy to gush about Savannah's artistic ability, the plans for her sister's art shop, and how well she gets along with Mark's daughter. However, when things became personal, the conversation dried up in a hurry.

There were some cryptic comments made during breakfast which make me wonder how well Shelby actually knows Savannah. Large chunks of their lives seem to be absent. I understand completely — I'd like to forget most of my teenage years myself. Still, I wonder what those missing years in Savannah's life represent, especially given her reaction to what happened yesterday.

Even though I didn't discover any earth-shattering answers in the puzzle that is Savannah, cooking her breakfast in my apartment was a calm oasis in the storm of my life.

I think I may just make it my mission to find new ways to surprise Ms. Savannah Lyons.

I move the bean grinder and find streaks of blood beneath it. I don't know why I even bothered to hire an outside crew to clean up the mess from yesterday's carnage. The advice my grandpa gave me when I was little rings true in my head. If you want a job done right, you need to do it yourself. I guess, in this case, I was hoping he was wrong — but the older I get, the more I think he's right. I have a hard time staffing my shop with good people. Natalie was one of the best workers I've had in a while. Losing her, even temporarily, will be a big setback.

A few hours later, I've sanitized the whole restaurant within an inch of its life and I begin cleaning and reorganizing the stockroom. I'm startled when someone pounds on the door — I thought I had made my 'closed' sign clear enough.

When I unlock the door, my first thought is, *seriously?* I thought I'd taken care of this; I already went down to the station and made arrangements with Tristan to turn over all the surveillance video. I can't imagine what else the cops would need from me.

I have to check myself to be polite. Interacting with police officers is not my favorite thing to do. I've had many run-ins with them and very few of those have been positive. It started when I was a kid and has improved little as I got older. There's something about me that makes them assume the worst.

"Mr. Moore? Do you have a few moments for us to speak to you?" the tall skinny officer asks. This guy must be a detective; he is wearing a suit instead of street blues.

I'm holding a dirty rag and a bottle of spray cleaner and my restaurant is completely empty — it's not like I can deny that I have time to talk with them.

I shrug. "Sure. Let me go put this stuff down. You guys want a cup?" I ask as I tilt my head toward the coffee bar and step back to let them into the shop.

"You got any of your vanilla roast brewing? I swear that's the best coffee I've ever tasted," the second officer says as he slides onto a barstool and plunks a laptop down on the bar.

"Not right now, but I could get one started if you're going to be here a bit."

"This might take a few minutes and we're due for a coffee break anyway," the detective says.

"Okay. Give me a second to wash up and I'll get one started," I say as I go to the restroom and wash my hands. Coming back to the bar, I flip the grinder on and grind some beans. After starting the coffee, I turn to the officers.

"I gotta ask — what warrants all this personal service? I've given my statement and I already turned over all of my surveillance tapes."

The other officer speaks up. "We are here about the surveillance tape, Mr. Moore. There are a few individuals who appear on the tape which cause us a bit of concern. We are wondering why they seem to frequent your establishment."

"Maybe because they like the coffee?" I respond, not fully able to keep the sarcasm from my voice.

"With all due respect Mr. Moore, we looked at your background and we believe there might be more to it than that. This is a mighty nice neighborhood for a little coffee shop. Maybe you've got a little business going on the side?"

"Shut up!" I snap reflexively. "Look, I don't care who you are. You don't get to come into my business and accuse me of stuff like that. My business is a success purely because I eat, sleep, and breathe coffee. I haven't had a day off in I can't remember when. The only reason I'm not working today is because my most talented barista was attacked in my shop. There's nothing shady going on here. I simply make good coffee and people like to drink it."

The detective leans forward, resting his elbows on the bar. "Mr. Moore, you must understand where we're coming from. Your past isn't exactly squeaky clean —"

I struggle to keep my tone civil. "No, I don't understand where you're coming from. If you'd taken a closer look, you would've seen the story of a thirteen-year-old kid who was thrown out on the streets because his dot-com dad cared a lot more about stuffing white powder up his nose and fighting with his ex-wife than he ever cared about his son."

As I place two cups of steaming coffee in front of the officers interrogating me, one of them mumbles, "I was not aware."

I hold up my hand to stop him from talking.

"If you plan to judge me by my past, you should at least know something about me which isn't in those idiotic file summaries."

"I'm not sure that's germane to our current investigation," the detective argues.

"We should hear him out. The man has a point. We're here because of what we believe about his past." The officer turns toward me. "Go ahead — I would like to hear the rest."

"Like any street kid, I did what was necessary to survive." I wipe down the bar, wishing I could scrub these memories from my mind. "Yeah, I did some petty shoplifting so I could eat, some panhandling for money, and some trespassing so I could find a place to sleep. I'm not proud of those days — but you do what you have to do. I never hurt anybody or did anything big until the night Ashlyn was killed."

"Who's Ashlyn?" the officer asks, as he sips his coffee.

"Back then, she was my only friend and the closest thing I had to family. We were both street kids with no one to call our own." I rake my hand through my hair and point to my gnarled t-shirt. "Apparently, she wanted to get me some new clothes because I had gone through a growth spurt and none of my clothes fit. So, she took a stupid crazy risk. One day I came back to our secret meeting place from a day of collecting cans and bottles and found her almost dead. She had cuts so deep, it seemed like I could see her bones. I don't know if a john did it to her or if it was her pimp." Even after all these years, I can't get the memory of her bruised, battered body out of my head. I have to take a large gulp of water from my ever-present water bottle before I can even form the words to complete my story.

"How old were you?" the detective asks.

"Just shy of my sixteenth birthday. I should've been getting my drivers' license and going to junior prom, not trying to save a teenage junkie's life."

"So what happened?" the officer asks.

"I broke into a pharmacy to get the supplies I needed to try to save her. It was mostly bandages and stuff, but I knew I'd need some antibiotics too because her whole body looked like someone had taken a meat cleaver to it. Well, I had the crappy luck of taking a bag of medicine which had a hand full of pain pills in it. So, the Oxy reads on my rap sheet like I'm some big drug dealer. All I was trying to do was save my friend's life — but it was too late. She died and I'm forever branded as a criminal."

"No wonder you're not a fan of the criminal justice system," the cop sympathizes.

"I think you left part of the story out," the detective says with a challenging gleam in his eye. "What about all your ties to known gang members?"

"By ties to known gang members, do you mean the outreach program for street kids I help out with? Uncommon Paths is a way out for kids who have nowhere else to turn and I'm only helping to pay back a little of my debt to the woman who helped rescue me from the streets. I refuse to apologize for that. Roberta doesn't discriminate against kids based on their gang affiliation. Plus, some of those kids were raised in gangs and weren't given a choice."

"I've crossed paths with Ms. Martinson before at law enforcement conferences." The detective nods. "She is a force to be reckoned with. She has done incredible things for juvies."

"If it wasn't for Roberta, who knows where I would be? I owe everything I am today to her." Honestly, there aren't enough words to explain the impact that one woman had on my life, but these two don't need to know the whole saga.

"I dunno, Moore, it seems a little too convenient. You have an answer for everything. You still haven't explained why your business seems to be such a popular hangout spot for the low-lives in our community —"

Lucky for me, the detective hastily intervenes. "Thank you so much for the coffee." He sticks his hand out for me to shake. "If we need your help to identify anyone specific on the surveillance footage, I will be in touch. I appreciate your forthrightness. It helps us put things in perspective. For the record, I understand why your coffee shop is so popular. I bring my wife here all the time and she positively hates coffee, but you make her a chocolate mint milkshake she raves about. I've already told you I'm a little addicted to your vanilla roast."

"If you're done schmoozing, we need to go talk to other suspects," the officer says as he stuffs his notebook back in his pocket.

After they leave, I make a mental note to call Roberta. It's been a while since we've touched base — even though I don't know what to tell her about what's going on in my head right now. She always wants to check in with me about how I'm feeling about my life but at the moment, I'm not sure I could even describe it all.

Last night was the roughest night I've had in a few years. Every time I tried to close my eyes to go to sleep, my mind played dark and dangerous games with my sanity. One moment I was holding Natalie's broken wrist waiting for the ambulance to arrive and the next moment I was holding Ashlyn's — dying a little inside when I felt her pulse gradually fading away.

I have been wrestling with my own personal failures the last couple of days. Why didn't I act faster? I know I'm not an MMA fighter or anything, but I know my way around a boxing ring and more than a few martial arts moves. So why did I stand there behind the counter like a statue while Savannah charged in like a fearless tiger? What does that say about me? I can tell you what it says about me — it says my dad was right. I'm a sniveling lightweight who can't handle life. If my dad was still alive, he would tell me to go cry to my mom.

I can't tell you how tempted I am to call her, but my mom has a slice of happiness in her life now that she's met Frederick. I don't want to rain on her parade. She has had enough heartache in her life without me adding one more drop. My dad's level of epic dirt-bagginess was only matched by his lack of awareness that he was one.

As much as my mom loves me, I think even she would be disappointed with how I handled myself yesterday. My mom is a big believer in knights in shining armor. I was anything but. I was like a little kid cowering behind the curtains while someone else came to the rescue and as a result, Natalie was severely injured and Savannah was traumatized. I don't know if I'll be able to come to terms with that anytime soon.

I write myself a note and stick it on my computer screen. I wonder what Roberta would think of Savannah. It would be fascinating to have these two women meet.

CHAPTER FIVE

SAVANNAH

"WHOSE IDEA WAS IT to put lime green paneling up in a business? Were they high? They must've been high, that's all I can figure out. This is ludicrous. What did they glue it with — a nuclear fusion gun?" I yell at the wall as I throw the crowbar at it in frustration.

"Knowing the former tenants, they probably were high. Based on the way they dressed, I suspect they may have been colorblind as well."

"Casey Moore! Are you *trying* to give me a heart attack? You are *so* lucky I just threw the stupid crowbar. If I hadn't, it would've been upside your head." I hold my hand over my heart. It's racing like the hooves in a wild horse stampede. "I really need to figure out a way to get the money together to hire Tristan," I mutter under my breath.

I fling off my headphones and walk up to him.

"I thought you agreed not to use your key anymore," I say, poking him in the chest to punctuate each word.

"You didn't answer when I knocked, so I thought something had happened to you again." He holds up a bakery box and a cup of coffee.

"Nothing happened to me. I'm wearing ear protection because I'm using power tools. What are you doing here? Don't you have a business to run?"

"I do. It's in capable hands — I hire lots of talented baristas. Anyway, I came over for your unbiased opinion. I'm trying out a few new recipes for scones and I'd like to know what you think."

"Are you sure this isn't simply a clever way to feed me?"

"I don't know. Do I need to? Did you eat breakfast this morning?"

"Yes, Mr. Smart-Aleck. I had a granola bar and a glass of orange juice. Thank you very much." I can't resist the urge to stick my tongue out at him, even though he brought me something which smells delicious.

Casey scowls at me. "You know … granola bars are just dressed up candy bars, right? But, I guess they're an improvement over eating nothing."

"You're mighty highfalutin about other people's breakfast considering you pedal caffeine and sugar for a living," I observe.

Casey grins. The man is utterly gorgeous with a smile on his face. "Point taken, but, if it makes you feel any better, these scones are organic and vegan."

I wrinkle my nose and make an exaggerated gagging sound. "You still want me to eat them? I don't think that's a great marketing strategy."

"Also a good point. Try to forget you know that when you taste them. I want to know how they compare with the type of pastries you usually eat."

"Why does my opinion matter to you? I'm only one

person. I don't even eat many pastries." I take the scone from the bakery box and take a small bite. "It's not as terrible as I expected it to be. When Shelby and I were small, my parents went on a health food kick — everything had sunflower seeds in it. To this day, I can't stand them … or anything else remotely healthy. So, that's actually a huge compliment."

Casey is looking at me skeptically and I realize I probably need to provide a more coherent answer. I study the scone a little more closely. "It's fluffier than I expected it to be. It could use a little more salt, but it's good."

"See? I knew it was a good idea to come over here. When I asked Samuel, the bus boy, the same question, he told me it didn't look like a pop tart."

"This isn't the same as yesterday's," I say as I take a sip of the steaming cup of coffee.

"Your sister told me over breakfast how much you like cinnamon rolls, so I decided to re-create one in your coffee cup."

"Why are you doing all this for me? I'm just another customer." I nervously fiddle with my hair. "I'm not even sure you can actually call me a customer, you never let me pay for anything."

Casey gently removes the coffee cup from my hand and places it on a nearby table. He grabs both of my hands in his and lets our arms drop between us. "Maybe I want you to be more than just another customer. Maybe I was looking for an excuse — any excuse — to come over and talk to you. Maybe I think about you way more than I care to admit and I wonder if you think about me too."

Like a feral kitten, I'm not sure whether I should stay or go. Every instinct I have tells me to run. Yet, my heart tells me to stay. Even though the only point of contact between us is our hands, I can feel strength radiating from him. Yet, at that moment, panic sets in and my brain overrules my heart.

"I want a lot of things in my life, but they rarely come true. Besides, you don't really want me. For a bunch of reasons, you don't really need to know, I'm a totally bad bet for you. There are a lot of women who are prettier, more educated, and a perfect fit for you. I'm better off not being in any relationships. I guess I'm just made to be a loner."

"Savannah, I'm not proposing marriage or anything, I'm merely suggesting we hang out for a while and get to know each other a little. We don't even have to call it a relationship. What's wrong with two people getting to know each other while they do a bunch of fun stuff?" Casey holds his hands out in a pleading gesture "It's a win-win for everybody, right? You're new in town and I'll get a chance to show you around."

I have to stifle a giggle — there's nothing wrong with Casey's persistence, that's for sure.

"For all you know, I'm some crazy cat lady who eats library paste and wears a foil hat while I wait for contact from life on another planet. Why are you so sure hanging out with me is a good idea?"

Casey draws me closer. His brown eyes have flecks of copper and gold in them. He tenderly kisses me on the cheek. "I think a better question would be: why don't you believe that you're worth my time?" He pulls away and squeezes my hands. "If you're free on Saturday, I'll pick you up at four in the afternoon. Dress casually."

Looking around my shop, I send one last panicked plea to my sister. "Are you sure this is a good idea? I still have so much stuff to do here. Why am I taking an afternoon off?"

Shelby holds her hand up and counts down on her fingers. "Well, let's just see, shall we? First, all work and no play make Savannah a very dull girl. Secondly, the flooring contractor told you to get out of here and let the glue dry without disturbing it. Third, Gainesville won't ever feel like home if the only two places you ever go are your house and your shop. Fourth, if you feel guilty imposing on Mark and me all the time, you need to make new friends. Finally, and this should go without saying, Casey is all kinds of nice … inside and out. You couldn't find a better guy to hang out with," my sister says, closing her fist around her fingers as she counts all five points down. "And come on, it's the weekend."

"What if I'm not so nice? You know better than most how we were raised. How do I even begin to explain it all to him? That's not even the tip of the iceberg. This is why I don't do relationships. There's no way to explain me. I've given up trying. If he knew who I really am, he would run so fast his head would spin. I don't know why I'm even bothering to go through the motions." I purse my lips in the makeup mirror and touch up my lip gloss.

"You should go through the motions because I've never met anyone who underestimates themselves more than you. You should go through the motions because things that are unexpected can be the best things ever. You need to go through the motions because you don't know what's coming next," Shelby insists emphatically as she fastens a dream catcher necklace around my neck and artfully arranges my hair.

"Easy enough for you to say — you have the perfect life. Everything went right for you, but that doesn't mean the same thing will happen for me. I don't have that kind of luck. I've come to the conclusion karma absolutely hates me."

Shelby hugs me from behind and rests her chin on my shoulder like she used to as a child. "You know, this is something I never thought I'd see. In my mind, you were always the fearless one. You were the first to go charging into any situation with your head held high and your heart on your sleeve."

I close my eyes against the nostalgic image I see in the mirror. I remember Shelby peeking over my shoulder when we were little as we did when we pretended to put on makeup like grown-ups. I'd give anything to have those days of innocence back.

A tear slides down my face as I fight the emotion of the moment. "Shelby, that person is gone. I don't know her anymore and I don't know if you or anyone else will like who I've become," I admit softly.

"You won't know for sure until you put yourself out there. It could be totally amazing."

At that moment, the dynamic between big sister and little sister comes back full force. It's as if no years have passed between us, let alone more than a decade and a half. Her absolute faith in me is heartbreaking. She still believes I control the sun, the moon, and everything between. She couldn't be more wrong if she tried. Yet, she has been through so much, I don't want to be the one to give her another crushing blow.

Tough

I reach up and awkwardly hug her head.

"I hope you're right, Sis," I murmur. "I really do."

CHAPTER SIX

CASEY

"DOING OKAY OVER THERE?" I glance over at Savannah. She is curled up against the door of my work van like a wounded dog. "I know you don't know me well, but I don't bite."

Savannah looks startled for a moment. She glances down at herself as if she's unaware of her body posture. Sitting straighter in the seat, she unclenches her hands, and takes a deep shuddering breath. Savannah looks out the window for a moment before she turns back to me.

"I'm sorry — I tried to tell you I'm not relationship material. I don't do this dating stuff. I'm not even sure why I'm here today. Maybe you should take me back home. I'll probably just ruin your day."

"Easy now… Nobody said we're getting married tomorrow or anything. Take a second to breathe. We're just going to go antiquing. I need to change the displays in the shop. I thought you might have a good time helping me find new treasures for Tough Breaks."

"I know nothing about antiques. I might like a cheap plastic knockoff. Her voice rises with panic as she twists her hair band between her fingers.

I shrug. "So what if you do? I don't know anything about this stuff either. I just pick what I like. If it looks cool, I try to get it for the shop. It's not like I'm a serious collector or anything. I used to go find things with my grandpa when I was little. He called it 'treasure hunting'. I guess you could say I've merely expanded my hobby a little."

"Are you serious? I would've never guessed. The stuff in your shop looks so cool! I thought it was a legitimate collection — like from a museum."

"Admittedly, it's gotten better over the years. When customers find out I collect random stuff, they bring in their own things they've inherited from family members. It's often odds and ends they don't know what to do with. Some of it I buy, but most people just give me stuff. Who knows? Some of it could be valuable. It started out as a way to fill a few empty spots in my restaurant, but the collection has taken on a life of its own."

"That's cool in its own weird way. I guess it's a good thing you don't collect something weird like spittoons, or something," she jokes with a tentative smile.

"Funny you should mention that — I think there are one or two in there. I inherited some guy's humidor collection and who knows what's in those boxes. There was a lot of tobacco paraphernalia."

"Maybe you should stick with toys," Savannah shudders.

I smile widely. "I plan to. Honestly, the little boy in me never quite grew up. Toys are my very favorite. Do you collect anything?"

As we stop at a stop sign, I watch as a wistful expression crosses Savannah's face followed by resolution and sadness.

"No, I didn't really collect much as a kid. My childhood was probably way different from yours."

"Different how?" I ask, curious as to why she shut down so dramatically.

"I don't talk about my past," Savannah states bluntly, leaving no room for misinterpretation.

"Ever?" I can't seem to leave well enough alone.

Savannah nails me with a look of exasperation as she blows out a puff of air. "Let me put it this way — it's so rare you shouldn't count on it happening. If it does, it would probably be under the influence of heavy-duty booze and you should question its truth and veracity."

"Veracity?"

"Just because I paint pretty pictures for a living doesn't mean I don't like to read." Savannah crosses her arms in front of her and glares at me as I park the van. "Where are we? I assumed we'd be at a fairground or something. I thought you said we were going antiquing?"

"We are. Mabel and Gretchen have a dairy farm out here. They have started up a successful estate resale business on the side. If they get in some cool stuff, they call me first and let me pick through the trinkets before they sell it off in lots."

Savannah glances around warily. "That's kind of them. What did you have to do to get such special treatment?"

I lean over toward her and whisper in her ear as if I'm sharing state secrets. "I order them tea from England and I make them special biscuits like Princess Diana's personal chef used to make."

Savannah covers her mouth with her hand as she giggles. "Casey Moore, you are so busted. I've got your number now. You may look tough with all your tattoos, but you're just a big old softy — nothing more than a marshmallow over a campfire."

Despite my best efforts, I blush bright red in response to her accusation. She's not too far off the mark. You would think I'd be tougher and a little more street-smart, given the way I spent my teenage years. Yet, somehow I'm still a sucker for someone in need and the fragile sort among us.

"Does it benefit my case more if I plead guilty or if I insist that I'm a rough and tough meanie?"

"It doesn't matter. I'm not looking for either type of guy. Even if you told me you were rough and tough, there's no way on this green earth I'd ever believe you. You forget that I watched you stand as still as a statue holding a woman's broken wrist and murmuring like a Zen yoga master to keep her calm for a good half an hour. That doesn't sound too rough-and-tumble to me."

"Maybe I'm just tough on the inside," I argue.

I'm not even sure where I'm going with this, but there's something about Savannah which makes me want to push and challenge. I don't want it to be easy with her. I want to explore all the outer edges of ideas and conversation. I know it sounds strange, but I guess I'm inviting it to be harder than it needs to be because I want to find out more about her and what makes her tick.

Savannah's brow creases as she thinks about what I said. Finally, she studies my face as if she's a detective looking for clues. She taps her bottom lip. "You know, you're probably right. I think you are very tough on the inside. It took exceptional courage to stand there and be calm in the middle of all that chaos and not let go of Natalie even though she was screaming and crying. You were a tower of strength. Most guys would have abandoned Natalie for a chance to show off and make a big splash — but you stayed focused on what needed to be done. You showed real mental toughness. So, I think you're absolutely right — you may have all these soft squishy relationships with everyone around you, but you're tough inside where it counts."

I squirm uncomfortably at her spot-on assessment of me. Tilting my head at the older women making their way toward us, I instruct, "Do me a favor, don't let those two know I'm a softy. I can't afford to give up any more ground in negotiations. Those two are tough as nails."

Savannah takes a moment to size them up. She reaches up and pats me softly on the cheek. "I'm sorry to break it to you, but those two have been in the game a very long time. You're not fooling anybody — but that's okay."

I consider her words for a moment and realize she's probably right. The two women currently motioning for me to roll down my window treat me more like a wayward grandchild than they do a worthy business adversary.

I turn to Savannah and shrug helplessly.

"Well, are you going to sit in your rig all day or are you planning to give me a hug?" Mabel demands in a loud voice as she taps on the window.

Savannah suddenly looks uneasy. "Can you give me a couple minutes, please?"

I squeeze her hand. "No problem. Let me go say hello."

"How are you doing Miss Mabel?" I ask, as I hop out and envelop her in a careful embrace.

"Well… I hate to complain, but not enough rich people have been dying recently and business is down a little. What's new in your life?"

Gretchen nudges Mabel with her elbow as she teases, "I think you're asking the wrong question. I think the most important question isn't *what's* new in his life; I suspect it be might be more like *who's* new in his life —"

Mabel looks over at Gretchen. "What on earth are you talking about?"

Gretchen laughs out loud. "I told you to get your glasses replaced; take a closer look inside Casey's rig."

Both women crane their necks to look inside the van as if there's just been an Elvis sighting at Graceland.

"Ladies, you want to back off?" I mumble in their general direction. "I'm trying to impress my date. This is our first."

"I'm not questioning your judgment or anything, but you do realize this is a dairy farm, right? I can think of more charming places to go," chastises Mabel under her breath.

I can barely control my laughter. "Nonsense, you ladies are the epitome of decorum and charm. I trust that you will help present me in the best light possible."

"You mean you don't want us to tell the young lady about the time you fell backward into a cow patty?"

"Well, it depends. Do you think the story will make me completely irresistible?" I walk around the van to open the door for Savannah. "I will leave it up to your discretion."

When I open the door, I notice Savannah has braided her hair — usually tumbling in wild curls across her shoulders — into a loose braid.

"You'll do great," I whisper in her ear. After I help her down from the van, I escort her over to where the women are waiting with openly curious expressions on their faces.

"Savannah, I would like you to meet my friends Mabel and Gretchen. They are pretty much always together, but you can tell which one is Gretchen because she usually wears something cat related."

"It's nice to meet you. Gretchen, you sound like me and my art themed T-shirts. I have so many of them, I'm running out of storage space," Savannah answers in a burst of nervous chatter.

Mabel steps forward and puts her hand on Savannah's forearm and escorts her toward what they affectionately call the furniture barn. "Well, honey it's your lucky day. I just got this beautiful chest of drawers in. It's the perfect size for T-shirts. All the drawers are exactly the same size."

"Miss Mabel, I wasn't exactly planning to shop for furniture today. I'm just a passenger on this date. I think Casey came to look for toys and similar things." Savannah looks around the crowded barn in awe.

"Oh don't be silly. Casey's been here often enough to know he should never come with a plan. You just go wherever inspiration takes you. You never know what you'll discover here. That's part of the magic."

Savannah looks nervous and bewildered. "I don't know if this is the right place for me. It's been a long time since I've believed in magic."

"Then this is exactly where you need to be. Perhaps you will find your missing magic here. Antiques have a way of helping you find the pieces of your past that you buried under piles of pain, hurt, and misunderstandings. They help you remember the good times in your life."

Savannah pales to a ghostly white and looks as fragile as antique glass. In a voice so low I can barely hear it, she says, "Sometimes, I can't remember any good times."

Her quiet admission settles like a lead weight in my soul. I didn't have an easy time as a teenager and young adult. In fact, I still have nightmares about it. After Ashlyn's death, the officials at the Youth Authority made me go to mandatory counseling while my public defender set about trying to clear my name. Even with all that on top of my parent's divorce and my dad's drug abuse, I still have some happy memories of my childhood. It wouldn't be a stretch to say before my dad became addicted to cocaine, my childhood was pretty great. I can't imagine how much worse Savannah's must have been for her to have no happy memories. That's just beyond sad.

I realize I've lost complete track of the conversation when I overhear Mabel say, "I don't know, dear, I think he must be trying some of his new decaf coffee again. He was kind of fuzzy the last time he tried going cold turkey from caffeine."

Before I can recover from my lapse in concentration, Gretchen tries to help fill my awkward gaffe by asking Savannah, "So, what kind of things do you like to collect?"

"These days? Nothing much other than bills." She shrugs.

Mabel looks confused. "Oh, come on, there must be

something you —"

"Well, I have a lot of art supplies, I suppose." She picks at the fraying edges of her cutoff shorts.

"Well, it's a start. But that's really no fun because that's kind of an occupational hazard for you, isn't it?" I tease.

"You never said there were any rules to this!" Savannah protests, as she throws her hands up in the air. "I told you this really isn't my kind of place. I don't know what to do here. I don't know what to do with you." She pauses as she struggles to take a breath. "I'm not even sure why you want to be here with me. I told you I don't do relationships. I'm so bad at this kind of stuff and now I'm embarrassing you in front of your friends." Savannah wipes away a tear and then whispers in a broken voice, "I'm so sorry."

Gretchen threads her arm around Savannah's waist and starts to gently lead her away from me. "Sweetie, you know what's good for stress? Baby animals are good for stress. We've got a few new ones in the barn. Lets you and I go check them out."

After the women are out of sight, I turn to Mabel. "Call me oblivious, but I'm not sure what I did wrong."

Mabel shakes her head as a sad expression crosses her face. "I don't know if I ever told you how Gretchen and I met. We weren't always farmers, you know. We used to be school counselors a lifetime ago and if you'll allow me to put my old hat on, I'd say it wasn't so much what you did wrong but a lifetime of wrongs stacking up against your girl."

"How do I turn those wrongs into rights?" I ask, as I sink my head in my hands.

Mabel walks over to me and pats me on the shoulder. "Casey, I like you too much to tell you anything but the truth. You can't make her past go away. You can only make her future look better."

"How do I do that when my very presence seems to make her so upset she can't breathe?"

"One word and gesture at a time until she can take a deep breath," Mabel says. "I know that's not what you wanted to hear, but it's what you need to hear. Make no mistake, your girl needs some right in her life. I think you might be the perfect person to deliver it."

"I hope so, Mabel. In a short time, she's come to mean a lot to me."

CHAPTER SEVEN

SAVANNAH

I CAN'T BELIEVE I nearly had a meltdown in front of Casey's friends when he is supposed to be here on a business trip. I haven't had an anxiety attack like that in years. For God's sake, I almost single-handedly apprehended a pervert and didn't bat an eyelash, but I can't go out on a date that would be approved by any church pastor anywhere? How lame can I be?

I smile at Gretchen as she walks around the stall, followed around by an overly pushy calf. She explained earlier that Popsicle was born with some sort of abnormality that made it difficult for him to nurse, so they're bottle-feeding him. Every time he sees Gretchen, he thinks she has food and follows her around. It was probably cute when he was little, but he's getting pretty big now.

As I'm watching their antics, something big and fuzzy bumps my thigh. I'm so startled, I have to stifle a scream. When I look down, I realize it's a dog. It's impossible for me to figure out what kind of dog he is with his square jaw and fuzzy coat. I've always wanted a dog, but it's never been in the cards for me. When Shelby, Owen and I were little, our lifestyle was too nomadic to support feeding another mouth. Some days, we didn't even have food to feed ourselves, never mind an animal. My dad always told us that dogs were parasites and there was no need to have one. I've always admired dog owners from afar.

With a tentative touch, I reach out and scratch the dog behind his ears. He lets out a big sigh that sounds like a moan. Gretchen stops what she's doing in the corral and looks at me with surprise.

"That's amazing. Usually, Blue doesn't let anybody touch him — especially, people he doesn't know. It took Mabel and me weeks and weeks to get him to the point where he was that relaxed around either one of us."

"Isn't he your dog? Why would he be nervous around you?"

"Oh no, honey. Blue's not our dog. We're merely fostering him for Dr. Stuart. He is our vet and he was looking for a foster home for this guy. Blue's story is so sad. His owner was killed in a car accident and Blue wouldn't leave his side."

My first instinct is to bury this giant of a guy in hugs, but I know from personal experience he would probably be overwhelmed. Instead, I just keep methodically stroking his ears. When I have to stop to adjust my purse strap, Blue nudges my arm as if to say, "Hey, you're forgetting something down here."

"Blue, knock it off, you're being obnoxious now," Gretchen teases. "You would think I didn't feed you this morning." Suddenly, Gretchen gasps. "Oh no! I forgot my pie in the oven. I get to playing with these animals in the barn and I forget everything else."

"Point me in the general direction, I can run there

faster than you can. Where do you keep your oven mitts?"

"I left them on the top of the oven after I put the pie in. Tell Casey where you are going, he can point the way. It'll be faster. I don't get around so quick these days."

Nodding, I stand up and rush toward the house. Much to my surprise, Blue gives a quick bark and follows me. As I sprint past Casey where he is still looking at toys with Mabel, I shout, "Come on, I need you to show me where the kitchen is."

While Casey is running to catch up with me, he shouts ahead, "See the bright blue door? Go through it and there'll be a mud room. The kitchen is to the left."

"Thanks," I yell as I kick my running into another gear. If there's one thing I know how to do, it's run. I'm not into those cute jogging suits and showing off at the gym or anything, but I can run in the street with the best of them. Lord knows, I've had to run before like my fate depended on it.

As I run faster, so does the dog. It's as if he is in tune with my emotions. Finally, I reach the cement stairs and a small stoop. I feel my heart beating out of my chest. I can hear the shrill sounds of the kitchen timer. When I try the back door, it's open. I look down at the enormous mutt sitting at my feet. He is waiting expectantly for a command from me. I take a chance and sternly say, "Stay." Blue immediately plants his bottom on the ground and watches me carefully in case I give another command.

Blue waits outside the door as I make my way through the mud room to the kitchen. To my relief, nothing smells like it's burning. I grab the oven mitts and pull the pie out. To me, it looks like a perfect apple pie —

the kind you see on the front of a cookbook.

I expected Casey to follow me into the kitchen. After I set the pie on a cooling rack and turn the oven off, I check the back door to see where Casey went. I find him in a standoff with Blue. Blue is blocking the entire doorway and is refusing to move. He is not snarling at Casey, but the hair on the back of his haunches is standing on end and it seems as if every muscle in his body is tense.

"I'm not sure what's going on. Blue has always been skittish around me, but it's never been like this," Casey says, quietly.

"I don't know either. I just met him a few minutes ago. Gretchen said he rarely takes to people, but he seems to like me." I reach my hand out toward Blue and he wags his tail. "It's okay buddy, you don't have to guard me against Casey. He's my friend."

It's almost as if I've flipped a switch in Blue. As soon as I say those words, he becomes like a puppy and wiggles and squirms. The tenseness disappears from his body and he nudges Casey's hand to get him to pet him.

Casey picks up a stick from the yard and throws it. Blue bounds after it with his tail flying high.

Gretchen walks up the steps and leans against the railing. "We've had Blue in our house for almost three months, and I've never seen that side of him. You two are the best therapy he's ever had."

I sigh with contentment as I watch Casey wrestle the stick from Blue's mouth. "I wish I could have a dog like him."

"Why can't you?" Mabel takes a picture with her cell phone.

"Me? I know nothing about owning dogs. I've never had any pets."

"Not even a hamster or a goldfish?" Mabel says with an incredulous look on her face.

I just shake my head.

This is why it's always so hard to explain my past to people. When I was growing up, my parents belonged to one of those doomsday cults which believed the world would end. We essentially lived like homeless nomads for years. My little brother was born with a terminal illness and my family traveled from town to town seeking every unconventional treatment and faith healer available. Soon, there was no one left except for con men and shysters who took advantage of my parents. Shelby and I had childhoods which had little resemblance to normalcy — there were no pets, birthday parties, family dinners, or sleepovers. I don't talk about my past because it's simply too much to dump on someone all at once. After Owen died, my parents took off before the police showed up. I watched helplessly as the authorities hauled my sister away in a police car.

Blue comes, drops the stick at my feet, and licks my hand. It's almost as if he can feel my internal turmoil. He waits quietly as I pick up the stick and heave it across the yard. The mangled stick does not go as far as it went when Casey threw it. Blue doesn't move. He is watching me with his gray-blue eyes while his tail is beating wildly against the muddy ground. I glance up at Casey with a worried expression. "Did I do it wrong?"

"I'm sure you didn't do it wrong, but I think he is waiting for you to give him permission to go get the stick. Blue has decided you're the boss."

"Really? Of all the people here, he's decided I'm in charge?" I don't even bother to disguise the shock in my voice. "Does he know that the only thing I know about dogs, I learned from watching Animal Planet?"

"No, and even if he did, he wouldn't care — and neither should you," Gretchen says. "Obviously, this guy has taken a liking to you. After all he's been through, that means a lot."

I take a breath and blow it out. I look at Blue. "Fetch."

With one simple word, Blue takes off like a rocket.

Mabel grins at me. "See, it wasn't so hard. You've got this dog-owner thing in the bag."

"Yeah, right. That was one word. I'm pretty sure it's harder than that."

"Blue is obviously attached to you and he is a good dog with great manners. You know, he's up for adoption. It's something to think about if you're in a place which allows pit bulls. He's not all pit, but he has some pittie in those genes somewhere."

Her words make my heart skip a beat. I know my neighborhood allows pit bulls because my neighbor has one he calls Belle.

Mabel turns to Casey. "When we saw this latest estate come in, we knew we had to call you. This guy used to be in advertising, so he had an impeccable eye for detail and a seemingly insatiable need to collect toys. There are some beautiful items."

Casey nudges my arm with his elbow. "Just in case you don't understand her code, that's Mabel's way of telling me she's going to stick it to me on the price."

"Hey, that's not fair!" Mabel frowns. "I'm just informing you of the condition of his beautiful toys. I've never taken advantage of you."

Casey looks chastised. "That's true, Miss Mabel, you haven't. I was just teasing."

Mabel shoots me a sideways glance and winks at me as she whispers in a stage whisper, "Some people are way too nice."

Casey blows out a breath. "That was downright mean. You had me going there for a minute. I thought for sure you were mad at me."

Mabel leads us to a different barn than we were in earlier. She turns on the buzzing florescent light and pulls a sheet off of a display. "If I was mad at you, would I give you first crack at this?"

I may not have had a lot of toys when I was growing up, but it doesn't mean I haven't watched television since then. I remember seeing some sort of documentary on these metal toys. I know they were exceptionally rare when they were made because of rations.

"Ladies, you treat me so nice. I'm not trying to be rude or anything; but are you sure these aren't stolen? These are museum-quality pieces. I'm no expert or anything, but I've seen a lot of used toys, and I can tell you they are rarely this dank," Casey says gleefully and then grows somber, as he tries to disguise his excitement over the toys.

"Dank?" Mabel raises her eyebrows at me.

"I think it's California-speak for awesome," I explain quickly.

"I worried about them being stolen at first too," Gretchen admits. "You know, I did a stint with juvenile offenders and I know how fencing works. I made sure we double, triple and quadruple checked these. I even called on a friend who works in insurance fraud for the state to help me verify all the paperwork. Everything was on the up and up and documented in photos."

"Well, that's totally amazing for your business — but, there is no way I can invest the type of money it would take to get these things. I recently put a bunch of new equipment into the coffee shop. I bet these are out of my reach."

"Normally, that would be true But the person whose estate this belonged to gave special instructions for its disposition. He wanted all of his things to go to someone who deserved them and who would cherish them as much as he did. He didn't want them to be sold off at some generic auction house or on eBay. In my book, that puts you back in contention. His family would rather get less money and have someone to take care of them. In the long run, they want his belongings to be seen and appreciated. What better place to do that than Tough Breaks?"

"Are you serious? I would make my whole coffee bar a display for just these items. It would be epic!"

"Wait a second, before you make plans, Casey," I caution. Looking around the area, I ask Mabel, "Did these come with their boxes? I saw on a television show that the boxes are sometimes more valuable than the toys."

"No, sadly if there were boxes we'd be having a whole different conversation," Mabel says with a wistful sigh. "I would be dealing with a high-end auction house instead of out of my barn."

"Even so, these are totally amazing," Casey is like a kid who just discovered a treasure trove of presents under the Christmas tree. "Do all the mechanics work on them?"

"So far, we've only encountered one with a broken spring."

"Wow. Just wow. Have I mentioned lately that you gals are my favorite people on the planet?"

"You may have mentioned that a time or two," Mabel admits smugly. "You are so good for our ego. Why do you think we have you come back here all the time?"

"Oh hush! Casey Moore, where are your manners?" admonishes Gretchen. "You're here on a date. You're supposed to be whispering sweet nothings to her, not to us."

I blush at the backhanded compliment. "It's okay. Really, he should be that flattering to you and more. It's extraordinary that you are giving him first shot at this stuff. It totally could go into a museum. I've spent a fair amount of time in my life wandering around in them, so I have seen many different museums around the United States. I can tell you these toys are as nice as any I've seen."

"I didn't know you were interested in collectibles," Gretchen says taking me by the elbow. "I have something I think you'll be interested in."

Gretchen walks me over to another display case. At first, when she pulls back the sheet I'm puzzled by the random collection.

"Isn't it extraordinary how they are all so different, yet they are all still music boxes?"

Unbidden, my thoughts fly back to a dark place. As

a child, Shelby, Owen, and I could not have our own belongings outside of a few religious relics. One particularly lean year, our shoes became worn and threadbare. Someone at the homeless shelter offered me a catalog from Sears to line my shoes. I had never seen such a magical book in my entire life. Most children would have gravitated toward the toys. I didn't. I found the housewares section much more mesmerizing. The idea that people owned towels, rugs, lamps, record players, and music boxes was astounding. I wanted nothing more than to own my own music box with a little pink ballerina in it. I did eventually have to tear up my Sears catalog to line my shoes and my gloves, I tried to preserve the part with the most beautiful pictures and only use the part which had car parts, tools, and other uninteresting things. I swore to myself that someday I would have the most beautiful house and it would be filled with music boxes, luxurious rugs, and the thickest towels ever made. Well, that was the plan anyway.

"Savannah? Dear, are you okay?" Gretchen asks with a concerned look. She helps me sit down on a nearby bale of hay.

Casey rushes over to my side and Blue presses his big body up against my thigh.

Like a swimmer coming up from a deep dive, I struggle to find my bearings. "I'm fine, I got a little claustrophobic there for a moment. I could use something to drink."

"Casey, if you want to run to the house, I have sweet tea in the refrigerator."

"I'll be right back," he assures me as he jogs toward the house. Blue stays parked by my feet.

Gretchen and Mabel watch Casey leave and Gretchen comments, "Casey's such a nice boy."

"That he is," Mabel confirms.

I jump at the sound when a van pulls down the long driveway.

"Oh shoot, I forgot they were coming today," Mabel says as she hits her palm against her forehead.

"Who is it?" I ask.

"Oh, it's nothing to concern you. We just have a group of gleaners come in. We love to garden. We are master gardeners in fact — but we can't possibly eat all we produce. So, every couple of weeks or so we invite people who don't have enough to come pick vegetables from our garden. It's no big deal, I simply forgot they were coming today."

Gretchen walks over to the case she was showing me and pulls out a large music box with beautifully constructed carousel horses. "I wanted to show you this one. It's my absolute favorite. I would keep it, but I'm supposed to be downsizing. Isn't it fantastic? Listen. By looking at it, you would expect it would play traditional music, but it actually plays *Send in the Clowns*. I love that someone had just a bit of a twisted sense of humor when they constructed this."

A corner of my mouth hitches up as I look at Gretchen with new respect. "Something tells me in another time, in another place, and under other circumstances, you and I would probably have been best friends."

"Who's to say that can't still happen?" Gretchen pats my shoulder. "When you get to be my age, you realize age is just a number and friendship is just friendship."

CHAPTER EIGHT

CASEY

NOT TAKING ANY CHANCES, I pack an entire cooler to take back out to the barn. I'm not sure what's going on with Savannah, but this is the third time I've seen her almost pass out. As I am about to go into the barn, I see an older gentleman staring intently at Savannah — a little too intently for my taste. I mean come on … I know she's beautiful, but there is appreciating her beauty and, then there's creepy. This guy passed creepy more than a few moments ago. I give him the stink-eye and he completely ignores me. Stepping it up a notch, I clear my throat and ask, "Can I help you?"

"No, that's all right," he mumbles, "Just here to pick food." He wanders off.

"It'd be nice if you could be a bit more respectful to the ladies," I call after him.

A feeling of relief washes over me when I turn the corner and walk into the barn. Mabel, Gretchen, and Savannah are laughing like old friends. She appears to be fine now. Blue is resting at her feet, completely relaxed.

"It looks like you guys are having a great time. This doesn't spell bad news for me, does it?" I quip as I open a drink from the cooler and hand it to Savannah.

She takes a long drink before she sets the bottle down between her feet and explains, "Not unless you are the deranged person who installed the doorbell in my house. It plays Broadway tunes."

"Seriously?" I ask as I hand bottles of soda to Gretchen and Mabel.

She nods. "Not only that — they are random."

"Oh, that's just cruel," I barely disguise my smirk. "It has to be somebody's idea of a practical joke."

"And they're out of tune." Savannah grimaces.

"Ouch! Why do you still live there?" I tease.

"Come on, Casey, you've seen my place. You'd live there if it was possessed by ghosts."

I grin. "The lady has a point. The doorbell notwithstanding, you guys have to go see her place. It's really nice."

"Boy, Gretchen, they sure do things differently nowadays. Methinks Casey is fishing for a dinner invitation. Doesn't it sound that way to you?"

"Geez, thanks, Mabel! I thought you were on my side here." I know I'm in deep trouble when all three women break out in uproarious laughter.

"Honey, if you need help from two old spinsters like us, you need to up your game. We haven't scored since the last time we won at bingo — and that was a good seven years ago," Gretchen says.

Savannah turns bright red. "Gretchen, I know we're new BFFs and all, but there is such a thing as TMI."

"Nonsense, dear. Honesty is good for your soul,"

Gretchen gives an exaggerated wink.

Savannah looks up at me with pleading eyes. "I think it's your gentlemanly duty to save me since they're your friends."

I pull her up to a standing position and nestle her against my side. "I'm sorry to break it to you, but it may be too late. I think these two already like you. They have decided you are their friend. That means it's pretty much a done deal."

"Could you at least tell them I'm a little shyer and more reserved than you are?"

"I hate to tell you this, I'm not sure I buy that, Savvy. You see, I had the great honor of seeing you truss up a guy like a Thanksgiving turkey without so much as breaking a fingernail. I think you're tough enough to handle two sweet ladies. It might take you a bit to warm up, though."

I watch as the color washes from Savannah's face again. I try to offer her my drink and she waves it away. "It's all right. I don't need it. It's just that I haven't heard that name in almost twenty years."

"Why?" Gretchen asks gently.

"My little brother used to call me Savvy before he died," Savannah replies hollowly. It's almost as if she's lost in the past.

Mabel looks over at me. "I think you should show her."

"Are you sure? It's an intensely private thing."

"It's all right," Gretchen assures me. "She has been in our shoes. She knows what it's like."

"Casey, what are they talking about?" Savannah asks

with a worried expression on her face.

"I know you haven't known me long. You have known Mabel and Gretchen for even less time. Still, there is one thing we all share in common. We have all lost someone important to us. When I discovered the journey I shared with Gretchen and Mabel, I set out to build them a place for reflection and meditation; a place where they can go and find peace — a place to let the pain go. They decided to call it the Garden of Tears."

I can tell Savannah has a million questions, but she is far too polite to ask them. I am at a loss of what to say because, on the one hand, I want to tell her every last detail about my life so she understands who I am and where I came from but I don't want to scare her away. This is, after all, our first date.

She doesn't really need to know how many of my layers consist mostly of dysfunction and pain. Yet, it seems dishonest not to tell her right up front. How do I begin to explain my relationship with Ashlyn and my parents? The person I was at sixteen bears little resemblance to who I am now, but he is in so many ways responsible for the person I've become. It is impossible to separate the two. I'm still waging a mental war with myself about how much of my story to share with her when she hesitantly wraps her long arms around her waist and holds them there.

"What a nice thing to do," she announces as her voice breaks at the end. Blue whines softly as he leans against her, trying to provide comfort.

"I consider it a penance for all the tears I caused my own mother over the years."

"Nonsense, it is a very special place to us — built by

an amazing young man." Gretchen insists. "Would you like to go see it?"

Savannah swallows hard. "Yes, I think I would."

It's been a good long while since I've been this unnerved. I have no idea what's going through Savannah's head right now. She has been totally silent throughout our whole trip to the Garden of Tears. I've been to formal Catholic Church services which have been more interactive and boisterous. I don't know if she's not talking to me because she hated the whole experience or if she wishes she was anywhere except here. Maybe she never wanted to come to the farm to begin with? Maybe she's not into me? Perhaps her interactions with Mabel and Gretchen have been too overwhelming? It's unlikely given the fact that his head is on her lap but maybe she secretly doesn't like dogs and Blue is invading her space? I just don't know.

Finally, I work up the nerve to ask, "What do you think?"

Before she can answer me, the Polaris hits a rut. Savannah bounces in the seat and nearly strikes her head on the windshield.

"Sorry," I mumble as I try to correct the path of the Polaris without over-steering. "I don't drive this thing very often."

"Everything on the farm is different from what I expected," Savannah tightens her seatbelt. "I definitely did not expect it to be this modern. I never expected the barns to be air conditioned like office buildings. I don't know, maybe I thought everyone rode horses or tractors like the old days. This is the first time I've actually been on a farm. I remember reading library books a long time ago as a kid. I didn't expect everything to be so mechanical. Gretchen was showing me the dairy operation. It's truly impressive."

"I felt the same way the first time they showed me the milking machines." I chuckle. "They run this place as efficiently as any corporation."

"The Garden of Tears you made for them is like an oasis. The stained-glass wind chimes are amazing. I do a little glass work myself but I'm not sure I would know how to make them shatterproof so they would hold up under those conditions. I am so surprised that Gretchen and Mabel have the patience to work on bonsai trees. It's another thing I've never seen done successfully in real-life. I've only seen them trimmed in the movies. The first time I ever saw *The Karate Kid*, I decided I wanted my own bonsai tree. When I was finally able to get my own, it didn't go so well. It didn't take long for my little tree to die. I simply don't seem to have the magic touch when it comes to plants."

"You should talk to Gretchen and Mabel, they know everything there is to know about plants, they can answer questions you didn't even know you had."

"I bet they probably could. They seem to know everything."

"Speaking of that, they wanted me to check in on the gleaners to see if anyone needs help to carry boxes with the hand truck. I can pull us over under the trees by the vegetable gardens. I shouldn't be long. Do you mind?"

"Of course not, it's been a long, emotional day. I need a chance to regroup with a little down time. I have

a book in my purse. Blue and I will just chill right here."
Savannah tucks her feet up under her as Blue lays his head
on her knee and closes his eyes to take a long afternoon
nap in the sun streaming through the dirty windshield.

CHAPTER NINE

SAVANNAH

It's weird. I thought I felt someone watching me before, but I'm sure of it now. I can feel the hair on Blue's back stand on end. I sit up straight in the Polaris and look around. I notice an older gentleman dressed in gray staring at me. Something about his hunched posture seems familiar, but it's difficult to tell because of the distance between us. When he catches me looking at him, he quickly walks away. A knot in the pit of my stomach tightens and inexplicably, I feel like crying.

I bury my face in Blue's neck as I hug him tightly. "I don't know what that was all about, but I would feel a lot better if we could go find Casey now."

Blue wags his tail and nudges my hand as he barks softly from his throat.

"Okay, I guess I'll take that as a yes," I respond as if it's perfectly logical to be having a conversation with a dog.

As soon as I move, Blue hops out and sits and waits for me to get out of the Polaris. As I grab my purse and my sunglasses, the enormity of it all hits me. I have no idea where Casey is. The farm is huge.

Overwhelmed, I sit on the running board. Blue lays his head on my lap expectantly. "I'm sorry Blue, I have no idea where to start."

I sigh dejectedly as I stroke his soft ears. After a few minutes, I start to feel edgy.

"What the heck — it always works on television, I might as well give it a shot," I mumble to myself before I stand up and brush myself off. I squat down and look into Blue's soulful eyes and instruct, "Blue, go find Casey."

Blue takes off as if he's been shot from a cannon. I have to run to keep up with him. When he runs past the Garden of Tears, things start to look a little more familiar. Gretchen and Mabel's house is up on the right, and their sprawling garden is down on the left. Blue comes to such an abrupt stop, I almost trip over him. Startled, I look around to see if I can find Casey. Unfortunately, I don't see him anywhere. Finally, Blue loses patience with my cluelessness and picks up a glove from the ground. I recognize those work gloves from the ones Casey had on this morning when he helped Mabel move a trailer hitch.

I shake my head at Blue. "Give me that!" He immediately spits it out in my hand as if he can't fathom a reason why it had ever been in his mouth to begin with.

"Very good, Blue. I see you found Casey's glove, but I don't see Casey." I try not to laugh at the comical expression on his face.

I hear a few people talking in the garden, so I scan the crowd for Casey. I'm frustrated and uneasy when I don't see him. However, that soon becomes the least of my concerns, because standing smack dab in the middle of Mabel and Gretchen's master garden is a woman I haven't seen since a couple of weeks before I turned eighteen.

Without warning, my knees buckle and I need to sit on the ground or I'm going to fall on my butt. Blue whines and curls his body around mine, acting as a natural backrest. He is as still as a statue as my body trembles. I'm tempted to examine the crowd again to make sure I didn't make a mistake — yet, even as I have that thought, I know I don't need to. All the puzzle pieces start to fall into place. Of course, my subconscious knew the man's body posture. I saw it every day of my life for the better part of two decades. There has been more trauma than my mind can even cope with between then and now, but there are just some things a person doesn't forget.

The question is why? Why here and why now? After ignoring Shelby and me for all these years, why pop back up in our world when Shelby has finally found some peace? The implications are almost too much to handle. I drop my head between my knees in an effort to control my breathing.

I hear muffled voices behind me as Gretchen exclaims, "Oh dear! Casey, you better come quickly, it looks like Savannah isn't feeling well again."

I look up so quickly that it makes me a little dizzy. Out of the corner of my eye, I see Casey drop a hand truck full of boxes on the grass as he runs toward me. "Savannah? What's up?" His face is tight with concern.

"Casey, I'm sorry but I need to go home right now," I announce as I struggle to get to my feet.

"Okay … but do we need to go to the doctor first?" Casey asks, running the backs of his fingers down my cheek before reaching his hand out to help me up.

"What?" I ask, momentarily confused by his question. "Oh, no, I don't need to go to the doctor. I just need to go home."

Casey's expression grows dark and his brows furrow. "It was that creepy guy, wasn't it? I had a feeling about him. I mean, who wears a sweater in this kind of weather? There was just something off about him. He couldn't stop watching you."

Oh, there is plenty off about George Lyons, but nothing like Casey's imagining. The problem is, I don't even know where to start. Part of the problem is it's not even all my story to tell. Shelby might not even want to know George and Nancy are back in town. I don't even know if she's told Mark all the details of our hellish childhood and I'm pretty sure she doesn't want me to broadcast it to everyone.

Blue leans up against my leg as if to remind me that he is a silent support system. I bury my fingers in his thick fur and take a deep breath. "It's fine. Nobody did anything to me really, I had a good time — but I need to go home now. I can't talk about it, I really can't. I'm sorry. It's nothing personal, I swear —" My speech trails off as I draw in a deep breath and then inelegantly hiccup like a small child.

Mabel steps between us and crosses her arms as she turns to Casey. "I know you want to know all the nitty-gritty details right now, but you need to stop being such a guy. You are just like my Harvey was. Whenever I was upset or angry, he would want to get to the bottom of it all. I always had to tell him that I wasn't like a car engine he could take apart and fix. Take your girl home and fix her a little tea. Cover her with her favorite blanket and put her favorite television show on the tube and let her get some rest. Things will look better in the morning," Mabel advises as she gives Casey a brief hug.

She picks up my purse and hands it to me. She squeezes my forearm. "Honey, if you need me, you just let Casey know. He knows how to get in touch with me anytime day or night."

Her kindness is so unexpected, I feel the need to reach out and hug her. I'm not sure who is more surprised—me or Mabel. "I will do that."

Casey takes a moment to shake both women's hands as he promises, "I'll try to be back later this week to work out the details. Thank you for giving me a heads up. I think the vintage toys will look great in my shop."

Casey puts his arm around my waist and pulls me close to his side, but remains silent as we walk back toward the Polaris. I'm grateful for the silence — but on the other hand, it gives my mind a chance to wallow in fear over what might happen. That's almost as hard as having to explain what's going on.

When we reach the van, Blue hops in and takes a perch next to the passenger seat as soon as Casey opens the door for me.

"Blue, I hate to break it to you — you live here," Casey says addressing the dog sympathetically.

Blue whines and sticks his head on the seat as if he's pleading his case.

I glance up at Casey with alarm. "What do we do now?"

"Well, it seems Blue here thinks he's your dog. Were

you planning to get a dog today?" Casey asks, amusement evident in his tone, his lips twitching with laughter.

"Well, no. Not really. I'm not opposed to the idea. But isn't it a complicated thing to do?"

"I guess we would have to ask Mabel. I think Blue's circumstances are a bit unusual — with him losing his family and everything. Let me text Mabel and see what she thinks." Casey says as he pulls out his phone and starts to text.

"He is a super sweet dog and I would certainly feel much safer with him around. Still, I don't know much about owning my own dog. I would hate to make things worse for him."

Casey helps me into the van and rests his hand on my thigh much longer than he needs to merely to be helpful. He leans his head in the door frame and says, "I don't see how you could make things any worse. You obviously have a soft spot in your heart for Blue. From what I've seen, the two of you seem to work well together. A person to love and a safe place to call home is always a great thing. You can always learn about dog training and keeping him healthy."

"I guess so. I feel so dumb because I haven't done this before. I mean, most kids have at least had a goldfish, I haven't even had that."

Casey shrugs. "So, you'll learn as you go along. Mabel and Gretchen are perfect role models. When they started this dairy farm, they didn't know anything about it. They were professional women from the education field."

"Really? You think I can do this? Honestly, I'm kind of attached to him. I know it sounds weird because we just met but, I'd hate to have to leave him here."

At that moment, Gretchen and Mabel walk up behind Casey. Gretchen smiles as tears leak from the corners of her eyes. "I had just about given up hope Blue would ever be truly happy again, but he seems to have found it with you. Goodness knows, we tried everything we knew how to do. He just never seemed to be comfortable here. You seem to have the magic touch with him. Still, I was afraid even though you had made a connection with him, you might not want him."

"Like I said before, I've always wanted a dog. I'm afraid that I might be too new at this," I confess as I stroke Blue's head. My heart races with excitement as I come to grips with the very real possibility I might actually get to take Blue home.

"Don't you worry about a thing. Stuart is such a nice young man. He graduated from veterinary school in Tampa and started a practice here in Gainesville. He's been involved in rescue work for a long time with his best friend, Mitch. Earlier today, I was telling him all about you and Casey and how much fun you were having with Blue. When I got the text message from Casey, I forwarded it to Stuart. He just wants you to come by the vet clinic next week and fill out some paperwork." Mabel writes something down on a piece of paper.

"That's it? That's all there is to it? How can it be so easy?" I ask incredulously. "Why would he let me adopt Blue?"

"Because I vouched for you. After I told him how well you and Blue have bonded, he thinks it's a good idea for you to see how things go. If they go well, he sees no problem with the adoption. Here's Dr. Stuart's name and phone number. This is the brand of food Blue eats. If you need help with a fence for your yard, I have a crew who can help get it built in a jiffy."

Her simple words take me off guard. I'm not used to being taken at face value. For a moment, I get lost in the emotion of it all and I have to stop and take a breath. I struggle to focus on the conversation at hand. "Oh, right, a fence. No, I think we're good. I guess we'll have to stop by the store to get food and bowls and stuff. Are there any pet stores open this late?"

"Yeah, that shouldn't be a problem." Casey grins. "I suppose you have yet to be introduced to pet superstores. There are pet stores like Walmart for pets. You can even take Blue inside."

"Hang tight, I'll go get you a leash for him," Mabel says as she heads toward the house.

"Okay, thank you. Thank you for everything. This has been an unforgettable day," I stammer.

"Sometimes, things work out in ways you least expect," Gretchen says. "You be sure to bring Blue for a visit, okay?"

"Of course I will," I promise reflexively. The honest truth is; I have no idea what will happen in the next few days. The last time I saw my parents, my whole world collapsed. Something tells me this sighting may yield similar results.

"What do you think of this?" Casey holds up a biker's costume designed for Blue to wear. "I think you should get this for him. You could take pictures and I'll stick them up in the shop."

Even Blue shakes his head no. "That would be a negative. Last I checked, Blue is my dog and not a child who I'm going to take trick-or-treating. Besides that, it's the middle of the summer. I know you've completely forgotten this, but I'm here to get dog food, a dog bed, feed bowls, a new collar — not one with spikes on it — and a few chew toys. That's it. You are a classic impulse buyer — marketers love you. I suppose your dog has every toy and gadget in this place."

"You'd be wrong," crows Casey triumphantly.

"I bet you I'm not. You know this place like the back of your hand." I challenge, narrowing my gaze and tapping my foot.

"I do know this place like the back of my hand because I have a cat."

"Hmm, a big tough guy like you with a fluffy kitty … like I said, you are nothing but marshmallows inside. I bet she's got a pink sparkly collar, right?"

"No, he doesn't have a pink sparkly collar. It's blue with spikes because his name is Aladdin."

"What does this mean for us?" I try to keep a straight face.

"What do you mean?" Casey asks with a puzzled expression.

"This might be a problem if Blue doesn't like cats." I look down at the big hunk of dog that has fallen asleep at my feet.

"If it becomes an issue, it will just be one more thing we have to tackle," Casey says with a skeptical look, as Blue snores. "Something tells me you may be borrowing trouble."

Borrowing trouble. That phrase haunts me the next few days as I wait for Shelby to come back from vacation. I am grateful to have Blue here as a distraction, but even though he helps keep my mind off of things, I still have important decisions to make. Still, Casey's words are a reminder that I might be making a whole lot out of nothing.

What if my parents' presence here means absolutely nothing? What if they didn't even recognize me? Chronologically, I'm almost twice as old as the last time they saw me. I feel like because of what I've been through during that time, my soul is incalculably older. If I'm able to speak to them again, would they even recognize the person I've become? Somehow, I don't think so. The parents I remember were judgmental and unforgiving toward outsiders. The things I have done to survive would not make them proud. Few people on this planet would be proud of the things I've done. I can barely stand to look in the mirror, so how can I expect my parents to be proud of me?

Once again, I'm stuck. I can't tell just part of my story without telling everything and nobody knows all of it — not even Shelby. I'm not sure I want to tell her because she's found her happily ever after, and I don't want her to hate life and everything in it.

CHAPTER TEN

CASEY

I USED TO THINK I had pretty good instincts when it came to women — but now I'm beginning to wonder if I have any intuition at all.

I knew visiting Mabel and Gretchen was an unusual idea for a date, especially a first date. I've had so many traditional first dates go south on me, I thought I'd try something different. It's awkward to try to talk at the movies or in clubs. Dinner can be a minefield if your date has different tastes in food. There is always the awkward bit at the end with the check. I always like to pay for first dates, but a few women find that offensive. Dating has become unexpectedly tough.

I thought things were going really well — especially when Savannah seemed to easily make friends with Gretchen and Mabel. The icing on the cake was when she and Blue became the best of buddies. Something happened and the day took a dark turn. Savannah won't tell me what went wrong. I have a hunch it had to do with that older man, but whenever I try to talk to Savannah about it, she just shuts down. I'm trying to be patient, but I'm frustrated because if I don't know what's wrong, I can't protect her.

I figured she must've been stressed out because of the formality of the date. I thought once we got back home on familiar ground, she would go back to being my friendly neighbor. Unfortunately, she didn't. It's almost as if she's pretending I don't exist. She doesn't even come over for coffee anymore. I've run out of legitimate excuses to go over to her shop to see how she's doing.

Just as I start cleaning up the tables to get ready for the lunch rush, Mabel and Gretchen charge through the front door.

"Welcome ladies. Do you want your usual or are you planning to branch out and go wild with some coffee?"

"Savannah was telling us that you make her some kind of coffee that tastes like a cinnamon roll. I'll try that," Gretchen says.

"I'd like to try the vanilla," Mabel adds. "I had no idea that coffee had come so far from the black swill I used to make my husband until Savannah started singing your praises."

I set about making the specialty coffee for my friends. "So, you still talk to Savannah?" I try to sound nonchalant.

"Oh, about every day." Gretchen chuckles. "She's worse than a new mama. I've never seen anyone so nervous about having a dog — but she's doing fine. Blue is such a good boy. Lucky for her, he has already had some obedience training."

A feeling of dread washes over me as I realize that Savannah has been speaking to everyone except me. "Did she happen to mention anything about me? About us?"

Mabel looks at Gretchen. "What's that saying that the kids always use these days?"

Gretchen chokes back a snort of laughter. "You mean, 'It's not all about you'?"

Mabel shakes her head in confirmation as she exclaims, "Yes! That's exactly the one I was thinking of."

I feel my ears turn red and I feel the need to defend myself. "Okay, point taken. I'm simply trying to figure out where I messed up. Things seemed to go okay, and then suddenly, they weren't. Savannah won't even talk to me now. She doesn't even come by for coffee anymore. I've barely seen her in a month. I thought we were good enough friends to be able to survive the first date at least. I just want to know what happened, that's all. If I hurt her feelings, I want to know what I did."

"Did you try to get all pushy and handsy at the end of the date?" Gretchen asks. "Mabel, do you remember what Sylvester did after the dance at our high school reunion? That was so disgusting. All I did was dance with him, and the guy thought that it meant he had license to do so much more."

"No, I did not get handsy!" I reply with a startled laugh. "I'm too much of a gentleman for that. Besides, my mom would box my ears if I even so much as tried. I helped Savannah fix up all the stuff that we bought for Blue and I set up her coffee machine so it would make her coffee in the morning. Then I gave her a nice chaste hug and told her that I had a great time and hoped she had sweet dreams."

"Well, that seems like a nice thing to do," comments Gretchen.

Mabel sighs. "Casey, I know this is hard to understand. But, this really is not about you."

"Did Savannah tell you that? What did she say?" I

look directly at Mabel and press for more details. For some reason, this seems vitally important.

Mabel sits a little straighter on the barstool. "Son, what kind of friend would I be if I went around blabbing my private conversations with everyone?"

"You're right. It wasn't fair of me to ask. I'm just trying to help," I admit, feeling chagrined.

Mabel pats my hand. "I know you have the best intentions, Casey. You will need to keep those in mind because things are going to probably get tough. Savannah's got a rough road ahead and she'll need you by her side."

Just as I'm about to flip off the lights and lock the doors for the evening, the front door bursts open. Savannah looks like she has ghosts chasing her. Even Blue looks upset and disheveled. I catch her in my arms and hug her tight. "Whoa, Savannah! What's going on? Are you hurt?"

She shakes her head but doesn't let go of me. I place my arm around her waist as I walk over to the front door and lock it. Blue follows us. "Let's go to my office. I've got a couch in there. Do you want a sandwich and some coffee?"

"I couldn't eat right now if I tried. I'm too freaked out." Savannah wraps her arms around her waist and trembles. Blue scoots closer. He's walking with his shoulder touching her thigh.

When we reach my office, I grab my jacket and place it around her shoulders. I squat down beside her and ask, "What's wrong? Please tell me … I'd like to help."

Slowly, she unwraps her arms from around her waist

revealing the cell phone she has clutched tightly in her hand. I cup her hand in mine until she releases the phone. "Just tell me it isn't real. It has to be a nightmare, right?"

I examine her phone to see if I can figure out what she's talking about and the only thing I see is her voicemails. I unplug my headphones from my phone and plug them into hers to see if I can replay the message.

When I do, it becomes apparent why she's so upset. As I listen to the vile message, the hair on the back of my neck stands up and my jaw clenches in anger.

"First of all, this is total bull-crap. I was there, remember? As far as I'm concerned, John Donelson should still be in jail. If you and Haley hadn't intervened, who knows what would've happened? He could've killed Natalie. 'Tortious interference with contractual matters' my butt!" I scoff. "I bet whoever this freak is, he got his legal knowledge from the back of a cereal box. Let him take you to court, I'll be there to testify for you every single day and so will all the people in my coffee shop."

"It's more than just that. Did you listen to the whole thing?" Savannah whispers in a broken voice. Her hand is shaking as she reaches out to stroke Blue.

"You mean the part about releasing information about your past to the media if you don't give him half a million?"

A tear slides down Savannah's face as she nods. "I don't have that kind of money; I've never had that kind of money."

I reach out and hold Savannah's hands in my own. They are ice cold. "Savvy, this jerk is bluffing. That's a cheesy line from just about every B grade movie everywhere. I wouldn't worry about it. Even if he had information about your past, everybody's got one. It's no big deal."

Savannah draws in a deep shuddering breath and blows it out. "Casey, I need you to trust me when I say if someone had access to my past, it would be a huge deal. Big enough that you and everyone else who knows me might hate me."

"Like I said, I've got a whole family full of skeletons living in my closet, I wouldn't be in any position to judge you I think you're worrying for nothing. I think whoever this is, is totally bluffing because if they were legitimate, they would identify themselves and not electronically disguise their voice. I believe that it's somebody taking advantage of a story they saw on social media. I bet you it's just some creep who thinks they can make a few extra dollars off your fear and anxiety. They probably think you didn't know anything about the legal system. They sure as heck don't know you have friends like Tristan and his father-in-law, Isaac."

"I didn't even think about Tristan. I only know him because of Shelby and Mark. I'm not sure it's okay to ask them for favors. He must get asked for favors all the time."

"I'm sure he does too because that's the nature of Identity Bank's business. It's what they do. But if I were in your shoes, it's the first place I would go. With Identity Bank's fancy computers, Tristan could probably get you an IP address which will tell you who issued the threats. Isaac has a ton of government contacts who could make sure that the guy can't get next to a computer for the next twenty or thirty years."

Savannah shudders and her jaw starts to tremble as she shrugs off my suggestion. "I think I should probably handle this one on my own. It'd be better for everyone involved if my friends and family don't know anything about what's going on."

It's all I can do to swallow my growl of frustration. I stand up and pace in front of the couch. I turn back toward her. "Are you sure, Savannah? What this person is doing is extortion, plain and simple."

Savannah hops up from the couch to a standing position, startling Blue. She stands chest to chest with me and throws up her hands in the air. "I don't have a choice in this situation. My choices were all taken from me a long time ago. I have to deal with what's left. Fortunately for me, I'm tough. So, I'll do what I always do. I'll cope. One second … one day … one month … one year at a time. Time moves on." Softy, she adds, "Life moves on."

Savannah calmly takes her phone from my hand and tucks it into her back pocket. "Thanks for keeping me sane there for a moment — but I have to do this on my own from now on." She glances down at Blue and snaps her fingers as she commands, "Let's go."

With that softly uttered phrase, I watch Savannah walk out of my life again. I don't know why I'm surprised, she warned me that she doesn't do relationships. Perhaps I should've listened a little better.

"Son of a hockey puck!" I roar as I smack my head on the top of my convection oven and manage to rip the delicate mesh filter I'm trying to change at the same time.

With far more force than necessary, I toss the mangled filter in the garbage and wash my hands. I know I need to get my head in the game, but I didn't mean it literally. I rub the sore spot on my forehead where it connected with the element. That'll leave an interesting mark.

Since Savannah left the store yesterday, I can't stay focused. I know she said she wanted to handle it all on her own, but can I actually sit around and do nothing while she's being threatened? Savannah is right on one count, there are no great options.

As I walk back over to the coffee bar and retrieve my phone, I can't help but wonder if what I'm about to do will destroy the tenuous relationship I have with Savannah. Yet, I have to do everything I can — even if it's not my favorite option.

With a pounding heart, I dig out a business card from my wallet and dial my phone. I can't tell you whether I'd rather speak to someone or get a voicemail box. As luck would have it, someone picks up the phone.

"Dylan Palmer, what can I do for you?"

"Detective Palmer, this is Casey Moore. I spoke to you the other day when you did a follow-up interview at my coffee shop."

"Yes. I remember. Do you have more information for me?"

"Not exactly." I sigh heavily.

"What do you mean by that, Mr. Moore? Are you trying to obstruct an investigation?"

Immediately, I sit straighter in my chair as I respond, "No sir. I don't really have many details and this isn't my information to share. I'm just concerned that one of the people involved in the case is receiving threats — probably related to social media coverage of this case, and I wondered if you could keep a little closer eye on her until it all blows over."

For several moments, I hear nothing but papers shuffling. I fight the compulsion to fill the awkward silence with sound and will myself to stay silent until he's finished.

Finally, he speaks again, "Who are you talking about? Are you talking about Savannah Lyons? Certain parties in this case are saying she was the aggressor. You are aware of that, correct?"

"Yeah, well, certain people believe the earth is flat too, but that doesn't mean it's true. I was there; I watched the whole thing happen. The truth of the matter is that my employee, Natalie, might have actually been kidnapped or worse had Savannah not been there to stop it. John Donelson is a sick pervert and doesn't care who knows it. Savannah and Haley stopped him in his tracks. I don't know why more isn't being done to stop him."

"Ever heard the adage 'money talks'? Well, John Donelson's mouthpieces all have loud megaphones — if you catch my drift."

"All I'm asking is for a set of eyes on Savannah. You don't know whether mouthpieces are all Donelson has at his disposal."

"I hear you. I'll see what I can do. Thanks for letting me know," Detective Palmer says. "Guys like Donelson make me miss my time on the traffic beat. Let me know if you come up with anything else, okay?"

"Will do," I promise solemnly, as I hang up the phone, hoping against hope I made the right call.

CHAPTER ELEVEN

SAVANNAH

"AUNT SAVANNAH, WHY DO you look like my dad does when he loses a case? I thought you were happy that your store is about ready to open? It looks much better without the green paint on the walls. I don't like the smell of new paint, but it will go away soon. You know, you kind of look like my mom did after she had to flunk a kid for cheating," my niece Ketki observes in her typical stream-of-consciousness questioning.

Maybe I should be offended about her blunt assessment of me but, she's totally right. I am a wreck. Between worrying about what I want to say to Shelby about what's going on with our parents and the fact that I am completely scared out of my wits about what to do about the situation with John Donelson — I am a complete and total disaster zone. I don't know if the creepy voicemail is tied directly to him or merely someone who wants to make a fast buck over the social media storm which arose over the scene at Casey's coffee bar.

I try to sound casual. "It's all right, Ketki. It's nothing for you to worry about — it's just grown-up problems." I throw her another bag of beads to sort. "Right now, I guess I should focus on getting my inventory ready," I suggest, trying to change the subject.

In typical Ketki fashion, she is not distracted or dissuaded. "That's what my dad always says when he doesn't want to talk about something. It's pretty silly because I'm almost thirteen years old — that's almost the same as being a grown-up. Sheltering me from a grown-up world is a stupid argument. It's not like I don't know what's going on. I have my own Facebook account and YouTube channel. I see what's going on in the real world. I know about the creepy guy — I was the one who discovered him, remember? You can tell me what's happening. I'm old enough to handle it."

"You make several good points. However, I can honestly tell you, I don't know what's happening with the creepy guy who's making all the threats against me. As far as I know, he's not in jail — even though he hurt somebody. The whole thing makes me sad, and it's stressing me out. I think if you hurt someone so severely, you should probably go to jail. It doesn't make any sense; I don't know if it ever will."

"I decided a long time ago that there are a lot of things which don't make sense and even though I'm super smart, I'll never make them make sense. When Mom got cancer, she proved it a thousand times." Ketki says as she braids and unbraids a section of her hair.

"I agree. That was a really hard time. Some good came out of it because Mark hired Tristan to find me," I add with a ghost of a smile.

"Yeah, and I found Tayanita. It's weird. She is my real mom, but she doesn't feel as much like my real mom as Shelby who's going to be my step-mom soon. Still, Tayanita is awesome. Dad is real relieved everybody gets along and he doesn't have to guess what my real mom is up to these days. He seems happy that she's doing okay. I just think it's cool everybody plays video games together on the same team — well everybody except Dad He doesn't play them. Dad says he's not coordinated enough to play. I think that's funny."

"I think it is kind of neat that you and your two moms have the same hobby," I comment with a smile.

"I think it's funny when my dad gets all philosophical and starts talking like a fortune cookie. He just says in his big, deep court voice, 'There is a season for everything and everything happens for a reason.' Isn't that corny?" Ketki asks with a giggle.

"It may be a little corny, but it doesn't mean it's not true." Tears gather in the corner of my eyes.

Ketki comes closer and awkwardly pats me on the top of the head. She looks right past me as she speaks. "I think you should talk to my mom and dad. They are both really good listeners. I always feel better after I've talked to them. Being all by yourself might seem like it's going to make you happy, but I don't think it will."

I give Ketki a brief hug. "That's the best advice I've gotten in a long while. Thank you so much. You are my favorite niece."

"Aunt Savannah, don't be silly." Ketki scoffs. "I'm your only niece!"

"Well, that may be true — but you're still my favorite niece. I love you," I assure her as I blink back tears.

"From this shopping list, I thought we were going camping or something. Where's the camping gear?"

Shelby shouts through the open screen door.

"There isn't any. You know me — I just like s'mores and junk food. Did you bring the wine?"

"Okay … now I want to know what's going on. Wine never used to be on our camping checklist." Shelby peeks her head out the door and looks at me with concern.

I shrug as I put more wood in the fire pit. "Gimme a break, Shel. The last time we had a sleep over you were like thirteen years old. Wine would've hardly been appropriate. You might appreciate it today though."

Shelby ducks back into the house and quickly returns with a tray of small bottles. "I didn't know what you like, so I brought a little of everything," Shelby explains when I raise a questioning eyebrow. "I hope we don't need it all."

I draw in a deep breath and swallow hard. "I hope not — but you never know." I spring to my feet and I start to fiddle with the food. I'm so nervous. I practically knock over the entire card table where Shelby is setting out the spread of food.

Shelby pats the seat on the porch swing next to her. "I don't know what's going on Sis, but I'm pretty sure marshmallows won't fix it. Come and talk to me. Stewing about it isn't making it any better."

"That's just the thing. I'm not sure talking about it is going to be any better. Once I open this Pandora's box, there is no going back. Do you understand? Our whole relationship is going to change. You'll probably hate me after this conversation. Are you sure you want me to talk to you?"

"You sound as pessimistic as Ketki. I don't know if it's because of her autism or because of her innate personality, but Ketki tends to ruminate on everything negative."

"I hate to break it to you, Sis. This is more than just a negative outlook. It's more than just theory. It's my life. There's a reason I don't talk about my past."

Shelby nods sympathetically. "I know it's hard. I don't talk about my past very much either. It's just too difficult to explain to people. Everybody automatically thinks of Warren Jepps when they hear about anything involving a religious cult. Our childhood was bad, but it wasn't quite that horrific."

Her words are like a knife through my heart. How do I even begin to go about dismantling her whole belief system? More importantly: should I? Is it fair to expose my little sister to the hell I've been through simply because it might make my life easier? Indecision makes me completely speechless as tears roll uncontrollably down my face.

"Oh God! Savannah, what's wrong? You have to tell me. Nothing is going to change the fact that you're my sister and we have already been through hell and back. Whatever it is, we can handle it together." Shelby gathers me into a tight hug.

I sit up and wipe my face with a paper towel as I warn, "You might change your mind after you hear what I have to tell you."

Shelby moves my hair out of my face and gives me one more brief hug before she says, "I'm here to listen, not to judge. Just pick a spot and start talking. I've been there. I know it's hard."

"I think Casey likes me," I blurt. I'm not sure who was more surprised at the revelation. That wasn't what I expected to say.

"Yeah," my sister probes, "and what does that mean?"

"It's not fair if he doesn't know all of it —"

"Okay, so tell him all of it," Shelby instructs softly.

"I can't. He'll hate me." I wipe my eyes with my sweatshirt sleeve.

"Sure you can. Just start at the beginning. Our parents were gullible people who had a sick, disabled child and wanted to believe that anything and everything would make him better. They didn't know how to be capable parents and they let other people's crazy ideas become more important than providing necessities for their children. In the end, they chose to follow a fanatical leader rather than watch out for the well-being of us. We haven't seen hide nor hair of them for over half our lives," Shelby says succinctly.

I unwind myself from the ball that I've shrunk into on the swing. I walk over and grab a couple of bottles of hard lemonade and bring them back to the swing. I hand one to Shelby and then open mine. Before I sit down, I take a long swig while I think about what to say. Finally, I just decide to announce it as if I'm ripping off a Band-Aid.

"Shel, that would be a nice summary, if it were true — but, I don't think that's the case anymore."

Shelby carefully sets down her drink before she looks at me and asks, "What do you mean?"

I sigh and wipe away a tear. I don't know why just talking about my parents makes me so emotional. They've been out of my life as many years as they were in it, but somehow I'm still screwed up over it.

"Remember, a couple weeks ago when I went out on a date with Casey?"

"How can I forget? Ketki bragged for days that she got to paint your fingernails."

"Well, we went out to this farm and I'm pretty sure Mom and Dad were there with a bunch of other people."

"Do you think they followed you to Gainesville? Did they know it was you?" Shelby asks with concern in her voice.

"I don't know. There's a lot of scary stuff happening in my life right now. I'm not sure what to think about it all. I just looked up and Mom was there standing in the middle of the garden."

"Did you say anything to her?" Shelby presses. "Was Dad with her?"

"Casey actually noticed Dad first—because he was staring at me. Casey thought he was being rude. I heard Casey tell him to knock it off, but I didn't see him. Later, I saw him from a distance, but didn't recognize him until I saw Mom and put two and two together."

"What did Casey say when you told him?"

I blush and hang my head as I mumble, "I didn't tell him. I just asked to go home."

"Why not? It's not like you planned for the parents we hadn't seen in almost twenty years to interrupt your date."

"I know, but how do I go about explaining the weirdness of our childhood without telling the whole story? I mean, I've sort of pulled my life together now, but I'm not like you. I don't even have a college degree and I'm older than you. I barely got my GED. He'll probably think I'm a pathetic loser who doesn't quite fit into society."

"That's ridiculous. You are so not a loser. Even back when we were kids, panhandling on the streets, we were not losers. You were the one who taught me that —"

"You don't understand," I say in a tortured whisper as I stand up and pace around my patio. "My story goes so far beyond panhandling. You don't know what I had to do in the years we were separated. You can't possibly understand. I don't want you to be able to understand."

I walk over to a Tiki torch that has burned out and use one of the other ones to re-light it. I check the citronella oil in the bug zapper as I slap away a mosquito the size of a quarter.

Shelby tries to draw my attention back to the conversation. "Savannah, I will love you no matter what. So just tell me. One word at a time if that's what it takes."

I can't look at my sister while I tell this story. I just can't. I take one of the skewers from the barbecue pit and place a couple of marshmallows on the end. I move a nearby lawn chair closer to the fire pit and sit down as I slowly turn the skewer.

"Savannah?" my sister gently prods.

Silently, I grapple with where to start my story. Finally, I ask, "What did you think happened to me when you were taken away?"

Shelby looks up toward the sky as she retrieves memories from long ago. "I just figured you, Mom, and Dad went on to have a happy family life without me. I thought that when Owen died, you were angry that it wasn't me who died instead."

I shake my head in disbelief. "I know you've told me

that before, but it still doesn't make sense."

"Cut me some slack," Shelby replies with a shrug. "The only day that I'd ever been more scared was the day Owen died. Nothing that happened the day our family blew apart made sense to me. I was still a kid. I was trying to put all the pieces together and I guess maybe I wanted somebody to have a happy family, even if I couldn't."

My breath catches in my side as if I've been running. I heave out a large sigh, "I wish that's what happened, but it's not."

"Oh Savvy," Shelby murmurs as tears roll down her face.

"It's so not. Our parents were weird, but I don't think they ever intended to be intentionally cruel. I just think they got so caught up in whatever Reverend Pratchett wanted them to do, they forgot to be parents. Unfortunately, they forgot to prepare us for the real world too. I might have been almost eighteen when Owen died, but I might as well have been seven."

"I was the same way. I was so unprepared to go to school. I didn't know anything about anything. You and Owen were my only friends, so I didn't know anything about how to make friends, how to dress appropriately, or even how to tell a joke. I made a lot of stupid mistakes trying to be popular. It's part of the reason I'm a skin cancer survivor. I tried to be one of the popular kids and spent a ton of time in tanning beds and sunbathing."

"Shelby, I don't want to tell you this story — do you understand? You could go a whole lifetime and not need to know what I'm about to say to you. But, if I tell one person in my life, it's only fair that I tell you too."

"Are you eventually going to tell Casey?" my sister

asks gently.

"I don't know yet. I haven't decided. A lot of it depends on how well this goes. If this blows up in my face, I may never tell another person — ever. I don't think you have any idea how scared I am. I've kept this secret for years. The only people who knew were my doctor and one undercover police officer."

"Oh Sav —" Shelby whispers with a break in her voice.

I hold up my hand, still unable to look at her. "Shel, please don't."

Shelby clears her throat. "Okay." She curls her feet under her and hugs her knees as she waits for me to continue.

"Mom and Dad split that day before you were even taken away in the police car. So, it was just me standing alone in the parking lot. I guess they left me behind because they thought I was an adult. I was in the garb Reverend Pratchett used to make us wear — you know the kind which covered us from head to toe with a scarf over our hair? It wasn't until after they had taken you away that someone figured out I was probably a little younger than they thought. So, one police officer hauled me into the station. Remember, we didn't have any ID back then? I couldn't prove that I was your sister, or that I was old enough to take care of you."

I glance down at the marshmallows and realize they're getting very brown. Shelby gets up and brings me a graham cracker and some chocolate. She silently takes the marshmallows off the skewer and makes herself a s'more. It's funny how nothing has changed, yet everything has changed in all these years. She still likes her marshmallows half-burned.

With a bittersweet smile, I continue my story. "There was no way I could prove I had been taking care of you and Owen for years. I couldn't get anyone to listen. They thought I was a mentally ill runaway. The only police officer who had any connection to what was happening to you went on vacation. He didn't make any notes about our connection in the paperwork. So, in your records, you didn't have any living relatives, and I had no documentation to prove I even existed."

"That's just so wrong," Shelby mutters. "What happened?"

"For a few days, they threw me into county jail. They accused me of loitering. I wasn't even sure what loitering meant back then. I was up one night writing with just the light from under the door and a guard caught me. I expected her to be angry, but she actually took the time to listen to what I was saying. She was the first person in days who was actually interested in hearing my whole story. After I told her what really happened, she found me a temporary space at a juvenile facility and helped me try to find some records to prove who I was."

"We didn't go to school, so it must've been hard to prove," Shelby says with a frown.

"You never got a chance to go to school, but remember I went to school for a little while before mom had Owen?"

"They were able to track your record down?"

"Yeah, but by the time they did, it was just a couple days before my eighteenth birthday, so they gave me a sack lunch and a couple of the guards pooled their lunch money and gave me twenty dollars and told me 'good luck'."

"That's it?" Shelby asks as her jaw goes slack.

"Pretty much. One nice lady who worked at the facility felt sorry for me and gave me a few of her daughter's clothes and the phone number of a church."

"If you didn't go to a foster home like I did, where did you go?"

"Are you sure you want me to go on? This is where the story gets rough," I caution.

"I don't know why you think I'll judge you for things which aren't your fault. You were just doing the best you could." Shelby reassures me, but I feel like every bone in my body is made of Jell-O.

"You know what's funny?" I ask, smirking at the memory. "Back then, I didn't even know enough to be scared. I figured if I had survived jail, the toughest part was over. I was still in mourning over Owen, I had just lost you and our parents. I figured everyone who I had ever known had left me. I thought it was a sign from God that I was meant to be alone."

"I was having the same thoughts with my foster family, but they were too busy to notice because they were trying to turn me into a replica of their dead daughter."

"It was just a mess all the way around, wasn't it?"

"Pretty much," Shelby says as she takes a swig of her drink.

"I kept thinking about how we made all those plans when we were little about what would happen when we were grown-ups — how we were going to leave Reverend Pratchett and go conquer the world. I was bound and determined to make this happen. Unfortunately, reality slapped me in the face. I was eighteen years old, but I was basically a fourth-grade dropout, I had no identification, I didn't know how to use a computer or even a telephone. The only job skill I had was begging for food and panhandling."

"Savannah, that's totally not true. I remember you helped Mom and Dad manage their money and you took care of Owen and me. Most of the time, we had someplace warm to stay because of you. The only reason I was able to catch up to my peers in school and go on to get a college degree is because you taught me how to read, write and do math. Don't you dare tell me you weren't qualified to do anything because it's a lie!"

"You remember it a little differently than I do. I recall it as a team effort between the two of us and we only survived because we had each other."

"Sav, you're not giving yourself enough credit. One of the main reasons I became a teacher is because of the way you taught me when you had nothing. You were simply amazing."

"I suspect you won't think the same thing in a few minutes, so remember that at one point in your life you looked up to me, please."

"Savannah —" she warns with exasperation.

"When you hate me, don't say I didn't warn you —"

"When I don't, can I say, 'I told you so'?" Shelby counters.

"Fine … whatever. Just let me get this over with," I snap, letting my nerves get the best of me. That's the problem with keeping things bottled up for so long. When you finally do let them loose, the results are unpredictable.

Gathering my courage, I pick up the story where I left off, "For a while, I was able to use the skills we grew up with. Panhandling, eating at church events or community picnics, behind restaurant dumpsters and grocery stores. I would sneak into the public pool or pretend to be someone's grandchild at a mobile home park and use the recreation center."

I stand up and warm my hands in front of the fire pit as I continue to retrieve painful memories.

"There was an unexpected cold snap, and I got sick — really sick. I wasn't able to make my usual rounds and stay clean. I began to look disheveled and dirty. I thought I would never get well. This lady, Esther Brennan and her husband Reggie, started bringing soup for me and a couple of other homeless people in the area. They said it was because of the holiday spirit. Esther took me to the doctor and got me some medicine because I had pneumonia."

"Oh no, you must've been scared. You don't like doctors," Shelby says under her breath.

"Well, you know me — I would've never told the doctor I was sick if I could avoid it because we don't do that. We don't go to the doctor and we don't ever tell anyone we're homeless."

"The doctor figured out you were homeless? I bet you were totally freaked out," Shelby says as she holds her hand over her mouth.

"He figured it out because Esther told him. So, he threatened to put me in the hospital unless I had someplace to go. Esther and her husband offered me a room in their house. I didn't want to go to the hospital, so I accepted."

Shelby shudders. "I don't blame you. As much as Mom and Dad taught us that medicine was evil and doctors would kill us, I wouldn't have wanted to go to the hospital either."

"Exactly. I was petrified about the prospect of seeing more doctors. It seemed like I hit the lottery at the Brennan's. It was like staying at a five-star hotel. I had a TV in my room and they brought me the most delicious meals I had ever eaten. Esther bought me brand-new clothes and shoes. I couldn't even remember the last time I had new shoes. If I wanted books to read, art supplies or anything else, it just magically appeared."

"When did your dream start to become your nightmare?" Shelby asks astutely.

"After a couple of weeks, I started to feel better as my antibiotics kicked in. I began to feel claustrophobic and confined in my bedroom, even as nice as it was. I guess it was not a big surprise considering we didn't live inside much as kids, but I was used to being able to roam as far I wanted to in a day and lying around all day watching television and movies wasn't really my thing."

"I can imagine," Shelby comments.

"At first, when I said I wanted to leave, Esther would come up with all sorts of excuses why I couldn't. Dinner was going to be ready, Reggie would be home or someone was coming over that she wanted me to meet. Initially, I gave into those demands because I was grateful they took me in. Yet, as I became more restless, it became more difficult for me to ignore my wanderlust."

"What did you do?"

"I came to the conclusion that it was time to tell the Brennan's thank you for their help and move on. All of a sudden I started feeling sick and dizzy again. I was so tired and weak I could barely eat. Esther told me that it was not uncommon to have a relapse of pneumonia. Of course, I didn't know any better, so I believed her. The weird thing is that I couldn't remember anything for hours at a time. Yet, when I was sick the first time, I didn't have those memory lapses. I couldn't seem to get out of the fog.

"The gourmet meals disappeared and were replaced by peanut butter and jelly sandwiches. The only thing that stayed consistent was my chocolate milkshake. Even the clothes started changing. At first, they were pretty modest — not Reverend Pratchett modest, but relatively modest for somebody who was still a teenager. All of a sudden, Esther decided it was time for me to grow up and find myself a man. So, she told me I needed to dress like a woman and not a prepubescent girl. It was a funny phrase for her to use since the clothes she bought for me were not much bigger than a child would wear. I could barely squeeze into them, but she took all the rest of my clothes away."

"Did you try to leave their house?" Shelby asks.

I shake my head as I respond, "No, Esther told me the doctor told her I had AIDS. Well, you and I heard about AIDS in the shelters growing up and we knew it would kill us, so I didn't want to spread it to anyone."

"That witch is pure evil," Shelby exclaims. "That's like mental torture."

I nod as I respond, "You have no idea. It wasn't long after she told me that little medical gem that Reggie started coming in my room at night."

"Oh no, please no," Shelby whispers.

"At first, I couldn't tell if anything was really happening or if it was just my imagination because of all the weird dreams and fogginess I had. Whenever I would tell Esther something weird was happening to me or that I was experiencing pain, she would tell me it was because I was dying. It wasn't until Reggie went to a Super Bowl celebration and got very drunk that I knew for sure. That night he was not careful. He was violent and left bruises and tearing. As awful as it was, I finally had validation that it wasn't all in my head."

Shelby starts to get up and come over to give me a hug. I put my hand up to stop her.

"There's more. I have to tell you the whole story," I insist.

She sinks back down into the swing and wipes tears away from her eyes.

"I tried to get help from Esther, but instead of helping me, she was just furious with Reggie. I thought she was supposed to be protecting me. I was still looking for the mother figure we lost when mom went looking for answers about Owen. Esther wasn't looking for a daughter; she was looking for a commodity. I was just an investment for her. She was furious that Reggie had marked up the inventory, so to speak."

"Oh my Gosh! Did you understand this at the time?" Shelby exclaims.

"Not as much as I do now, I just knew that something was drastically wrong. I needed to get out of the situation. But I was trapped—like literally trapped. They installed a door at the top stairs which didn't have a doorknob. They kept it locked from the outside with a deadbolt. Once they had me trapped, and I had been 'broken in', they let up on the drugs. Then I started having terrible withdrawal symptoms. I practically tore off my own skin, I itched so badly and I started throwing up blood. They were mad at me because I lost a bunch of weight and didn't look very good."

"Well, I can't say I feel sorry for them. They were keeping you hostage and raping you!" Shelby states emphatically.

"They didn't see it that way — they saw my sexual servitude as a way for me to pay them back for all the things I had taken from them. Esther was always complaining about how much I owed her."

"Pfft," Shelby scoffs. "Clearly they had more than just a few screws loose — they had a freaking hardware store running amok."

"Somehow they devised a scheme to auction off my virginity. I'm not sure how they pulled that off since Reggie had already taken it. Although, I'm sure I was a pretty convincing terrified virgin. When Mic Ricard purchased me, it was the first time I'd ever been conscious during a rape session."

"You're kidding me! You were just sold? Like a puppy?" Shelby asks incredulously.

"More or less," I confirm. "The scary thing is that Mic looked like your next-door neighbor and probably acts like him too. He was an official with the Federal Aviation Administration. It was his job to fly all over the nation to inspect planes and give safety training. He had a wife, a daughter, and twin boys at home. As far as I know, they were a completely normal family and had no idea that he kept me locked in an apartment on a mountaintop in Colorado."

"Colorado? How in the world did you get to Colorado?"

"Mic had all sorts of connections in the airline industry. He simply disguised me as a sick cancer patient and pretended I was going to a special hospital on a mercy flight. Then, he told people I died."

This is the hardest part of my story by far. I take a deep breath and a swig of hard lemonade before I continue, "I could count them. There were seventeen days every month that I didn't get raped — but they were random. I never knew when I would hear his car coming up the drive. I lived in fear of it every hour of every day … day in and day out."

"Oh, Savvy, I'm so sorry I wasn't there to help," Shelby says in a low, hoarse voice.

"Never, ever wish that again. I wouldn't have wanted you within two thousand miles of that man. I would've died before I would've let him near you," I rebuke sharply.

"I have no doubt you would, I'm glad you didn't have to, though. How did you escape?"

"Not surprisingly, with all that sex, I ended up getting pregnant. However, as these things sometimes go, I lost the baby. Of course, I didn't get any medical care because I didn't exist. So, I bled for a long time. Mic got impatient with me and decided to look elsewhere to fulfill his sexual needs. He hired someone from an escort service and brought her to the cabin in Colorado. He was not gentle with her either, but what he didn't know was that she had worked as a magician's assistant in Vegas and could get out of any lock. When he had to take an emergency call for work, she escaped and hot-wired his car. The police department sent an undercover officer to rescue me."

"So … what happened to all those people who did this to you?"

"I have no idea. For years, I ran without stopping, I talked to nobody, relied on no one except myself, and believed in nothing. Then, two pushy guys who wouldn't take no for an answer told me I had a pesky little sister who loved me and missed me. They made it clear if I didn't hurry up and get to Florida, she might just die. That had a way of changing my perspective real quick."

"I love you too, Savannah. Nothing you said today changes that. I admire your strength and resolve even more. I would venture to guess Casey would feel the same way. I don't understand why you think he wouldn't," Shelby answers firmly.

"Casey thinks I'm tough. If I was really tough, I would've gotten away from the Brennan's and Ricard a lot sooner than I did."

"I don't think Casey will see it that way at all. I think he's going to be astounded by your strength, grace, and perseverance. If he isn't, he does not deserve you."

"That's easy for you to say," I argue. "Tell me … how exactly do I go about mentioning in casual conversation, 'Oh, by the way, I used to be someone's sex slave?'"

Shelby places her hand on my forearm. "One word at a time works — one word at a time."

CHAPTER TWELVE

CASEY

I CAN'T BELIEVE IT'S already past six o'clock at night. Putting the last coat of finish on this display case is taking a lot longer than I expected. All my brush strokes are showing through the finish. It's really frustrating. At least the weather is nice enough to do this outside as long as the bugs don't get into the varnish. The alleyway behind Tough Breaks and Paint Your Art Out is a good place to set up an impromptu workshop because there isn't any vehicle traffic here since the bank changed its drive-through lane.

As I'm painting, the back door to Paint Your Art Out opens, and Savannah emerges carrying a large bag of garbage to the dumpster. She looks like she's had a rough day. For lack of a better term, she appears wilted. I jump up to help her with the trash, but before I can put my brush down and move through all my D-I-Y crap to get to her, she's already thrown it in the dumpster.

We walk side-by-side over to my new display case. "Casey, this turned out so great. It's beautiful! I love the mahogany color. It'll look so sharp in your shop." Leaning over the case, she grins as she remarks, "Cool, you added the extra LED lights. Will you be able to hide the wiring?"

I point to the hidden compartments I built behind the kick plate. "I guess all the time my dad thought I was wasting in shop class has paid off," I remark, somewhat sarcastically. "Honestly, though, I'm having a little trouble with the finish. It's not going on as smoothly as the guy at the hardware store said it would. I don't know what I'm doing wrong."

Savannah picks up the can of varnish and reads the instructions. "What are you painting with?" she asks, raising her eyebrow in question.

I walk over to the makeshift table I set up with sawhorses and an old door and pick up the brush from a cracked coffee cup. "This," I answer, holding the brush up in the air.

She gives it a cursory glance. "Well, there's your problem. Just a minute, I'll be right back." Once again, Savannah is gone almost before I can blink. Even Blue is looking a little bewildered over by the back door of her business.

It doesn't take long before Savannah emerges with two brand-new paintbrushes in her hand. "See, the texture of these bristles is finer and designed to hold onto the varnish better. The bristles won't leave as many marks on your finish."

"Thank you, but why two brushes? I don't know if I'm that coordinated," I tease.

"I haven't had the chance to paint anything smaller than a wall in a while. Today is as good a day as any. I thought maybe you could use a hand." Shelby twists her hair around her hand until it's coiled tight like a rope and then quickly ties it in a knot on the top of her head. She takes one of my pencils from the table and sticks it through the knot. "There — much better. Getting varnish out of hair is hard work. I've had to do it more times than I'd care to admit. Are you ready to get started?"

I'm completely mesmerized by her efficient, graceful moves. So much so that I'm a little slow on the uptake.

"Casey? Are the fumes getting to you already?" Shelby asks as she pours varnish into an empty paint tray.

"No, I'm just admiring the view." I regret the words immediately because they sound trite.

"Casey, you're a polite guy, but you're also a tad vision impaired. I look like I went through the steam cycle at the laundromat while I was upside down. It's been a hard day. I still can't get my air conditioner to work correctly. Still, it was charming of you to try to be kind."

"Hmm, you must be talking about someone else because I see no one here who remotely matches that description. To me, you always look ravishing."

"Ha — see, now I know you're lying." Savannah points her brush at me. "You might as well call me resplendent or exquisite like some cheesy dime store novel. I am sweaty, stinky, and sticky. Lucky for you, those are the perfect qualifications I need to help you paint your cabinet, so do you want the front side or the backside?"

Hiding my instinctive smirk with a dust rag, I wisely confine my comments to neutral topics, "Since you obviously have more experience with the paintbrush than I do; I'll let you do the cutting in around the glasswork in the front."

"That sounds doable to me." Savannah takes a large empty bucket I use for shortening and turns it upside down to use as a stool as she begins the tedious detail work. "I can't believe how well this is put together. Where did you learn how to do this?"

"Why, Savannah, that sounds suspiciously like a compliment. Are you flirting with me?" I tease with an exaggerated wink.

Savannah blushes bright red as her head dips and her long lashes brush her cheeks. "If I was, would it be a bad thing?"

"Not in my book … never in my book."

Savannah draws in a quick breath and blows it out slowly before she says quietly, "I'll definitely keep that in mind. However, today I'm not in any shape to do any flirting, so I'll just say I meant that as polite conversation for now."

My brain is busy turning over Savannah's words and trying to sort out the mixed messages they contain. I decide to play it safe and honor her request to treat it as small talk as I begin to tell her my story.

"I went to an uppity private school when I was younger. It was one of the many things my parents disagreed on. My mom wanted me to go to a school that was artsy and well-rounded and my dad wanted me to go to one focused only on math and science. The junior high school had a shop class which was pretty unusual. Most kids made small jewelry boxes and that kind of stuff, but I wanted to make my mom a dresser. My teacher said I could do it as long as I made up the plans."

"Wow, that's a lot to expect of a kid," Savannah remarks as she dips her brush in the varnish again.

"For some kids, maybe. Remember, my dad was an executive in Silicon Valley—I had tons of friends who had access to super complicated computer programs, so it didn't take me more than a couple hours to design my mom's dresser on my laptop and print out schematics."

"I bet your teacher was totally impressed."

"Not so much," I answer dryly, as I remember the showdown with my teacher. "He was kind of ticked off. Mr. Allen figured I wouldn't be able to do it — he would be off the hook so I would be stuck making a jewelry box like all the rest of the students. Once I was able to design the dresser, he had to keep his word and let me build it."

"Good for him for keeping his word. A lot of people wouldn't have."

"After I actually got started on the project, he was totally into it. He said it was the nicest thing anyone had ever made in his class."

"What did your mom think of it?" Savannah asks as she continues to add varnish.

Savannah has no idea how her small talk is stomping all over landmines in my heart. Of course, at the time I had no way of knowing my dresser would symbolize the beginning of the end of normal in my life either — but that's what happened.

My gut twists as I recount the story. "At first, Mom said it was too fancy for her to use. She was afraid to touch it. She thought that if she got fingerprints on it, the dresser would be ruined. She said it was so pretty that it looked like a piece of art. It was the first time anyone had ever told me that I had an artistic flair for anything. I was so used to being praised for being good at math, science, and computers. I didn't even realize that I could be good in anything artistic or working with my hands. I remember feeling about ten feet tall because I made my mom smile."

"That's the best." Savannah whispers. "I can only imagine how proud you felt."

Swallowing back a flood of emotions, I struggle to continue, "Finally, I convinced her to use the new dresser. I helped her clean up a spot in her bedroom and we were moving things from her old dresser to the new one. We found a false bottom in one of her drawers and underneath it was a bunch of white powder in a baggie with needles, razor blades and a burnt spoon."

Savannah gasps in shock.

I nod grimly. "From my mom's reaction, I could tell the drugs were not hers. Finding them made everything we had been going through with my dad during the previous six months or so suddenly make a ton more sense. I remember thinking at the time that I wished I'd never made the dresser. After that day everything in my life changed."

Savannah sets her paintbrush in the jar of paint remover and moves her bucket over closer to me. "What happened? I thought you said your mother loved it."

I grimace as I recall the pivotal day, "My dad was one of the first people to realize computers would be a huge deal outside of the industrial environment. He wasn't a computer programmer himself but he knew all about consumer products design so, with laptops coming into their own, my dad became a hot commodity. Everyone wanted a piece of him and they basically were throwing money at him. For a while, he rode the wave and things were good — but it got out of control and he started using drugs. At first, I think it was merely a way to fit in or maybe it had something to do with staying awake all the hours he needed to keep up with his job. Either way, it quickly grew out of control and the drugs ruled my dad. What used to be a brilliant man who knew the ins and outs of computers like no one's business became an angry, sullen person we couldn't recognize."

"How terrifying," Savannah shakes her head.

"When my mom found the cocaine, it was like the match that lit the forest on fire. It completely demolished what was left of our family. My dad walked in on us shortly after we discovered it and while we were talking about what to do about it. He was sure my mom was using his drugs. He pulled a knife on us and threatened to cut my mom's tongue out like they do in the movies. This went on for hours until he finally crashed."

Savannah nods sympathetically.

"In the morning, my mom decided to send me to school to protect me, in case my dad woke up from his stupor. I remember not being able to concentrate on a single thing all day — I just sat and stared into space. All I could think of was the knife he held to my mom's throat. I was afraid I would come home and find my mom lying in the middle of the living room floor with her throat slashed."

"I would have been terrified too."

"I didn't even bother to wait for the school bus, I just ran until I got close enough to town to take a city bus. When I got home, my worst fears were realized. There wasn't anyone there, including the housekeeper who usually came on that day. It was the eeriest feeling ever. My mom — and everyone else I knew — were completely gone."

Savannah holds up a trembling hand over her mouth

as she whispers, "Oh no."

I nod. "Uh-huh. It turned out that the housekeeper had just gone to go visit relatives. Eventually, she came back, but my mom had disappeared. All of her belongings had been packed up and the dresser I had made for her was demolished."

"What did your dad say?" Savannah asks in a shaky voice.

"After that happened, it was several days before my dad actually appeared. When he did, he looked terrible — as if he had been high the whole time. After he finally crashed back to earth, he tried to pretend nothing had happened. He drove me to school and went to basketball games as if nothing was out of the ordinary. This pattern continued for about six months."

"Wait! What?" Savannah sputters. "Didn't you ask about your mom? Didn't people notice she was missing?"

"If they did, it never filtered down to me. One of the weird things about being super rich is people assume you're weird and crazy anyway. They don't ask very many questions. I guess it's considered rude. It was so isolating for me. I felt completely alone. Even my teachers who could see that suddenly I wasn't doing very well in school didn't bother to ask me any questions or follow-up with my dad. I guess they figured I was the spoiled son of a McMillionaire. That's what they called us in my neighborhood because we had new money instead of old money — therefore I couldn't have any real problems."

"That's just crazy!" Savannah exclaims with a huff.

"That about sums it up. Anyway, we were bouncing around pretending everything was relatively normal and one day I accidentally made a comment about wishing my mom would come home for Christmas. That made my father come unglued. He threw me up against the wall and got right in my face and told me that he had made my mom disappear and he could make me disappear too."

"What did you do?" The color drains out of Savannah's face.

"That night after my dad passed out in his usual routine, I packed up as much stuff as I could carry and I took off in search of my mom. I figured unless my dad hired an assassin to kill my mom, there was no way he would do it himself. He had a hard enough time killing spiders in the bathroom, there was no way he could kill my mom. Or at least that's what I hoped. So, I took off in search of my mom."

"Oh, Casey!" Savanna exclaims quietly under her breath.

"At fourteen years old, I became a homeless drifter living on the streets, and at sixteen I watched a junkie die," I reveal. "I don't know why I told you all of that simply because you asked me how I learned woodworking, but there it is. This is the ugly truth about the guy next door. Life isn't so pretty and perfect, even when it seems to be on the surface."

Savannah takes in a deep breath and wipes her hands on a rag. "You're preaching to the choir, Casey, preaching to the choir."

CHAPTER THIRTEEN

SAVANNAH

FOR ALL THE HASSLE that the move from Georgia to Florida presented, there are a few upsides — besides the coffee shop next door. The biggest one is probably this studio. My old shop didn't have any place for me to work. It was basically a storefront. Here, I have my own private studio. I feel a little pretentious calling it that since I don't have any formal training as an artist. Actually, I have no training at all to speak of. Every once in a while, a manufacturer will have a workshop or two when they introduce a new product, and I'm always quick to go to those if I can. I've learned everything else from library books.

I take my place behind the potter's wheel and throw some clay. There's something incredibly soothing about this ritual. I have an old-fashioned wheel. I have to keep it going with a trundle using my feet while I shape the clay with my hands. The rhythm calms my mind. As Nora Jones streams through my headphones, I get lost in shaping the clay. I don't have any grand plan for what I want to make today, I just let my body decide what the clay is going to make.

I feel Casey's presence behind me. Startled, I stop the

wheel, causing my piece to collapse.

"Oh geez, I'm sorry. You didn't have to do that," Casey says as he squeezes onto the bench behind me and wraps his legs on either side of mine.

His bold move takes my breath away and I can't move. Usually, I am fiercely protective of my personal boundaries. I have an encyclopedia of ways to tell people to back off and get a life. Yet, from the moment we met, Casey seems to have a way of eroding those boundaries. I can't remember the last time I was this close to someone by my own volition.

Casey seems to instinctively know I am at war with myself over his place in my life. He holds perfectly still to allow me to get used to his presence.

One breath in, one breath out, one breath in, one breath out. It's all I can permit myself to focus on. If I let my mind go anywhere else, it goes to deep, dark places I never want to visit again. There's a reason I haven't allowed anyone close to me in years. I trust no one. Over the years, I've gotten pretty good at pretending to be a normal and functioning member of society like a regular person as long as everyone stays about four feet away. Yet, Casey isn't feet away. He isn't even inches away; he is actually touching me. It's overpowering. Even as I try to force myself to calm down and breathe through my panic, I realize it's not all terrible.

The warmth of Casey's chest against my back seeps through my body. I've been cold and alone for so long, I've forgotten what it's like to find comfort in the touch of another. As I relax, I instinctively take a deep breath to fill my starving lungs with much-needed air. When I do, I'm reminded again how much I love the way Casey smells. He smells like everything home I've been searching for my whole life. A little coffee, a smidge of cinnamon, and a lot of something else I can't identify but know that I really want.

I release a contented sigh and settle back against him as for the moment I'm allowing my present to win the victory over my past.

It's not until I feel Casey exhale that I realize he's been holding his breath as well. "Good afternoon," he murmurs against my ear. "What are you making?"

I have this inexplicable urge to laugh like a sorority girl. I don't giggle as a general rule, but something about the question and the situation makes this all seem so much sexier than it should be.

"I'm just throwing pots," I answer with what I hope is a casual shrug.

"That's cool. I've always wanted to try that. I've only seen it in the movies. Will you show me?"

"Do you mind if you get dirty? This is not a tidy process."

"It's okay — it's the end of the day anyway. I'm just planning to go home and shower."

Without warning, visions of Casey taking a shower pop into my head. It has been an extraordinarily long time since I have had fantasies about a man, any man. I've gotten used to the fact that my past has driven out any hope of a normal future. I can't help but grin to myself as I ponder this development. Maybe, there's hope for me after all.

"Okay, don't say I didn't warn you."

I dip my hands in a bucket of warm water and re-wet my lump of clay as I start to pump the trundle again.

I try to concentrate on forming the clay and get lost in my process again, but it's hard when I can feel the steady beat of Casey's heart against my shoulder blade. I lean forward and reposition myself—that seemingly innocent movement causes my hips to slide backward. Suddenly, all the danger I'd conveniently forgotten comes roaring back to the surface.

Every nerve cell in my body goes on red alert, and I began hyperventilating. Casey places his arms around me in an attempt to help me — yet that gesture makes things so much worse. Finally, he pulls his hands away and says helplessly, "Savannah, you know I would never hurt you, don't you? I don't do that kind of thing. *Ever.* I thought you knew that about me."

After I've broken away from Casey, I attempt to collect myself and rebuild my carefully crafted walls. I begin randomly rearranging things in my store to disguise the fact that I'm minutes away from collapsing into a fetal position and watching reruns of Little House on the Prairie until I can no longer stay awake. Right now, I'm not even brave enough to look at Casey Moore, let alone talk to him. I'm so upset that my teeth are chattering. Blue comes over and stands beside me and leans into my thigh as he often does when I'm anxious. Yet, even his comforting presence is not enough. Today, I am struggling even with the basics like breathing. Crap. I thought I got over this garbage a long time ago. Just when I think I'm tough, I'm not.

I chance a glance over at Casey, and I watch as he rakes his fingers through his hair. He looks torn. "I came over to invite you out for dinner, but it doesn't look like that'll happen anytime soon. Everything I do seems to hurt you. I can't keep doing that to you." Lowering his voice to a whispering plea, he adds, "You know where to find me if you change your mind." As he walks toward the back of my store, he pauses and looks back over his shoulder. "I really like you, Savannah. Maybe someday we can work out all the glitches. I hope you call me. I really do."

A few moments later, I hear my heavy metal door clink shut. I have held it together as long as I can. It's a good thing I have closed down my business for the day because my knees are no longer willing to hold me up and I collapse in a puddle of tears behind the counter. Eventually, I have no more tears left, and Blue is whining at the door to be let out. I have no choice but to gather my wits about me and be a proper pet parent. Taking a deep breath, I struggle to my feet and give myself a mental pep talk. *Come on Savannah, you've been through worse than this. One breath, one inch, one step, one day. You can do this. You are tough.*

Shelby and are I hanging out on my patio again but, this time it's for a Labor Day party. I didn't realize people actually celebrate this holiday, but Ketki insisted that I had not had a proper housewarming party when I moved to Florida and this party would serve as a two-for-one deal. I'm nervous for a couple of reasons.

This is the first time Stuart will be doing a hands-on evaluation of my home environment with Blue. I met him at the vet clinic once, but now he is coming to the party today to see how Blue and I interact. There shouldn't be any problem, but weird things happen to me all the time.

The whole gang from Ink'd Deep is supposed to be here. It shouldn't be any big deal either because I met them all during Jessica's bachelorette party and wedding, but it's another thing to have them all around my house. I don't have a lot of close friends — okay, honestly I don't have any except for Shelby and her stepdaughter Ketki, so the concept of simply hanging out with a bunch of friends for a barbecue is a little terrifying for me. I don't even have to worry about the food. Jessica and Rogue have taken care of that because it's my housewarming party. Yet, somehow, I'm still a nervous wreck.

I'm pacing around my small patio when Shelby steps in front of me. "What's wrong with you? This is neurotic, even for you. This is supposed to be a party, and you're acting like you're about to be brought in front of a firing squad."

I smile weakly at her description. "It's ironic you would put it that way. I sorta feel that way. Shelby, how do you do this? How do you pretend that any of this stuff feels normal after all the stuff we've been through?"

"Are you asking how to allow yourself to be happy when you're not sure you deserve to be?" Shelby asks astutely.

"Exactly," I answer a little too quickly. "All of this stuff is for the people who had normal childhoods with white picket fences—those who haven't been screwed up by life. I feel like a giant pretender."

"Did you ever stop to think that maybe it's the people like us who've had starts rougher than most that need this stuff more than everyone else? This fun, lighthearted friendship and the unconditional love of the people around us helps us overcome the bad stuff."

"Do you think it's even possible to put all our history behind us and forget it ever happened?" I'm unconsciously hugging myself and scanning the crowd for Casey.

"Forget that it never happened? Probably not. Put it into perspective? Maybe so," Shelby pours me an iced tea. At my skeptical look, she continues, "It's true; before I met Mark, I was totally convinced I would spend the rest of my life alone lurching from one catastrophe to another. Not a lot of good had ever happened to me. I met Mark under the worst possible circumstances. Even though I never planned to fall in love with Mark, it happened anyway. Despite all the bad stuff. It was the best thing that ever happened to me. It didn't erase all the awful things, but I guess it helped to make them seem not as important."

"Are you suggesting that what I went through doesn't matter?"

"Oh Gosh, no! Never in a million years. What you went through matters more than I can say. As far as I'm concerned, those people should be publicly castrated for what they did to you."

"If you don't mean 'not important', what do you mean?" I demand, my voice breaking with emotion. Blue nuzzles my hand to comfort me.

"Blue is a perfect example of what I mean. Letting him into your life was an improvement, right?"

I reach down and stroke Blue's ear. "Yeah, it's great to have someone who's always there when I need a shoulder to cry on—even if it is furry."

"Being loved unconditionally by people is like that

too. Mark is always there for me whether I'm having a phenomenal day or whether I just need to dissolve into a puddle of tears and be held. It took me a long time to accept the fact that Mark loves me either way. I don't have to pretend I'm doing okay when I'm not."

"I'm pretty sure Casey knows most of the time I am not doing okay. These days I seem to be closer to a complete emotional breakdown than actual sanity. Things have been really hard. First, there was the attack on his waitress, then Mom and Dad came back into town and then there was the incident in the shop the other day."

"What incident?" Shelby asks with a curious expression.

I groan in frustration. "Didn't I tell you about it, Shel? Oh Gosh! It was awful. I felt so stupid."

"I'm sure it wasn't that bad."

"No, it really was. Casey came over to invite me to dinner and I flipped out right in front of him."

Shelby puts her hand up for me to give her a high five. "That's awesome! Did you say yes?"

I frown and shake my head. "We never got that far because of my stupid meltdown."

Shelby comes closer and puts her arm around my shoulder as she walks me over to the porch swing. As soon as we both settle in, she rocks it gently. "Okay, start from the beginning. What happened?"

"I don't even know where to tell you where the beginning is. Casey is a lot different from who I expected him to be. Did you know his parents are rich? Or, at least, at one point they were."

Shelby shakes her head. "He doesn't come across as

a rich snob to me. He seems more like one of us."

"He is in more ways than you might think. He said he spent several years out on the street as a runaway. Casey's watched someone die."

"He said that today?" Shelby asks, struggling to follow the story.

"No, he told me a while ago when we were painting his display case he made."

"So, when did you have your meltdown?"

"A couple weeks ago when he came to ask me out for dinner."

"I don't understand."

"You and me both. Casey came over to my studio when I was making pottery. He sat down behind me. I thought I was okay with it … until I wasn't. It's like my brain short-circuited or something. I couldn't even reason with myself."

"Did you explain all that stuff to Casey?"

Tearfully, I shake my head. "No. What answer could I possibly give that would make any sense without having to tell him about everything? I can't even look the man in the eye right now — let alone tell him my deepest, ugliest secrets. What am I going to do, Shel? Please tell me."

CHAPTER FOURTEEN

CASEY

I FLIP THE INVITATION over in my hands for what must be the hundredth time. It's from Savannah's niece, but the barbecue is at Savannah's house. Is there some secret meaning behind this invite or is it simply a friendly get-together? I just don't know. After I think about it for a moment, I realize that I know someone who could help me figure this out.

Digging my cell phone out of my pocket, I make an unorthodox phone call. I hope my friend doesn't think I'm totally nuts.

"Identity Bank, this is Tristan."

"Tristan, this is Casey Moore. How are you today?"

"Fine. Are there problems with your system?" Tristan asks immediately.

"No, I called about something more personal. Did you — uh — get an invitation to a barbecue at Savannah's house?"

Tristan chuckles. "Yeah, not only that, my wife and mother-in-law have been making tamales for days. We are going to eat spectacularly well. I'm looking forward to it. Why? Is there a problem?"

I'm not sure how to proceed from here. It's not like Tristan and I are the best of friends. We've done a few business deals and watched a game or two at the local sports bar. I must've lost my marbles thinking it was a good idea to call him — but, he's on the line now, so I forge ahead. "This will probably sound like a stupid question, but I'm trying to figure out why I was invited."

"I'm assuming it's because you're Savannah's friend," Tristan answers.

"I'd like to think that's true — but some days I actually don't know. Some days Savannah acts like she would just as soon have me drop off the face of the earth."

"Oh, so it's like that, huh? Rogue was like that when we first met too. I had to convince her not all men were terrible — especially not me."

"So, what you're saying is that I may not be completely sorry-outta-luck?" I try not to sound too hopeful.

Tristan laughs out loud. "Look, I don't know what to tell you — except you got an invitation from Ketki and she seems to have an intuitive sense for this kind of stuff. It's supposed to be a fun barbecue with lots of great people and tons of food. Maybe you guys will get a chance to talk to each other without the pressures of dating. It's worth a shot."

"Thanks. Maybe I'll cruise by later."

From the look on Savannah's face, I don't think she expected to see me here today. It's hard to tell what she's thinking. Her expression seems to contain happiness, dread, and fear all at the same time. I don't know what I did to upset her so much. She hasn't been into the coffee shop and I haven't had an opportunity to apologize for upsetting her. I tighten my grip on the gift bag in my hand. Hopefully, this will smooth the way.

I wish I had a better idea how to fix what's wrong between us. One moment everything seemed fine in the next moment it wasn't. Maybe it's all my fault, after all, it was a little presumptuous of me to share her pottery bench. Still, we have held hands before and I've had my arm around her waist. I'm not sure if that's the problem at all.

Maybe I misread the whole situation and she doesn't like me. Perhaps she doesn't approve of the way I grew up in the time I spent as a teenager. Or maybe I blew my chances the very first day when I wasn't the one to rescue Natalie.

Just as I'm about to say hello to Savannah, a teenager slides between us. Very carefully, she extends her hand to me, although she looks right past me. "Hi, I'm Ketki. Thank you for coming to Aunt Savannah's party. Do you play video games? I play video games. I play a lot of video games. Would you like to see my computer? Aunt Savannah said it was okay if I brought it today. So, I'm not being rude. If you don't play the same games I play, I can set you up a profile and an avatar."

I smile at her stream of questions as I ask, "How much espresso have you had today, Ketki?"

"Oh, I don't drink coffee. My dad is super careful about my diet because of my autism. I don't really like coffee anyway, so it's not a huge deal."

"You'd be surprised how many people don't like

coffee. It's all right though because I serve lots of stuff at my restaurant. To answer your questions: I do play video games — mostly the racing ones. However, it's been a while, so you'll probably beat me. I'd be happy to play some games with you after lunch if that's all right with you. I haven't seen my friends in a while and I'd like a chance to catch up first."

"Yeah, you and Aunt Savannah need to talk. She looks pretty stressed."

"Noted. I will catch up with you later, Ketki. It was nice to meet you."

Ketki turns to Savannah. "Be nice to him. He's a boy and sometimes they can't help but be stupid."

"Ketki! That's not very fair. Women can be pretty dumb too. Mistakes usually happen on both sides it's not fair to blame only one gender."

She rolls her eyes at Savannah as she counters, "Aunt Savannah, have you talked to any thirteen-year-old boys recently?"

"Well, no. I'm not sure if I've ever spoken with a thirteen-year-old boy."

"Exactly." Ketki crosses her arms. "I'll see you guys later," she says as she runs from the room.

"She's right you know," I blurt at the same time that Savannah asserts, "I'm right, you know."

Savannah laughs. "Go ahead."

"Ladies first," I gesture in her direction.

"No, that's all right. I'll let you go first," Savannah acquiesces.

I hand Savannah my gift. "Please consider this my apology if I was stupid. I didn't mean to offend you, make you feel uncomfortable, or do whatever I did to create distance between us. I'm sorry I was a jerk."

Savannah takes me by the hand and leads me into a back bedroom she has set up as an office. She points to a large recliner and says, "Please sit. I need to explain a few things to you. I should've done this a really long time ago. You probably have a right to be angry with me because I didn't share. I'm sorry. I hope you understand why I didn't — but that doesn't make it right."

I motion for her to sit down beside me, but she resists. "I'm sorry — it's not personal — but I can't. This will be hard enough as it is." She paces across the room, as she follows the edge of a small rug.

"Savannah, if it will hurt you to tell me this, do I really need to know? I don't want to cause you unnecessary pain." I watch emotions flicker across her face like an old eight-millimeter movie.

"Casey, please don't give me an easy out," Savannah pleads. "I've been trying to work up the courage to tell you almost since the day we met. I feel like such a chicken for keeping secrets."

My heart drops to my feet. The last person I knew who keep secrets from me died in my arms. History simply cannot be repeating itself. Karma cannot be that cruel, can it? I make a conscious effort to unclench my jaw and keep my body language neutral.

"Savannah, you know I've had my share of secrets. I know how hard it is to share them. If you need to stop, just say the word and I'll understand. Believe me, I've been there."

"For the love of everything that's holy, I hope to God you've never been where I've been. I wouldn't wish it on my worst enemy let alone someone I like as much as I like you."

Her words are like razor blades to my soul. The small part of me which wants to be happy she's acknowledging that she likes me is being stomped out by the gigantic monster of the words not yet said. Sadly, I know they're coming.

A thousand puzzle pieces fall together in my mind as I look back over my time with Savannah over the last few months. You don't survive on the streets long without learning how to read people. The signs were there. Apparently, I didn't want to see them, so I looked the other way and found other explanations for her actions. I, of all people should have known better. I should have done better.

Savannah sees the expression on my face and exclaims, "Oh my gosh! You know."

"I don't know anything for sure. I can make an educated guess based on my experience. I lived on the streets for several years, I know what happens out there."

"How could you even know my story?" Savannah whispers. "Is it written on my forehead or something?"

"No, of course not. We travel in the same circle of friends. When Shelby beat cancer, she caused quite a stir in local media. Some media outlets liked to play up the orphan aspect of her past. The day that Tristan met you at Shelby's house so you could reunite with her, he rescheduled an installation job with me. Even though I didn't know you yet, I was aware of your presence and I inadvertently became aware of your background because I knew of Shelby and Mark through Ink'd Deep."

Savannah's eyes meet mine as they widen and a

horrified expression crosses her face. "Do you suppose everyone knows my story? Crap! I try so hard to fit in. You don't even know how difficult it is to pretend to be normal when you're me."

"Savannah, look at me please," I command firmly. "Listen, no one can tell simply by looking at you. The only reason I had any clue was because of our conversations and watching you has become my favorite hobby."

"That's a little creepy, Casey." Savannah stops pacing and stands in front of me.

I shrug. "I suppose in some ways it might be, but I find you beautiful, fascinating and confusing. If you're not telling me how you're doing, I spend an inordinate amount of time trying to figure it out from your body language."

Savannah narrows her eyes at me and shakes her head slightly. "To borrow a phrase from Ketki, 'That's just weird.'"

"To avoid any confusion, why don't you tell me what you think I need to know?"

"You understand that when you find out how messed up I am, it'll probably be the end of us, right?" Savannah wipes her eyes with a Kleenex. Her hands are visibly shaking.

"You have no way to know that. I'm a pretty understanding guy. I've been through a lot myself. You can't make those judgments without telling me first. It's not fair."

"Listen to *me*, Casey!" Savannah growls in a frustrated voice. "Don't talk to me about fair. There is no fair in life. If life was fair, I wouldn't have been pulled out of school in the fifth grade and dragged all over the country while my parents followed some wacko con artist who thought the world would end in Y2K. I wouldn't have had to raise my little sister and little brother on my own with no money, no house, and no guidance. If life was fair, my brother wouldn't have been born sick or my parents would've been smart enough to take him to the doctor instead of every crazy person they could find to take their money. If life was fair, my brother wouldn't be buried in the mountains somewhere."

"I'm sorry. I didn't mean it that wa—" I explain as I begin to move toward her.

Savannah holds up her hand. "I'm not done yet. You want the story? Let me tell you the whole story."

I swallow my protest and sit back down, bracing myself for the worst.

"If life was fair, my parents would've actually been parents and stood up and fought for us when the police separated us and took Shelby away when she wasn't even a teenager yet. If life was fair, I wouldn't have been left standing in the middle of the parking lot and then tossed in jail as if I was a common criminal. If life was fair, I wouldn't have been thrown out on the streets like a stray dog left to fend for myself. If life was fair, I wouldn't have lost my virginity to a pedophile while his wife watched."

Savannah has to stop to throw up in a nearby garbage can. In truth, I want to be right there hurling with her. The rage coursing through my body right now has my adrenaline levels off the chart. My hands are shaking as I'm holding her hair back as she is puking so violently the only thing coming up is green bile.

Eventually, Savannah's nausea subsides and I help

her over to the couch. There is a soft knock at the office door and I get up from the couch to check it out. I'm surprised to see Ketki on the other side with a tray.

"I brought this for Aunt Savannah. I heard her throwing up. It's some ginger ale and her favorite cinnamon tea. There are some saltines too," Ketki explains. "Casey, be gentle, but make her tell it all, okay? Even if it's making her sick," she adds in a whisper.

I nod. "Thank you. I'll do my best."

I walked back over to the couch with the tray in my hand. "Ketki brought you something to help you feel better."

"It is funny. People assume because of Ketki's odd speech pattern and hand flaps that she must be stupid and unable to understand the world around her. I think she understands more than all the rest of us combined. Sometimes, I think she can see everything written on my heart and soul."

"I haven't been around her much, but from what I've seen — I suspect you're right," I concede. "Would you like ginger ale or tea?"

"I'd like some tea, please. I'm not sick. I'm just overly emotional. This is not easy for me. When I told you I don't talk about my past. I wasn't kidding. The only other person on the planet who has heard the whole story is Shelby — and I only told her this summer."

"Oh wow, that's a hard burden to carry. I'm sorry it happened to you and that you were alone."

I pour Savannah's some tea and sweeten it with sugar before handing it to her. She takes a couple of sips and then sets it down.

"Ketki is right. I've come this far; I need to tell you

the rest of the sordid truth. I have to warn you, it's about as bad as it gets. If you want to bail on me after this, I don't blame you. It's ugly and it makes *me* ugly."

I just stare disapprovingly at her. I don't even know what to say to a comment like that.

She blushes. "Shelby looked at me the same way when I told her that."

"… and how has Shelby reacted to the story?" I ask.

"She's been great — nothing but supportive."

"Why would you expect any different from me? Am I really that much of an ogre?"

"No! It's just that you're a guy — and guys can be weird about this stuff."

"I don't know about your opinion about guys. First, you call me stupid. Then you call me weird. A guy could get a complex —" I tease lightly.

"*Touché.* I can only hope that you react as well as Shelby did. It's tough stuff and not for the faint of heart."

"Consider me forewarned. If you don't want to tell me, that's fine too. Like I said, I'm not interested in hurting you any more than you've already been hurt."

Savannah gets a faraway look in her eyes and curls up into a ball. "I don't think that's possible. You see, after the Brennans were done with me, they sold me to Mic Ricard. They pretended I was a virgin and sold me to the highest bidder. He was a sick son of a b. He kept me hostage on the top of the mountain in Colorado for nearly four years. He sadistically raped me on all but seventeen days out of every month."

"You know these guys' names and they're still running around free?" I ask, unable to keep the shock and razor-sharp anger from my voice.

"I don't really know. After I was rescued, I didn't stop running until Tristan and Mark tracked me down to be with Shelby during her cancer treatment."

"Those sickos could still be out there!" I argue before I censor my words. I want to kick myself for being so insensitive and blurting the first thought that comes to my head but fear and outrage overrule my common sense.

Savannah abruptly stands up and stalks across the room. "What makes you think I don't know that every second of every day? Think back to where I sit in your restaurant. Have you ever seen me sit with my back to the door? Have you ever seen me go into my shop after dark and not have the door locked? Do you see me go anywhere and not have my keys in my hand ready to defend myself? How many times have you come up beside me and almost been clobbered?"

"Savannah, you can't be vigilant your whole life and protect your kids."

"Well, well, here we go. Here's the rest of the ugly truth," Savannah announces with an ugly sneer. "Thanks to my rapists, I'm likely to never have another child."

Having spouted off without thinking before, I decide to wait to see if she'll tell me what she means.

Finally, she gives me a skeptical look and says, "Wow. Either you're too polite or too scared to ask me … so I'll just tell you. Right before I was rescued, I miscarried an unplanned pregnancy from Mic. Because I didn't get any medical treatment through my whole ordeal I developed pelvic inflammatory disease. The medication I take to control it makes it unlikely that I will ever get pregnant."

It takes a few more moments for me to control the anger boiling inside me enough so I can speak without scaring Savannah. I may only be a 'stupid boy' as Ketki puts it — but even I understand what a huge loss that is for Savannah.

I slowly walk over to where Savannah is standing. I reach out and lift her chin so she's looking me in the eyes. "Savvy, I'm sorry they took so much from you that you can never get back. You're right, it wasn't fair and nothing I can do will ever make it fair. But, there's one thing they won't take from you — my respect and admiration. You had it on the first day we met and you have even more of it now. That won't change. Those monsters did not get that and they will never get it. What they did to you doesn't change how I feel about you, do you understand that? I think you are simply amazing."

CHAPTER FIFTEEN

SAVANNAH

I GRIP CASEY'S HAND tightly as we walk up the stairs to my sister's home. It's amazing how a few words can change everything and nothing at all. I expected my entire world to fall apart like a crumbling sandcastle at high tide—but that's not what happened. Casey is still right by my side, and my sister loves me as if nothing ever happened.

I squeeze Casey's hand and smile up at him. "You're being such a good sport about this. Not everyone would be all right with hanging out with family members for a date."

"Are you kidding? Ketki showed me pictures of her gaming cave, it's the stuff of legends. Any self-respecting gamer would want to hang out there. I'm honored she invited us."

"Be honest with me — there's a very real possibility I'll be ditched for Ketki and a game controller today, isn't there?"

Casey looks down at me. His eyes are surrounded by laugh lines, and his smile is bright. "That's not fair. I promised never to lie to you, so you've got me boxed into a corner. I've got no choice but to tell you that you're probably right. Inside every grown man who can operate a computer, I think there's a kid who cut his teeth on Nintendo."

"Oh, relax. I won't take your Mario Brothers membership card away." I smirk. "I'm just happy Ketki has found another kindred spirit. I always feel out of place when I come over because although Shelby can compete with her like a champ, somehow I never picked up the knack."

"No worries. I got you covered," Casey assures me as he shows me a mysterious grocery bag.

"I'm afraid to ask what you've got in there," I respond with a grimace.

"Only the key to Ketki's heart," Casey brags smugly.

"If you got pizza in there, it's going to be a colossal mess."

"Not if you make pizza my way."

"I'm afraid you're going to vastly outshine me in the kitchen too. I get by, but my cooking skills are nothing to brag about. I doubt Ketki will be overly impressed—"

"Come on, we'll make it together. It's gnarly."

I laugh at Casey's California slang, yet another word sticks out too. Together. I'm still not used to that concept. I've been alone for so many years, I never thought together would ever apply to me. After I lost my family, I never thought I would ever see any of them again. I *never* expected I'd be hand-in-hand with a man. Not just any man, a very tall, handsome man who pushes all of my boundaries and buttons. Yet, as much as he challenges me, he has made sure I know he's in my corner.

The other day, my air conditioner finally gave up the ghost, even after the landlord assured me it had been completely serviced and properly repaired. Rather than take over the situation, Casey called around and located a few reputable general contractors for me, but he let me interview them. After I had chosen one, he stood silently by my side as I met with Mark to draft a letter to my landlord. We informed Oscar that I would be deducting the cost of the repair from my rent. Coincidently, we were having dinner when my landlord finally returned my call about the matter. Casey's calm and steady hand on my knee was all I needed to hold my ground in the face of my landlord's less than charitable threats. Not surprisingly, when faced with a second letter from my soon-to-be brother-in law's law firm, Hunters Crossing, Oscar quickly backed down.

When I asked Casey about it later, he told me when he reunited with his mom, she told him during the divorce and custody fight over him, it wasn't the lack of money which totally demoralized her, it was the fact that his dad completely stripped her of the ability to make any decisions. He doesn't want me to feel the same way.

Considering the volatile stuff I laid in his lap, he's done a pretty good job of keeping a lid on his macho tendencies. I can tell he'd like to go after Mic, Reggie, and Esther. I don't think Casey quite understands that after so many years of putting as much distance between them and me as humanly possible, I don't relish the thought of inviting them back into my universe—even if it does mean jail time for them.

As I always do, I take a deep breath to prepare myself for interacting with other people. It's incredibly frustrating for me because it doesn't even seem to matter if it's people I want to be with, I'm still frightened. My heart beats a million miles an hour and my palms are sweaty. Casey notices my reaction, and he gently squeezes my hands. "Not going anywhere. I'll be here until you ask me to leave."

Shelby's front door flies open and Ketki runs out onto the porch. "Where's Blue? I want to show him the spot I made for him so we can all play video games together. I hope it's big enough for him because he is a huge dog. But … I think it is."

Ketki's antics make me smile as I tease, "Well, hello to you too. I'm so glad I can provide a taxi service for my dog today."

"That's a very funny joke, Aunt Savannah. Did you bring anything for me to eat?"

"Well, Casey brought —" I reply as Ketki grabs Casey's hand and drags him into the house.

"Guess what Casey?" she announces excitedly. "Tristan says we can play his new prototype game today. I've run through it a bunch of times, but he wants somebody who's never played before to give it a shot. So, he said today was a good day to practice it."

"That's cool," Casey says, dropping my hand to give her a high five. "What's it called?"

Ketki looks at Casey with disbelief on her face. "Don't you know anything about secret testing? We can't talk about the product name. That's radically against protocol. People might steal Tristan's hard work. For now, we just call the game P4K."

"Ketki, how long have you been helping Tristan with his video game business?" Casey asks.

"I dunno, I guess it's been close to two years since I

signed my first NDA."

Casey looks at me quizzically as he mouths, "She signed a NDA?"

Ketki looks back and forth between us with a look of pure astonishment. "Wow! He is a real noob. I thought everybody knew about nondisclosure agreements."

"Kiddo, you might have a leg up on the legal jargon, given the fact that your dad is an attorney." I set the sack of groceries down on the kitchen counter. "Are you guys planning to eat or play video games first?" I knew it was a silly question the moment it passed my lips but, for some reason, I asked it anyway.

Casey and Ketki look at each other and announce in unison, "Play!"

I grab a bottle of soda and a quilt and settle in beside them as I listen to my niece explain the game to Casey. Ketki abruptly turns to me. "Are you sure you don't want to play? It's super fun. I'm going to video chat with some other players today. That's one of the cool new features Tristan incorporated into this new game. We won't all be avatars anymore; we'll be able to talk in real time as we're playing. It'll be so rad."

"Isn't that a little dangerous?" Casey asks. "You don't want people to know where you live and what you really look like online."

Ketki shrugs as she responds, "I know, but Tristan has done all sorts of filters and backtracking of IP addresses so players can't figure out where other players are located."

A shiver travels down my spine. "What about what you're revealing on camera? Wouldn't somebody be able to guess where your house is based on what's inside?"

Ketki ponders that for a moment before she responds, "No, I don't think so. You know the technology that Snapchat uses to put all sorts of silly filters on your face? You know? The one that makes you look like a dog or a princess? Well, Tristan developed something like that to completely block out the background behind people when they are playing this game. You can put yourself in the middle of a castle, a battle scene, or one of the pyramids. It's super cool. I like it because it means I can play in here and the players don't get all distracted by my other gaming systems. When I Skype with other players, a lot of times they want to talk about my other games— especially when they see my vintage stuff."

I take a moment to look around the library which doubles as Ketki's gaming room and once again I am astonished to see how well decked out it is. It puts many arcades to shame.

Casey whistles under his breath. "I can understand why they would feel that way. I'm a little jealous of your digs myself."

Ketki changes all the batteries out of her game controllers and fiddles with the resolution on her monitors before she answers Casey. "When I was little, I used to think this stuff would make people like me more. Now I know that's not true. These days, I try to focus on making it matter less."

"I have to say, you rock," Casey praises with a wide smile.

"Yeah? Some days I suck at it. People can be really mean," Ketki replies succinctly. "Are you ready to play P4K? The object of this game is to build a survival camp before the rival team. But every action you take to destroy your rival team will adversely influence your own team.

Every nice thing you do for your rival team will be magnified in your own team."

Abruptly, she looks at me. "Oh snap! What time is it?"

I glance down at my cell phone and respond, "Just past 7:15, why?"

"I was supposed to meet E-Glam Gram and Big Joe Joe in the chat room at seven. They're probably waiting for me."

Casey leaned forward on the couch and claps his hands together with excitement before he grabs one of the controls. "Let's get this show on the road. I have never been in on the development of a game before. This is the bomb!"

Ketki giggles. "Hold your horses! I don't even have a profile set up for you yet. What's your favorite screen name?"

Casey looks back at me and winks. "Well, some folks call me Folgers 911."

Ketki nods slightly as she types it into the gaming console. "Clever. I like it." She turns toward me and asks, "Aunt Savannah, are you sure you don't want me to set you up one too?"

I shake my head as I take a sip of my drink. "No, I'm good. I'd just slow you guys down. I'll simply watch."

I wait with anticipation as a series of intricate graphics come up accompanied by dramatic music.

"Nice tunes!" comments Casey.

"Jade's husband, Declan, wrote that. He got a contract with Aidan O'Brien to write some songs. Isn't that cool?"

Suddenly two cave-like structures come up on the screen. "Oh, there they are. I wonder what backdrop they'll choose. I like outer space, so I chose to float through space. Casey, in case you can't tell, I'm Stones," Ketki instructs as she clicks through a bunch of screens.

"I put you in ancient Greece, but if you'd like to be somewhere else, that's cool too."

Ketki's words fade out as I focus on the images on the screen. At first, I can't even speak. I just blankly stare, unable to believe what I'm seeing. Finally, I'm able to find my words. "Ketki, you actually know these people? Have you played with them before? Do you know their names?" I ask sharply, sounding like a machine gun.

Ketki quickly closes the screens and mutes her microphone. "Geez! Way to be rude." She rolls her eyes at me and gives me an angry look. "I told you who they were. That's E-Glam-Gram and Big Joe Joe. I don't know their real names, only Tristan and Marcus know that kind of stuff. We've been working on the prelims for this project for months."

I jump off the couch and squat down in front of Ketki so I am between her and the monitor. "Ketki, this is probably the most important thing you will ever hear from me. I need you to listen to me. Do you understand?"

"I'm not retarded! I have autism. I thought you knew the difference," Ketki throws her control down on the couch.

"I'm not saying this because of your autism, I'm saying this because you are my niece, and I love you."

"What's going on? Why did you stop my game?" Ketki asks stubbornly.

"I don't know what's going on — but I think it's

more important than your game. Take a second to look at your aunt's face," Casey instructs gently.

Ketki uncrosses her arms and flexes her fingers as she tries to control her hand flaps which get worse when she's emotional. She searches my face for clues. "Aunt Savannah, is he right? Is there something wrong?"

I stand up and sit down on the couch pulling Ketki down next to me. I shift my position until I'm facing her. She is watching me with trepidation. I'm sure she believes that she's in trouble, but there is no way to convey the gravity of the situation without giving that impression. I feel horrible for that, but I have no other choice. I look at Casey helplessly as I struggle to find my words, but he doesn't understand what I need from him because he doesn't know what I'm about to say.

"Remember when Casey was asking you about the potential danger of meeting people face-to-face in your game?"

Ketki nods solemnly.

"That danger isn't merely philosophical now. The people who you've been playing with are extremely evil people who victimize young girls and they should have been in jail a long time ago."

"E-Glam-Gram and Big Joe Joe are criminals?" Ketki asks incredulously. "I don't understand. They seem so nice. They were always interested in everything I do in school. They didn't care that I'm a huge computer nerd or that I collect feathers and stones."

"Yep. That's exactly how they operate."

"How do you know this? Maybe you made a mistake. You didn't see my monitor for very long — maybe it's not them. Did you see them on television or something?

Sometimes those mugshots can be misleading."

The more agitated Ketki gets, the more her hands flap, and the odder her speech pattern becomes.

Finally, I reach out and place my hands on her shoulders as I bare my soul. "Ketki, I know. Okay? I know them and I know their names aren't actually E-Glam-Gram and Big Joe Joe. Their names are actually Esther and Reginald Brennan."

Ketki holds stock still. "Really? You mean they lied?"

I nod carefully. "Yes. They lied and much, much worse. They are known pedophiles."

Ketki's jaw goes slack as my words sink in. "Are you telling me even with Tristan's firewalls, a couple of pervs got through? Tristan'll blow his top!"

"That's exactly what I'm telling you. You can't play the game until Tristan figures it out. Do you understand me? It's very important. Don't even log on. Esther and Reggie are the most dangerous people I have ever met in my life," I struggle to swallow because my mouth is so dry. My fear is a palpable thing and I fight to keep it at bay so I can focus on helping my niece. Yet, with every second that passes, my panic grows.

Ketki's body stiffens before she scrambles off the couch. "I don't know where Tristan is, but I know where Mom and Dad are. I think we need their help." Ketki drops her controller on the floor and runs from the room.

As soon as she's gone, I curl up into a ball and start to shake. I am so glad Casey knows my secret and I don't have to explain my near catatonic state or try to cover for the fact that I've checked out of reality for the moment.

Casey picks up one of the baby-soft blankets Shelby

learned to crochet during her cancer treatments. Without saying a word, he walks over to the couch and gently scoops me up and places me on his lap as he wraps us both in the blanket. For several minutes, Casey just sits there and absorbs my pain. He says nothing because there really is nothing to be said. What can he say when the monsters who haunt my dreams are haunting my reality too?

CHAPTER SIXTEEN

CASEY

What just happened? Okay, that's not exactly what I mean … I can figure that much out by myself. What I can't understand is the how and the why—and the how in the heck am I supposed to help Savannah now?

Savannah isn't a particularly small woman; she is nearly as tall as me and quite strong, but at this moment, she seems fragile and delicate in my arms as she trembles uncontrollably. I'm unable to do anything but silently hold her as tears stream down her face and into her hairline. I concentrate on slowing my breathing down, hoping she'll follow suit. I try not to think of all the things I'd like to do to her rapists. Since I now have names and faces to go with the images I've built up in my imagination, my mind is spinning with ideas, and none of them are especially wholesome or legal.

One thing is surprising. From the moment she told me her story, I've tried to visualize who these people might be. I haven't talked to Savannah about this because I don't want to upset her, but her nightmares have become mine. In the moments before I drift off to sleep, I wonder about the animals who savagely robbed her of her innocence. Today, I found out those animals look just like everyone else. They could very easily be one of the couples who play bingo with Mabel and Gretchen. That thought is enough to make my heart stop.

As I run my hand in small circles across Savannah's back, I realize her breathing has slowed and she has stopped sobbing. I pull her hair back from her face and examine her. "Are you going to be okay?"

"No, I don't know if I'll ever be okay. They were a couple of mouse clicks away from my niece. Do you understand that? *They could've gotten Ketki.* I don't know if it was an accident of fate or if they targeted her. Those sickos never stopped, they're just working on another generation using new technologies. This time, it's not soup, it's video games." Savannah's voice climbs as she becomes more upset. "Casey! They almost got her." She starts to tremble violently again. "They almost got her. No one would've known what happened to her. What if we wouldn't have been here when she first played the game? What if I hadn't recognized them?"

I gently stroke her hair. "You can't go there —you'll drive yourself crazy. I know it's hard because I did that after Ashlyn died. I tried to think of all the scenarios I could've done differently to save her — but it didn't change the fact that she was dead. Right now, Ketki is okay and they can't victimize anyone else in the game because the game isn't live yet. It's only a prototype, remember?"

Savannah struggles to sit up and I hand her a napkin from the coffee table where we had set up snacks earlier. As she collects herself, I say, "It's been a long time since

I've had anything to do with the programming end of things, but back in the day when I used to play around with this stuff, an opportunity like this is a gold mine. When you find a vulnerability before the release date, it's like a Christmas gift wrapped in gold leaf paper."

"Casey! Shut up! That's Ketki we're talking about, they could've gotten my niece," Savannah shouts.

Mark and Shelby burst through the office door. Ketki trails closely behind holding an iPad.

"Actually, I've got Tristan here on FaceTime. He tells me it's a little more complicated. They wouldn't have been able to get too far with the information they had, but it was still too close a call for my taste," Mark explains in a rush.

"Ketki, you mentioned they were really interested in your problems at school. What did you tell them about those?" I ask, fearing the worst. I know how people are at my coffee shop, I can only imagine what she might be tempted to share at the computer keyboard from the privacy of her own home.

"I told you, my dad taught me about all this stuff a long time ago. As far as those jerks are concerned, I'm a junior at Ridgemont High School and I'm dating the most popular football player on campus and we are planning to go to college at the University of Texas in a couple years."

Shelby lets out a gasp of surprise. "Wow! I didn't know you were such an accomplished liar."

"They lied too!" Ketki insists defensively. "At least I didn't lie about what kind of person I am. I fibbed for a very good reason."

"You're right. You did. Your dad asked you to

disguise your identity when playing role-playing games and you did exactly what we told you to do. I am so grateful that you paid attention to our instructions. In this case, it might have saved you from a lot of trouble. For the foreseeable future until Tristan tells you it's safe, do me a favor and play only your old school games which don't require an Internet hookup, okay?" Shelby says as she puts her arm around Ketki and kisses the top of her head.

Ketki nods slowly. "No problem. It's so creepy that I might just go back to playing chess against Dad in the real world." Looking down at her tablet, she asks Tristan "What are you gonna tell the gaming club?"

Through the speakers, I hear Tristan respond, "I've already made P4K unplayable. I'm the only person who can put it back on line."

"It royally sucks that the bad guys are winning. P4K is a great game, they shouldn't be able to take it away from us. Evil shouldn't win all the time," Ketki declares, her voice rough with frustration.

"I totally agree with you. There are a bunch of folks in this room who don't want to let that happen," I say, pointing to everyone in the room and looking directly at the iPad. "Today's development was a setback for sure, but you have to give us some time to come up with a plan. I promise you we'll be on it. None of us want those guys to get off lightly."

"What if they go after Aunt Savannah again?" Ketki asks as she chews on her bottom lip.

"It might have been a coincidence. We have no information to indicate the creeps were targeting me specifically," Savannah says as she gamely tries to reassure her niece.

"But, you don't have any information that says they're not. You live in a super safe place. I think you should go back there. Besides, I don't feel much like playing games tonight. I want you to be protected from bad guys," Ketki awkwardly pats Savannah's face. She turns to me and declares, "I'm counting on you to keep her safe — you are her boyfriend, right? It's like your job."

"I'm planning on it. As her boyfriend, I do consider it my most important job right now." After she scampers off, I look down at the iPad she left on the coffee table and ask Tristan "Is it all right if I come into Identity Bank next week?"

"Sure, I'll be in town."

"Mark, you may want to sit in on this," I add. I turn to Savannah. "Do you want to be there?"

Savannah holds up her hand. "No thank you, I've dealt with Esther and Reggie enough to last a whole lifetime. If I never see or talk about them again, it will be soon enough."

Savannah hugs Shelby. "Please tell Ketki I'm sorry it had to end this way. Hopefully, soon, we'll have a family get-together where my past doesn't come back to haunt me."

After all the turmoil, I drove Savannah home. As we walk to the front door, and gather her hair up and pull it away from her face as I thread my fingers through it and tilt her chin up. Gently, I place my lips on hers as I tenderly kiss her good night. After several moments, I reluctantly pull away and unlock her front door.

"Where are you going?" Savannah tugs on my shirt collar. "I liked you where you were." She captures my lips in a deep and thorough kiss.

"Just trying to be a gentleman here." I maneuver us through the door. Savannah kicks off her shoes at the door. I remove her purse from her shoulder and help her out of her jacket as she pulls me by the hand toward her couch.

"Maybe I've decided I'm sick and tired of playing by the rules." Savannah backs away from me and, in one fluid movement, pulls her shirt over her head.

"Are you s-s-sure?" I stammer at the unexpected sight. Under any circumstances, Savannah is enough to take my breath away, but standing in her living room in nothing more than a barely-there lacy black bra and a pair of threadbare Levi's is just naturally erotic.

When she nods, her wild blonde hair tumbles into her face in a riotous mass of blonde curls. "Yes, I'm sure. I'm totally sure. I have spent more than half of my life running from these people. I've avoided every possibility of a relationship for almost two decades. I have watched as every person I know has fallen in love while I don't even have any friends."

It's a good thing she doesn't expect me to say anything because I am totally speechless.

She stalks over to her purse and grabs her hairbrush as if we have this conversation every day with her standing around in lingerie. She brushes her hair in long angry strokes.

"I can't believe I wasted all that time trying to protect myself. Darn it, Casey! I could've had a normal life. I could've gone to school, had a boyfriend and a regular job at McDonald's. I could've worked with kids or at a nursing home. I could've gone on dates with handsome guys — or not so handsome guys if that's who I fell in love with. I could've gone dancing or on picnics or gone to the fair. I didn't have to let them ruin my whole life!" she exclaims as she nearly tears her hair out by the roots.

I walk up behind her and carefully remove the brush from her hand and gently wrap my arms around her while I rest my chin on the top of her head.

"Savvy, stop this, baby. You had no way of knowing that. You did the best you could. You survived. That's all anyone could ask of you—especially you."

I sit down on the fireplace hearth. I position Savannah on a big throw pillow between my knees as I brush her hair in long even strokes. There is something innately soothing about this activity. She is like a cat who has found a patch of afternoon sun.

After she starts to relax, I continue, "You are one of the most extraordinary people I have ever met and I have met a lot of people. I know people like Esther and Reggie, I know what kind of scams they run. I know how life is on the streets. I didn't learn that crap from books. I lived that life for more than three years. You develop some weird, paranoid habits while at the same time having to trust a whole underground system of checks and balances which don't exist in the normal outside world. If you never lived it, you don't understand it. If you've lived it, you never forget it."

"So, you understand how stupid I was to be a victim. I, of all people should have known better." Savannah groans out loud. "They must've thought I was the easiest mark ever. I bought everything they said hook line and sinker. I was still buying it almost twenty years later. The only thing that woke me up was seeing them going after Ketki. Well, that ends today. I'm claiming my life back."

"I'm proud of you," I say squeezing her shoulders. "But what does that have to do with us? Why this?" I ask as I run my thumb along the lacy edge of her bra.

Savannah reaches up and grabs the brush from my hand and flings it over on the couch. "Oh my gosh, I can't believe you're making me do this the hard way when all I really want is you."

Of their own volition, my fingertips do a slow dance up and down her arms. "Do you really want me or would just anyone do?"

"Okay, that's a little rude," she answers with exasperation. "No, I'm not just looking for something with a heartbeat. I've had a crush on you since the very first day I met you and everything I've found out about you since has only reinforced that crush. Of course, I want you." She pulls out of my arms and spins around to face me. She licks her lips the way she does when she's nervous. "Somehow, I thought this would be easier. I mean, I haven't done this in a while — but I was under the impression men thought about sex all the time and if I offered it, you would jump at the chance."

"Trust me when I say wanting you has never been the issue."

"So, why are we even still talking about this?"

"Because I don't want you to regret this decision tomorrow. I care about you too much to be something you do just to scare away the ghosts of your past. I want to be your future," I explain.

The light fades from Savannah's eyes and I wonder why I am fighting so hard to do the right thing. It's not rocket science — I want this woman like I've wanted few others. I haven't so much as looked at anyone else since she showed up in my life. So why doesn't this feel like a no-brainer? Why can't I just take the easy way?

My eyes roam over her, taking in her lithe, lean body bathed in the soft light of the reading lamps. As enticing as I find her body, it is her face which captures my attention. She looks shattered.

Standing, I pull her up into my arms. "It'll be all right. I hate seeing you in this much pain. What can I do?"

She reaches up and kisses me on the chin. "Please love me. Remind me what it's like to connect with someone and feel whole again. Don't let them take that part of me too. I trust you, Casey. I know you would never hurt me. We can sort out what it means for us on another day, but for tonight, I simply want to get lost in us and forget I ever had a past. Is that too much to ask?"

I swallow hard and try to tamp down all of my logical arguments as I respond, "You know me. I'm the ultimate people pleaser. I'd never want to let a lady down."

CHAPTER SEVENTEEN

SAVANNAH

"Why didn't you tell me?" I demand.

"Why didn't I tell you what?" Shelby slides a fried peanut butter and banana sandwich on my plate.

"That falling in love with Casey would change everything," I admit with a sigh.

"If you'll recall, I did try to tell you. You told me you were impervious to love and that it would never strike you — you said you were immune."

"I thought I was, and then Casey … happened. I don't think I'll ever be the same. Before he came into my life, I was completely independent, and now I'm not. I think about him all the time. I wonder if he's happy or sad, I wonder if his coffee shop is doing okay, I worry if he doesn't have enough customers or if he has too many, I worry if he looks too tired or if he seems like he has a cold. It's just crazy."

I tear my sandwich into bits and stick a bite in my mouth. "Do you know what I did the other day? I waited for him to call. *Me*, Savannah Lyons, sat in front of my phone and waited a whole hour for him to send me a text message or call. I don't do that garbage." I scowl at

Shelby.

She smirks with amusement. "Welcome to the world of being a couple. That's what we do. You guys *are* a couple, right?"

"Oh yes, we are very definitely a couple. There's no mistake," I admit as I turn bright red.

"Uh-huh, I see why you're so stressed out now," Shelby smiles knowingly.

"What?" I demand. "What's that look for? What are you talking about?"

"Oh, I just remember what it's like. We spent so much of our time growing up expecting things to be bad — mostly because they were. When you fall in love with the right person and things are suddenly as right in your world as they can ever be, it's just hard to make the adjustment. You wait for things to go wrong. You look for small annoyances and blow them up huge because you can't bear to look at how much happiness is in your life."

I gasp before I practically scream, "It's like you're reading my mind!"

Shelby covers her ears. "Take it easy and tell me what's going on."

"It's like you said." I shrug. "That first night was perfect. It was better than anything I had ever read in any of those books I used to sneak at the library — you know, the ones with the super cheesy covers?"

"Even better than the stories we used to make up about how knights in shining armor would rescue us from all the bad things in our lives?" Shelby says wistfully.

A tear leaks from the corner of my eye. "Yeah, even

better than those, because Casey is human. He was so scared he'd make things worse for me that he was beyond careful. I've never had anyone pay so much attention to how I felt —ever. Casey was tuned into every movement of my body and breath I took. It was almost spiritual."

"How did you do with the whole situation?" Shelby asks gently.

"Better than I expected, actually. In some ways, it feels like all the stuff that happened to me was so long ago it involved a different person. It's not always that way, but if I can keep it in that frame of mind, I do better."

"I imagine so," Shelby murmurs under her breath.

Ignoring her, I continue spilling my thoughts, "I guess I was surprised to discover having someone else touch my body feels good. I had never really had that before. You know how we were raised. Before I was abducted by the Brennans, I didn't have a chance to have a boyfriend."

"Well, there was that one kid — what was his name?"

"Camillo Durrill — oh yes, the kissing bandit. He wasn't really my boyfriend, he was just a reckless drifter who fancied himself a lady's man. I think he was all of fourteen. Still … even if I stretch my imagination, he was not my boyfriend."

"I remember wishing he was my boyfriend. He was cute!" Shelby grins.

"Camillo was cute, but he was no Casey," I concede. "Casey is somehow making it possible for me to like myself again. I haven't been able to in a couple of decades. In fact, I don't know if I fully believed in myself since the day we had to leave everything behind and say goodbye to everything normal."

"So, what's the problem? Does Casey remind you too much of the past?"

"No. Not really. Everything he does is so respectful and honest, it's nothing like the deceit and rape I experienced before. Like I said, it was like happiness, peace and pure joy wrapped up in one experience."

Shelby is trying hard not to laugh at me. "Gee, that sounds just awful. I don't know how you endure such hardship."

"Okay, fine. I'm being ridiculous — but what happens when Casey changes his mind?" I throw my hands in the air. "If experience has taught us anything, it's that people lie. People lie all the time. Casey may not mean to, but what happens when he gets tired of dealing with my crap?"

"Who's to say he'll get tired of dealing with you? You are one of the most generous, smart, amazing people I know. Why would he get tired of you?"

"Get real! I'm also paranoid as heck, scared of my own shadow, have about as much relationship experience as your average twelve-year-old, and have the social development skills of a mushroom growing in the shade. I don't exactly scream girlfriend material."

"Did Casey say any of this stuff?" Shelby asks incredulously. "If he did, he and I are going to have a few words."

"No, of course, he didn't. He didn't have to."

"So, let me get this straight: you have an amazingly hot, sweet, attentive, guy who thinks you hang the moon and make the sun shine and you're planning to preemptively wreck the relationship because of something he might think about you someday down the road because of your own insecurities?"

I nod slowly. "Yep, that about sums it up. I think it's probably better for everyone. Then, nobody gets hurt. I might as well nip this in the bud, don't you think?"

"No! I could see the two of you had something from the very first time he brought you breakfast. To back away from something potentially scary now would be totally idiotic. I will admit that Casey has the power to hurt you. Everyone we let close to us does, but that doesn't mean he's going to on purpose. He could be one of the really good guys. They are out there. Mark is one, Tristan is one, Declan is one, and don't forget Isaac … If you look around, we are surrounded by great men."

"What if he's not—"

"Savvy, what if he is? What if he's everything you've ever wished for in your wildest dreams?"

"Bye, Cassidy. Thank you for coming to my class," I say as I help one of my most dedicated students on with her coat. "I hope you'll come again." I smile as she skips down the sidewalk. Teaching second-graders the art of pottery has been more fun than I could possibly imagine. They aren't afraid to try anything.

Unfortunately, the cleanup isn't quite as fun. I am in the middle of wiping down all my equipment when Gretchen and Mabel rush through the doors of the shop.

"Savannah, we're sorry for interrupting you. Are you busy right now?"

I look around the shop and comment, "Not as busy as I wish I was for a Saturday afternoon, but I'm doing okay. What's up?"

"I don't know how to ask this, do you?" Gretchen says to Mabel.

"However you do it, I think we should hurry," Mabel responds with a worried look on her face.

My heart sinks. "What's wrong? Did something happen to Casey?"

"No, child, not as far as we know. We're not even sure this relates to you, but we think it does — so we have to ask," Gretchen says tentatively.

"Oh, for Pete's sake, just spit it out," Mabel directs.

"Okay, so, you know we have the gleaners come every couple of weeks. Well, one of them wasn't doing very well today and she collapsed in the middle of my potato field. Just right there. One minute she was up and the next minute she was down. So, we brought her to the hospital—"

"What Gretchen is taking her own sweet time to tell you, is that this lady, Nancy, is asking for you. She claims you are her daughter. Now, we took a good long look, and we suppose it's possible. You do look a bit alike."

"Is she going to live?" I ask. "What did the doctor say is wrong with her?"

"I don't rightly know," Gretchen responds. "With those newfangled health care laws, they won't tell us much."

"Did they tell George?" I ask, trying to wrap my brain around it all.

"George?" Mabel asks. "Oh, you mean the strange little fellow with her? I don't know. Last I checked, he was refusing to step foot into the hospital, claiming it was possessed by the devil."

I roll my eyes. "Yeah, that sure sounds like my dad."

"So, they are your parents?" Gretchen asks with a confused expression on her face.

"Why didn't you say something?" Mabel demands. "We would've invited them into the house for something to eat. You treat family better."

"We aren't exactly that kind of family," I try to explain.

"Well, that might change now because your mom clearly needs you," Gretchen advises.

"Give me a moment to shut everything off and let Casey know where I'm going." I start flipping off lights around the shop.

"I'll text him. I'm sure he'll want to be there," Mabel offers.

"Oh, I don't want to bother him, he's in the middle of a big promotion at the coffee shop. He's probably slammed with business right now."

"Nonsense, the only place that boy will want to be is right beside you."

I haven't seen my mom this close up in years and what strikes me is how fragile she looks. Although her skin is tan and leathery from all the sun exposure over the years, she is very thin — too thin. There are deep purple splotches under her eyes and her lips are dry and cracked. As hard as my life has been all these years, I suspect hers has not been much easier. The nomadic life is a constant grind. I wonder where they've been keeping themselves and how they've stayed alive. I wonder if this is the first time my mom's ever been hospitalized or if this is just one of many. Shelby's cancer was a wake-up call. She could have been the first in our family to get it, or it could be a family legacy, I have no way of knowing.

My mom's eyes flutter open. "Vanna? Is that you?" she asks in a whisper. I have to lean down and place my ear next to her cheek before I can hear her. Her use of my childhood nickname makes me sway on my feet. Only Casey's steadying hand on the small of my back keeps me upright.

"Yeah, Mama, I'm here." I fight back tears.

"Where's Bee?" she asks with a cough.

Her question brings me up short. I was in such a rush to get here I didn't even think about calling Shelby. "I'm not sure. Today is one of her teaching days. I haven't had a chance to call her yet."

"I sent her fiancé a text message. They will be here as soon as Mark gets out of court," Casey answers in a calm, confident voice.

From the doorway, I hear a gruff voice. "So, not only did my daughter have the bad sense to get involved with a heathen, she had to go and choose a common criminal as well?"

My heart races as white-hot rage travels through my veins. I whisper to my mom, "I'm sorry, Mama, this won't be pretty — but his words about Bee are ugly."

She blinks away tears. "They almost always are."

I whirl around on the man who is technically my dad. If it were not for the eyes staring back at me which are virtually identical to my own, I might as well be talking to a stranger.

Casey threads his fingers through mine and gives my hand a squeeze as he says softly, "Breathe."

His soft encouragement reminds me that we are in a hospital room and this is not the place for a full-blown showdown. Still, I feel like I need to say something. Shelby deserves better. Heck, even I deserve better. He doesn't know us any better than we know him.

Gripping Casey's hand even tighter, I solemnly address the man I used to adore and call Daddy, "Look, I know who you are, but I don't really *know* who you are anymore. That means you don't know me either. You also don't know my sister. You lost the right to have an opinion in our lives when you left us to fend for ourselves in a strange city in the middle of a parking lot when we were still kids. You know what? You lost the right to have any say in our lives long before that. Unfortunately, no one paid attention to what you were doing. So, Owen, Shelby, and I paid the price for your inability to make logical, sound decisions."

"Listen here, you don't talk to your elders that way —"

"With all due respect, sir, I think Savannah has earned the right to talk to you any way she pleases. If I were you, I would consider myself lucky that she's even in the same room with you. If I were in her position, I'm not sure I would have made the same decision."

My dad glances over at Casey with disdain as he takes in his intricate tattoos. "Who are you? Another mouthpiece of the devil?"

Casey smirks. "I suppose I've been called worse. Actually, I'm here because I love your daughter and I thought she might need someone in her corner."

He pivots sharply toward me as he barks, "You and your sister are such a disappointment to me. All that time we spent trying to raise you in a godly fashion and you go find criminals and heathens. We tried to keep you separate from all the riffraff, but you found it anyway."

The complete ludicrousness of the situation is not lost on me. My whole childhood was spent trying to protect my parents from one con man after another. The idea that they were protecting Shelby, Owen and me from anything is laughable. Shelby and I were the reason they had anything to eat or a shelter to sleep under. They were so busy trying to follow the strange and bizarre edicts of Reverend Pratchett that they couldn't be bothered to see after the basic tasks of everyday living.

I can't help but laugh out loud. "You have no idea what you're even saying. Do you even know what Shelby has been up to in her life?"

When my dad shakes his head, I continue. "Well, let me tell you what my little sister has been up to since you watched her being hauled away in a police car. Oh, wait … you didn't watch her be hauled away. You split before that ever happened. Anyway, Shelby managed to pull her life together and get a degree in advanced mathematics and elementary education. She now teaches kids who are too sick to go to public school. Do you know why she does that?"

My dad just stares at me as if he's daring me to continue — but I am on a roll. Nothing will stop me now.

"Well, your youngest daughter almost died of skin cancer when you guys weren't anywhere to be found to support her. So, she used her advanced college education — the education you forbade her to get — to help kids who otherwise wouldn't be able to go to school."

"My Baby Bee is a teacher now?" my mom asks softly. "I always wanted to. But then I got married and my plans changed. I always thought it was a wonderful profession."

"Don't worry, Shelby will soon have brats of her own and she will forget all about any career ambitions. All women do," my dad comments.

At the moment, I'm struggling to remember why I ever loved this man. He seems like a stranger to me. I can't remember why I ever thought we had anything in common.

"Actually, Shelby is raising a daughter. She is raising Mark's daughter. Ketki is a beautiful teenager and loves Shelby like a mom."

"Ketki? What kind of name is that?"

"Ketki and Mark are Cherokee," Casey answers.

"Oh great, my daughter is probably raising some other man's child because he's too drunk to do it himself."

"Dad! You have no idea what you're talking about. Can you just shut up until you do?"

"Well, you said the guy was in court —"

"I did. The reason Mark is in court is because he is an attorney. He owns the firm, Dad." I answer, clamping my jaw shut.

"I never trusted lawyers anyway, they're all corrupt."

I throw my hands up in the air. "I give up. You are bound and determined to think whatever you want to believe. If you want to believe the worst about Shelby and me, feel free. We have functioned just fine for more than half of our lives without you in it; I expect we'll continue."

My mom lets out a sob. "Please don't say that. I don't want him to behave this way."

I glance down at my mom, who looks like a shell of her former self. If I can't win an argument with my father, I guess my mom has little or no chance. I let the matter drop for now.

"Mom, what do they think is wrong with you?"

"Well, I guess I got a little dehydrated in this heat and got myself a kidney infection and some kidney stones."

"Can you believe they want to keep her in this place because she can't pee right? It's nothing a little church service and a little water won't take care of."

Casey sees the color flare in my cheeks and wisely intervenes, "Mr. Lyons, I'm getting a little claustrophobic in here; let's say you and I go take a walk."

My dad claps him on the back. "I'm glad to see you're a man after my own heart. I've never had any use for these quack doctors and hospitals. I think it's a waste of money."

As I watch them walk from the hospital room, it's all I can do to bite my tongue and stop myself from giving my honest opinion of what I think of the whole situation. When I turn back around, I notice that my mother has fallen back asleep. I pull up a chair and sit down beside her. I grasp her hand and whisper, "Oh Gosh! Mom, how can I help you?"

My mom's eyes never open, but she whispers quietly, "More than anything, I want a house; a real house with walls, windows, doors, and a roof. I want something to call my own. I want to stop moving. I want to have family dinners and a place to keep books and clothes. I want to make friends and plant a garden. I want to grow marigolds and daffodils. I would like to plant a lemon tree and make a lemon meringue pie from lemons right outside my front door. I want to meet Shelby's daughter and her fiancé. I want your boyfriend to tell me what it's like to get a tattoo."

I smile through my tears. "I'm sure as soon as Shelby and Mark get here, we can make all those arrangements. I guess the only thing you'll have to decide is whether you want to have a place with or without Dad."

My mom sighs as she confesses, "I don't actually know today. Can I wait to see if that foolhardy man comes to his senses and decides to act like a reasonable human being?"

I stroke my mom's cheek. "Sure thing, Mama. I just want to see you get better and be happy."

Chapter Eighteen

Casey

It's a good thing my shop is quiet today because Tristan and Mark brought the meeting to me. It's turning out to be significantly more complicated than I ever expected. I knew the crap would hit the fan when we started dealing with the Brennan's, but I had no idea things were going to erupt with Savannah's parents.

Things have become so uncomfortable; it's like we are all holding our breath to see what happens next. For the time being, Savannah's mom is staying in the little cottage behind Jade's parent's house. Shelby used to live there before she moved in with Mark. George is angry that Nancy wants to change their lifestyle, so he has elected to stay on the streets. I don't know Savannah's mother well enough to understand whether she is upset or relieved by his decision—but she already looks healthier. Mabel and Gretchen have adopted Nancy into their inner circle and she is making a few friends.

I hang up the closed sign and take a hot pot of coffee to the back table where Mark and Tristan are seated. "Is black okay with everyone?" I ask, as I hear a knock on the front door.

"Oh, I forgot to tell you — Isaac is joining us," Tristan says as he shuffles his papers.

Instinctively, my stomach tightens when I hear those words. I've hung around this group of guys long enough to know if Isaac Roguen is involved in a case, something serious is about to go down.

I rush to unlock the door. "I wish I could say I'm happy to see you, but something tells me you're probably not bringing good news." I escort the former Federal law enforcement agent to the table.

"You're honest, *amigo*. I like that in a man. It makes my job much easier." Isaac shakes my hand before he takes a seat next to his son-in-law.

"Did you get any results from the search warrant?" Tristan asks his father-in-law.

Isaac looks both intense and glum at the same time. It's a disconcerting expression. "I did. The news is not encouraging. The threat is closer and wider than we thought."

"Isaac, I need you to put that in plain old English for me," Mark says in a lethal voice. "How much danger is my daughter in?"

"We don't have evidence which indicates Ketki was specifically targeted because of her identity," Isaac answers carefully.

"In other words, you don't have evidence that she wasn't either, correct?" Mark asks astutely.

"Well, obviously, Ketki's close, personal relationship with one of the Brennan's former victims gives us a great deal of concern."

The way Tristan forms that sentence catches my

attention. "*One* of their former victims? You mean there are more?"

Tristan nods tightly as he responds, "Several. Over many decades."

"Son of a —!" I roar. "You know, this will destroy Savannah. She will feel guilty about each and every victim regardless of whether it's her fault. She says she thought there were other victims even younger than herself, but she was never certain because they kept her drugged."

"That's what I hate the most about these kinds of cases," Isaac comments sadly. "Even if we catch the bad guy, the damage is already done."

"These perverts hurt my family and scared the crap out of my daughter. Just tell me where to find them. I don't care if I lose my law license over this, it'd be worth it." Mark stretches out his arms and cracks his knuckles.

"I'd advise you to stand down—we've got the resources to deal with this correctly—but, they are close. Too close. We suspected they were bouncing their IP addresses around. So we got a more detailed search warrant to allow us to ask more specific questions of their Internet provider. It turns out that they are not playing any games. They are in the state."

I look at Tristan directly. "You still run that charity which grants people their lifelong dream if they've worked hard—*Identity something...* ?"

He looks confused for a moment "Yeah, Rogue is still on the board of the Identity of the Heart Foundation. I didn't know you even knew about that stuff."

"I've been following your career since you were in college. I might run a coffee shop now, but I'm still a techie at heart. You run your business and your life the way I wish my dad would've run his. I keep up on all your charitable stuff," I explain.

"That's fascinating, but what does it have to do with anything?" Tristan asks.

I stick my hand in my pocket and fish out my keys. I stand up and walk over to Tristan and drop them in front of him on the table. "Do me a favor. Please try to make sure someone gets this shop who truly needs it. Maybe a single mom somewhere who is escaping a bad marriage or maybe a recovering drug addict who is clean and sober and can't find a job anywhere else. I want somebody to have the chance to start over in life like I did."

Mark's brows furrow. "Are you giving Tristan your business lock, stock, and barrel? Why in the world would you do that? Didn't you just get this place a few years ago?"

"I need to get Savannah to a safe place and I can't be in two places at once. If Tristan gives my business to someone who really needs it, it will at least be a win for somebody."

Mark clears his throat uncomfortably. "I'm not sure you need to go this far. Perhaps you could simply sublease your business or hire a manager or sell franchise rights to your restaurant. What you're planning seems like career suicide."

"I understand what you're saying, but in order for me to protect Savannah, she needs my undivided attention. I can't be trying to salvage my business and save her at the same time. I made that mistake once and I don't intend to make it again."

"So, that's it? You're planning to give up everything

you've built?" Mark asks. "No backup plan? No Plan B?"

"I have little choice here. I have loved three women in my life. Well, that's not exactly true. Technically, I guess it's been more like two women and my best friend who happened to be a girl — but I managed to let two out of three of those women down. I wasn't technically in a position to save my mom from my dad's physical, emotional and mental torture, but it never stopped me from feeling responsible for what happened to her before my dad crashed and burned."

Mark stops drinking coffee. "But —"

I hold up my hand to interrupt his speech "In many ways, I guess I also feel responsible for my dad's descent into addiction. I know it's stupid, but there's a part of me that wonders if I had only been more like him, would he have been more interested in me and less interested in drugs?"

Marcus shakes his head at me. "I can tell you from my own experiences with my brother, they don't much care what we do — it's pretty much all about the strength of the addiction."

I nod my head in agreement as I respond, pointing to my head. "I know that too … up here. When I was sixteen years old, I wasn't able to keep my best friend Ashlyn away from drugs. She came on to the streets addicted and she died addicted. She took terrible risks to stay high even though we talked for hours about what drugs did to my family and countless friends. On the day she died, she was doing stupid things to earn money to get me new clothes. I should've been taking care of *her*, not the other way around."

Isaac stirs his coffee slowly. "I'm sorry, son.

Unfortunately, that story is all too common, but it doesn't make it your fault."

"I love my mom and Ashlyn was the only friend I had in the world for three years, but my feelings don't begin to even approach what I feel for Savannah. She is terrified of the Brennan's."

Isaac looks at his phone and frowns.

"If the Brennans are anywhere near here, I need to get her as far away from Florida as possible. If that means giving up everything I've built here, so be it. I can rebuild. I've done it before, I'll do it again. None of this is as important to me as she is."

"I understand how you feel, I would probably do the same thing for Shelby, but how will you survive?" Mark presses.

"I've got a backup plan. I'd rather not use it if I don't have to because my dad had a hand in making it, but I will if it means keeping Savannah safe. My mom had the foresight to squirrel away some stock in Apple and Microsoft back when Steve Jobs and Bill Gates were not such household names. Normally, the stock just sits there because I don't actually consider it mine, but it technically is. If I have to tap into it, I will."

"Nice," Tristan remarks. "But what about Savannah's business? She just reopened it, and she won't want to turn around and close it again."

I shrug. "I didn't say my plan was without flaws. I don't know how this will unfold, I just know I need to get her out of here. You guys haven't heard the whole story and it's not mine to tell. Let me tell you; it would give you nightmares."

"Where will you go?" Isaac asks me.

I look at Isaac for a long time. "I don't think I should tell you. It would be safer for everyone involved if no one knows where we are until these creeps are caught."

"Fair enough," Isaac responds pressing his lips together in a grimace. "Just leave us contact information so we can reach you."

"Okay — now I have to go home and tell my girlfriend who hates to be uprooted that I'm taking her to a mystery location for an undetermined amount of time for reasons I can't fully explain. That ought to go over really well."

"I have no great advice for you other than try to make it sound as romantic as possible," Mark suggests.

I roll my eyes. "Gee thanks. Is that the best your sharp legal mind can do?"

"Hey man, I gotta work with what I'm given," Mark quips.

"Me too — but it doesn't mean that this won't suck big time."

"Take good care of my soon-to-be sister-in-law. Shelby and Ketki love her to pieces. They pretty much worship the ground she walks on."

I respectfully shake Mark's hand. "Trust me, they are not the only ones. I will do everything in my power to keep her safe. That's the only reason why I'm making this move."

Tristan blows out a deep breath. "I hope she trusts you enough to understand that you are doing this because you love her. It won't be easy on your relationship."

I shoot him a sideways grin. "For some reason, we seem to specialize in tough."

CHAPTER NINETEEN

SAVANNAH

"CASEY, THIS ISN'T FUNNY!" I peer out the window anxiously. "Why can't you tell me where we're going? The last time someone did this to me, they kept me hostage for almost four years. Don't you understand why this is freaking me out?" I pace up and down the aisle of the small plane.

Casey stands up and guides me back to a seat. To call them airline seats is a bit of a misnomer, they are more like recliners in the sky. "Savvy, relax. You know these pilots. This is Tristan's decked out private plane. It's one of the most bizarre perks of having him and Rogue as friends. I still can't believe he lets us borrow this baby whenever we need it. Rogue told me you met these pilots when you and Shelby went to Jessica's wedding. Tristan's people would never hurt you, okay? *I* would never hurt you."

"Then why can't you tell me where we're going? Why are we leaving Florida? This is crazy. Who packs up their entire life and disappears? Oh, wait my parents did. They went and followed a crazy person. Is that what we're doing? Are we going to go wander around the country for twenty years?" I ask sarcastically.

Casey laces his fingers through mine and kisses the back of my hand. "I know I'm asking a lot here. Still, I need you to understand I love everything about you and I want to do everything I can to keep you safe — even if what we need to do seems extreme. Don't you trust me?"

I can read the terror in Casey's eyes as he looks at me. "Against every instinct I have, I do trust you. Despite the odds, I've fallen in love with you. Still, I thought we agreed that it wouldn't do me any good to run."

"I know what I said. That was before we found out Esther and Reggie were within a few miles of you. I can't risk your safety. I held my best friend as she died. I will *not* let someone else get hurt on my watch."

"Wait! You mean to tell me they're actually in the state of Florida?" I feel a couple beats behind the conversation. "What did I ever do to them? I was only a skinny teenager, with no education or skills. Why are they still after me?" I ask, nearly crushing the bottle of iced tea in my hand. After a moment, a sickening thought occurs to me and I blurt, "Casey, if I'm in danger, Ketki isn't safe either. What about her? Who is protecting her?"

Casey runs a soothing hand across my shoulders. "Arrangements are being made for Ketki and your sister. I don't know what their plans are — just as they don't know ours. If we are clueless about what's going on, there is nothing for us to inadvertently let slip in conversation."

"Oh no, I just found Shelby. Does this mean I'll never see her again?" Panic makes my voice squeak as I sob under my breath.

"No, I don't think there is a chance on earth that'll happen. Isaac and his people are on the case. They've practically adopted Shelby and consider Ketki to be their granddaughter. They want these people caught. I still don't know what exactly Tristan and Isaac do, but they've got more connections than I've got coffee beans."

"But you don't have any coffee beans anymore! You gave your coffee shop away. Who does that? Have you lost your mind? The last person I saw do something like this wandered around the country for almost two decades. My mom has fought to get a house for years. I would say you don't understand what it's like, but you do know. So, why are we doing this again? How will we live? I don't have any marketable skills. Nobody will hire me in the real world. I only have a GED. I can't compete with young kids flipping burgers at a fast food joint. The last time I had a real job, I sold shoes at a mall, and I was terrible at it. How will we survive, Casey? Do you have any answers for that or will I have to beg for food again?"

"I know it's hard to understand why I can't tell you anything right now. Please trust me when I say I've got it all covered. There are parts of my past I can't explain to you."

"Yeah, I know you told me you grew up rich and then your dad became a junkie. It happens," I snap.

Casey sighs and scrubs his hands down his face. "Up until then, my parents were good people, smart people, people who did well in business. So, they made solid decisions about my future," Casey looks pensive as he gazes out the window.

"So, what are you trying to tell me?" My voice vibrates with frustration. "I suppose you're going to say you got secret money hidden all over the world and you're the heir to some oil fortune somewhere," I remark dismissively.

Casey cringes. "Oil, no. Stocks — more than my fair share. Mansions, not so much. Dad blew through our money … literally."

I can't help it, I laugh out loud. This is too absurd. "So, let me get this straight; you are … like … rolling in the dough, but you spent several years homeless, and you bust your butt every day from sun up to sundown to work in a coffee shop. It's a nice coffee shop—but it's still a coffee shop… and you don't have to?"

"Yeah, that pretty much sums it up," Casey admits with a crooked grin.

"Why?"

"For a long time, it was just a reaction to my dad's implosion. The way I saw it, we were happy before we had money and the more money we got, the unhappier and more addicted to drugs my dad became. So, I figured if I could steer away from the money, I could stay away from unhappiness. Of course, I learned I was wrong the hard way. Even when I avoided money, I couldn't escape tragedy. Still, I wanted to prove I could make it in my life without money."

"How did you do it?"

"Fortunately for me, there was a woman named Roberta who saw through all of my grief and anger over Ashlyn's death. She helped me work through it in a healthy environment. Work through it, I did — the hard way. I worked at the stables for one of the therapy horse programs for people with disabilities. I mucked out stalls and fed all the animals. After that program closed, Roberta moved me to another program. I stacked cans and unstacked cans, and arranged bottles and sacks of food for local food banks until I never wanted to see another food product again in my life. But, it taught me that my problems were not as big as many other peoples'. It gave me a rock-solid work ethic."

"How'd you come to own your own coffee shop?" I ask, curious about his sudden openness.

"After I proved my worth at the food bank, Roberta got me a retail job in a restaurant. By that time, I was old enough to work as a bar back. So, I began working at one of those family restaurant pub combos. I was grateful for the chance to interact with all sorts of customers. On the other hand, it was really hard for me because we had customers who were alcoholics and struggled with addiction like my father. I had to stare it in the face again. I was offered an opportunity to go to bartending school — you know, like the one in Cocktail with Tom Cruise?"

"Impressive." I smile.

"It should've been. It definitely was an opportunity for promotion — but, it didn't really feel that way. I felt like I would be enabling people to be just like my dad. Eventually, I made the difficult decision to turn it all down."

"Wow, that must've taken real guts." I fiddle with the label on my bottle. "I'm not sure I would've had the strength to stand with my convictions in the face of the opportunity to make that much money."

"I know, it was hard for me too. I second-guessed myself for a long time. My boss at the restaurant was not happy with me—in fact, he demoted me back to dishwasher."

"What a scumbag! You had your reasons."

"That's okay, I got the last laugh in the end. Later, I saved his bar from bankruptcy and turned it into a family diner." Casey smiles. I can tell he is lost somewhere in the past.

"How?" I ask, confused by all this new information.

"Around that time, I tracked down my mom. She told me about the trust fund he had set up for me when I was a baby. All the money became mine when I turned eighteen, but I didn't know it even existed. I was furious at my dad because he had somehow removed my mom's name from all of their joint accounts and left her basically penniless during their divorce. Yet, here was this huge sum of money my mom could not touch which would've made her life so much easier."

"Did your mom have any idea where you were? I'm not a parent, but I was pretty much the same as a parent to Owen and Shelby. I fought so hard to keep Shelby that they thought I was crazy. They almost put me in the psych unit because I put up such a fuss about being separated from her. I can't imagine simply walking away from my own child."

"Oh, trust me. My mom never really walked away. My dad had all the power in the relationship; he made all the money and had slowly stripped my mom away from any responsibility. She didn't have access to any of the banking. It was so extreme that she couldn't even go to the grocery store. Piece by piece he had taken away her autonomy. So, when he kicked her out over the drugs, she was powerless to fight back. He had even taken her identification just to prove he could strip her of her personhood. Of course, back then I didn't really understand all of it because I was still barely a teenager."

"Wow, that's harsh." I understand full well what it's like to not be able to prove who you are.

"I only knew they had gotten into a huge fight and my dad had pulled a knife. I was clueless about most of the rest of it until years later when I was an adult."

"How did you guys ever reconnect?"

"It's not quite as random as how you reconnected with your parents, but almost." I chuckle softly. "I saw a news story one day about adoption reunifications. I was feeling frustrated because I figured there was no chance I'd ever get my hands on my mother's personal information to do a search. I spent a couple of weeks being totally bummed out about it. I decided maybe a change of scenery might do me some good. So, I wrote to the GED program and the high school I attended when I was in Roberta's program to get proof of my education to put on my resume. It was a completely routine thing to do. I expected nothing extraordinary to happen. Whoever was working in the school office goofed, and sent me my entire school record including copies of my parent's drivers' licenses. There was also an application for extra protection from police to keep my dad away from the school. I was never even aware my mom was trying to keep me safe."

"How did you feel when you discovered that?"

"I knew Dad's drugs were causing trouble, but I guess I didn't know how deep his issues were. In some ways, finding the application for protection made sense and finally provided an explanation. I could never figure out what sent my dad into a tailspin. That would've been something which would've enraged him. He was all about keeping up appearances."

"Oh, I see," I answer, not really seeing at all.

"I used the confidential information I got together

with my computer skills to track down where she was working. It was a good thing I did. She thought my dad had done something desperate to get rid of me too. She assumed he'd actually killed me. She tried to contact the school to see how I was doing and because I had run away, they had no information for her. For many years, she thought I was dead."

"Oh my gosh, how awful for her. I guess maybe our stories are much more alike than I thought they were. For many years, I believed everyone in my life might be dead too. It's an awful feeling. So, why doesn't your mom live near you now?"

"My mom probably would have followed me to Florida except she fell in love with Frederick. He owns a surfing school in California. There's not a lot of surfing in Gainesville."

"It's too strange to me that you ended up on opposite coasts after being separated for so long."

"That's not exactly my mom's fault. Back then, I was still running from everything in my life. I wanted to put as much distance as I could between my past and my future. I thought I could outrun my grief over Ashlyn and my rage against my dad. Of course, there aren't enough miles on the planet. But ... I was young and stubborn. I was eager to get my life restarted and didn't want to listen to anybody who told me to take my time and grieve."

"I hope this doesn't sound callous, but you seem far more well-adjusted than me, how did you pull it all together?"

"I owe all that to Roberta. Even from across the country, she held my feet to the fire and held me accountable. At first, I was ticked off because I thought I had done it all and paid my dues. But, she was on me like a rash until I grew up enough to realize that I didn't actually know what I thought I knew," Casey says as he shakes his head at the memory.

"I know, I think you might be underestimating your skills, I've seen what you can do. You're a pretty impressive businessman."

"Oh, you should've seen me a few years ago when I was trying to figure it all out. I made some real bone-head mistakes. I was more bluster than brains."

"So, how did this Roberta help you?"

"She made me sit on the other side of the table. She challenged me to expand Uncommon Paths and replicate the program in Florida."

I draw in a breath, I wasn't expecting that answer. "That's a big responsibility."

"That's what I thought too. But, I didn't want to let Roberta down. She had had faith in me for so long. She had taken me from the streets where I was covered in Ashlyn's blood, held my hand when they wanted to charge me with her murder and traveled with me to Florida when I first hung my open sign in my own shop. Roberta has been by my side every step of the way, so there was no way I wanted to disappoint her."

"What did you do? How do you prepare for something like that? Don't most people in those positions have massive amounts of college?" I sit forward in my seat as I pepper Casey with questions. This is a side of him I rarely ever see. He plays the friendly store owner who serves coffee with such ease — it's easy to forget it's only a dimension of him.

"Well, I read. A lot. Everything I could on drug addiction, suicide, gang loyalty, family dynamics, adolescent development anything I thought the 'real professionals' might be reading. Roberta helped me out by sending me all the journals she got as part of her job as director."

"While I was waiting for our building to be renovated, I flew back to the headquarters of Uncommon Paths and met with several of the veteran counselors. I went through the process as if I was a client. This time, I was more honest about the impact of my dad's drug addiction had had on my life and how devastated I felt about not being able to save Ashlyn. Once I realized admitting my weaknesses didn't make me less of a man, the puzzle pieces came together and I felt much stronger."

"That's amazing. So, you built a program to help a bunch of kids in Florida?"

"It's nothing like Uncommon Paths in California. We simply don't have the funding." Casey grimaces.

"Wait ... I thought you said you were loaded, or something —" I interject.

"I already tried that. Roberta won't take my money. She says I may need it someday."

"That's it? You just gave up?" I ask with more judgment than I mean to. "Sorry to sound so awful about this, but the whole time I was growing up, my siblings and I would just pray that someone — anyone, would take notice of us and be a hero. No one ever did. I used to hide from them and cry myself to sleep. You know the weird way I cry — under my breath and silently? I learned to do that when I was younger so I wouldn't scare Owen."

Casey puts his arms around me. "You'll never know how much I wish I would have been around to rescue you. But, to answer your question — no, I didn't give up the dream. I merely had to scale it back. I have twelve-step meetings for drug and alcohol abuse at the shop several times a week, the community policing task force meets there, and so does a group from the local high school that's trying to stop bullying and helps to retain students. I was trying to make Tough Breaks a safe place in the community for everyone," Casey explains with a sigh.

"You gave all that up for me?" I cry. "There are members of the community counting on you. It's just wrong. I'm just one person! You can't sacrifice all your good work to save me. That's crazy."

"No, it's not crazy. If I lost you, none of the rest of it would matter. Having you in my life has highlighted all the rest of my priorities and shows me why they are so important."

Casey's words stop any protest that was about to form on my lips. I don't think I've ever been anyone's top priority. I can't remember the last time I truly mattered to someone — except maybe Shelby and Owen. I am at a complete loss for words. I open my mouth to speak, but no sound comes out. I can do nothing but cry as Tristan's plane touches down

Chapter Twenty

Casey

Umm, that didn't go well. Tears are streaming down Savannah's face. She looks like I've just done something horrible to Blue. As she huddles in a blanket, while the pilot taxis to the gate, I'm left to wonder what I should do next.

In my head, I had scripted the way I would tell Savannah how I felt about her. I completely blew my plan. Although I know she has a tendency to be skittish and nervous, I thought we had made real progress. This was not the reaction I was hoping for. I reach out and try to make some contact with her.

Much to my relief, she grabs my hand and squeezes it tight.

"Savvy, I won't lie. You're scaring me here," I murmur. "You gotta tell me what's going on, please."

"I'm scared," she mumbles from under the blanket.

"Me too, baby."

"Something tells me we might be scared of different things." Savannah sits up in her seat and runs her fingers through her hair. I can see her hand is noticeably trembling. "My whole life, people have been telling me they love me and then leaving me, or doing unspeakable things to me."

"I never plan to do anything like that to you." I say in a strangled breath of surprise.

"Casey, I know that in my head. The logical part of me understands. The grown-up Savannah Lyons, who runs a business and is a capable adult and who functions in society reasonably well, gets it. I know you love me and that you are as near to a perfect guy as I am ever going to find."

"I don't know if I'm all that —"

"*But*," she continues with emphasis.

I brace myself for what's coming next. Whatever it is, the tear tracks on her face tell me it's not good. Maybe I jumped the gun and shouldn't have said anything about the way I feel. Honestly, I thought we were on the same page. A chill goes up my spine as I realize that maybe, just maybe, I completely misread the whole situation.

"But what?" I prompt wanting to get it over with.

"Deep down inside me, there is an eighteen-year-old, the one who thought she could conquer the world but who had her hopes completely obliterated by people who took from me what only I had the right to give away. Those people told me they loved me. They promised to watch out for me and keep me safe too. I don't know if I'll ever be able to believe those words and take them at face value again — and I hate myself for my weakness."

Now it's my turn to be speechless. I don't even know what to say in response. I can't tell her that I can make her past go away because I can't. I can't tell her not to feel the way she feels because it would be wrong. Right now, I can't even tell her that everything will be all right because I have nothing to indicate that's true.

I elect to ask her a question instead. "Do you mind if I ask you which side of yourself you would rather believe?" I ask with trepidation, not entirely sure I want to know the answer.

"I would give anything to turn off my fear and be able to trust everything will be fine. I want to believe in the happily ever after that Shelby and I used to write as kids. I want it to happen for us, but I'm not sure I'm brave enough to believe."

"For now, is it all right if I believe enough for both of us?" I ask. "I'm not ready to throw in the towel on us quite yet."

When the plane comes to a stop, Savannah stands up and gives me a hug and a deep kiss, catching me completely off guard. I always thought it was an artistic embellishment in movies when the character's knees would buckle during a passionate kiss, but if the tall leather seat had not been propping me up, I would've been nothing but an unfortunate grease spot on Tristan's very expensive carpet.

"What was that for?" I stammer as I pull away and catch my breath.

Savannah looks a little crestfallen. "What's wrong? Didn't you like it?"

I caress her cheek as I capture her face between my hands and kiss her again, "Savvy, I couldn't have loved it any more and not embarrass myself. I'm just confused."

"So am I, Casey." Savannah swallows hard and bends down to pick up her purse off the seat next to where she was sitting and clutches it close to her. She starts to file off the plane and then stops, turns around. "I was trying to show you that I will try to listen to the side of my brain which tells me everything will be fine. I'm going to stomp on the part that is afraid. That's all I'm trying to do. I'm not trying to confuse you, I promise."

Placing my hands lightly on her shoulders, I give them a light squeeze. "Savannah, you're not the only one who is a little confused in this situation. This is all new to me too. We've got time to figure it all out as long as no one gives up."

"I hope we do have time. Esther and Reggie are not playing with a full deck. I worry about what they could do."

It's far smaller than I remember. I suppose it's because the last time I saw it in person, I was only about seventeen. Everything else has been handled through online transactions and through my eminently capable real estate attorney. As I glance around the yard, I'm pleased to see the maintenance company has been keeping it in good shape since the last tenants moved out.

Savannah is watching me with wide-eyed fascination as I unlock the door. "Are we just going to walk in? Do you know the people who live here?" She peers through the window. "Wait. It doesn't look like anyone lives here — so why are we here?" She sounds a lot like her niece.

"A lifetime ago I used to call this home," I say with a grand gesture of my hand. I have an urge to carry her over the threshold even though this is not the time for it — there's nothing romantic about what we're doing.

Savannah's jaw goes slack. "Is this your parent's house — or yours?"

"No, this house is one hundred percent mine. I don't even have to say it belongs to the bank." I reply, not even trying to disguise my brag. "It used to be my parent's house, but my dad tried to renegotiate the terms of the loan to get more drug money and then fell behind on what was actually the fourth mortgage on the property. By that time, no one wanted to touch it because my dad was such a bad credit risk and it fell into a state of disrepair."

"Oh…" Savannah's lips form a surprised O.

"When I located my mom and found out about the trust fund, one of the first things I did was purchase the house back from the bank and repair it so my mom could move into it. She did briefly, but then she fell in love with Frederick, and the house became mine again."

"What happened to your dad?" Savannah's eyes are full of sympathy

"Eventually my dad's drug habit got so bad he tried to sell the intellectual property of the companies he was working for to make money through back channels. He eventually got caught for corporate espionage. When they started investigating, they realized the extent of his drug problem and the fact that he was trafficking in drugs to help support his habit. So, he got some federal time."

"But, that was years ago, wasn't it? Where is your dad now?" Savannah asks as she catches onto the hesitation in my voice with precise and laser-fast speed.

"I don't know. I assume he's dead. After I finished up working with Roberta, I never looked back. I figured if I knew where my mom was, my dad's location didn't matter a whole lot."

"How does it feel to be back in your old house? Are

you haunted by memories?" Savannah asks me as we step over the threshold and stop in front of a sheet-covered couch.

"I don't know, I guess we're about to find out." I grab her coat and hang it in the coat closet.

"What do you mean?" she asks with a puzzled look on her face

"I haven't been back here since I was a teenager," I explain with a shrug.

"You own a house you don't live in? It's just sitting here empty?"

"Up until my renters got military orders, I had someone in here, just not family members."

"Hmm, I think I found you less intimidating when I thought you were simply an employee behind the counter at my neighborhood coffee shop. Now that I know you've got this really complicated back story, an important job, and you're a real estate guy on top of it all, I'm feeling a little outclassed," Savannah says as she looks down at her toes.

I lift her chin up and point it at me. "There's no reason to be intimidated. I'm not anything all that special I'm merely coping with life one day at a time the same as you."

"Well, you seem to be coping much better than I am. I don't do anything particularly extraordinary with my life."

"I happen to know that's not true," I argue as I kiss her forehead.

"What in the world are you talking about?"

"You know all sorts of people come in my coffee

shop, right? Well … one of my favorite customers happens to be Charlita Sanchez."

Savannah turns bright red. "Oh, that. It's no big deal. I just think it's great that she has started over again after what her boyfriend did to her. I wanted to help."

"The students in Miss Sanchez's class would beg to differ. They love to come to your shop for art class. The fact that you offer classes free of charge to Charlita's students is extraordinary. In fact, I would say you have a few marshmallow tendencies of your own."

"I guess maybe I do, but don't tell anybody," Savannah averts her gaze.

Suddenly the front door opens behind me, and I instinctively cover Savannah with my body.

My mom takes in the view before her with a look of horror.

"Since when do I get that kind of greeting? I know it's been a long time since you've seen me, Son, but really—I'm not so scary. I brought you guys something to eat. I thought you might be hungry. The last time I flew on an airplane, they didn't even give me any food."

I break away from Savannah to give my mom a brief sideways hug. "We do appreciate you, Mom. It's just that everything in our lives is incredibly stressful right now and we were not expecting to encounter anyone. That's why we overreacted."

Savannah steps forward and extends her hand to my mom, "It's nice to meet you. I don't even know what your name is, I'm sorry. I know nothing about what's going on. I assume we are in California."

"Chandler Edward Moore, did you kidnap and drug this woman?" my mom accuses. "You better have a good explanation."

I groan. "Geez, Mom! Did you really have to go there? I've been going by Casey since I was about seven years old. You know this."

"I notice you didn't answer my question. Why doesn't this lovely lady know where she is? Why didn't you tell her you were coming home to visit your mom? Are you embarrassed about Fredrick and me?"

"No, Mom! That's not how it is at all. I didn't want to talk about where we were going or who we were planning to go see because I didn't want anybody to know. There are some people who might be after Savannah, and until they are caught, I want to keep her as safe as possible. Nobody knows I bought this place because I purchased it under a shell corporation. It can't be tied to me. Most people in Florida don't even know I'm from California. So, I figured this was probably the safest place for her."

"Oh, I see. Is someone working on your mess back in Florida?" my mom asks with concern in her voice.

"Yes, ma'am. Casey has the best people working on it. He is taking excellent care of me, I promise. You raised a good boy here." Savannah smiles at my mom.

"Aren't you a polite one? By the way, my name is Hazel, Hazel Hughes. Sadly, I didn't really have much to do with the way my son turned out, he did it pretty much on his own. Pulled himself up by the bootstraps, my son did. I'm so proud of him. I don't think he even knows."

Savannah's eyes tear up. "I think he does, I really do. I can tell you that the way he lives his life is something you could be proud of every single day."

Although Savannah's words fill me with hope we will

be able to figure this all out, they also make me feel really uncomfortable. I'm not used to hearing people tell me how great I am. I mean, they might like coffee, but that's a different thing than hearing that you're an awesome human being.

I clear my throat and announce, "Mom, you're totally right. I am absolutely starving. What did you bring me?"

"How does Grandma's meatloaf recipe sound?" my mom asks with a smile.

"Like a gift from heaven!" I pick up the box she sat on the ground.

"I made you the fruit salad you like with all the marshmallows too. Lord knows, you got a thing for marshmallows. If I didn't know better, I'd say you might be made of one."

Savannah winks at me. "See? What did I tell you? Even your mom knows."

CHAPTER TWENTY-ONE

SAVANNAH

Looking around the facilities at Uncommon Paths, I am completely blown away. It's part classroom, part medical clinic, and part cool hang out center for teens of all descriptions. It's like its own little bustling city. I think back to my childhood when I was trying to support my siblings and keep my parents out of danger. A program like this would've probably saved my life—or at least prevented much of the pain I went through.

Roberta catches my bleak expression as she comes back with a cup of hot coffee. "Painful memories?"

"More than you can imagine," I admit.

"Oh, I doubt that very much. You'd be surprised at what I can conjure up. I came from the streets — just like these kids. I was every stereotype you can think of. My parents and brothers were in a gang and I was sold into prostitution. It was as bad as you imagine. I even had a strung-out pimp with a flashy car."

As I take in the well-appointed woman in front of me dressed in a lawyer-like business suit, I can't put the two things together in my mind. "Really? You're not simply making that up to make me feel better?"

"No, I'm not. I would never do such a thing. My story is authentically my own. Would you like to see the track marks on my arm?" Roberta asks.

I have to turn away from Roberta for a moment to collect myself before I turn back. "I'm so sorry. I didn't mean to imply you were lying. It's just that I've had people take advantage of me before by pretending they'd been in my shoes. It's hard for me to separate reality from fiction. Your story was so similar to my own, it stomped on a few buttons for me."

Roberta chuckles. "Don't worry about it, you can't live through what we lived through and not have a few buttons. If you did, I wouldn't call you human."

"How do you do it?" I study Roberta and her quiet confidence. "How can you look at me and all the other street kids and not relive every second of your own story in horrifying detail?"

"Honey child, that's what drives me to do what I do every day. Because if I can rescue one child from the streets before something truly awful happens to them, then I make a dent in the ugliness."

Her words hit me hard. What have I been doing to help stop the cycle from happening again? The honest answer is not much. I've been surviving in my own little cocoon and I've been running. The incident with Ketki underscores the fact that the danger is not over.

"What can I do to help?" I blurt in a voice stronger than I feel.

"Well, let's see, what do you like to do?" Roberta smiles broadly.

"I probably wouldn't be useful in your office — I seem to have the worst luck with computers and other technology. I don't know what it is, but we don't have a good relationship."

"That's okay. I have other people who volunteer to do that kind of thing. What makes you special?"

"I don't know how special this makes me, but back home I run a pottery and painting business."

"In our book, that makes you very special. Our resident artist went on maternity leave, and we haven't had anyone to work in the arts field for a while. The kids miss it. Painting and drawing are good therapeutic outlets."

"I'm not a therapist or anything; I just like to draw and do crafts."

"We make do with what we've got available around here, and the fact that you are an artist and a survivor will mean a ton to these kids. Don't sell yourself short."

I can't believe we've been here for six weeks already. Isaac suggested that we adopt new identities, just to be extra cautious — so I have become Astrid Jones, and Casey is River James. It's been hard to remember to call him that, but it's been liberating because it separates me from who I once was in a very tangible way.

My other challenge has been how to completely hand over Paint Your Art Out to one of Rogue and Ivy's friends from art school. I still don't know if it'll be a permanent or a part-time thing. I'm trying to be as casual and copacetic about the whole situation as Casey, I mean … River, seems to be, but it's not working very well. In the back of my mind, I keep obsessing over how I'll restart everything once this nightmare is over.

My cell phone buzzes at the same time a student comes up to my easel. I briefly check, expecting it to be a message from Casey, but what I find there instead is a naked picture of me taken when I was about nineteen.

Before I can close the picture down, Kelsey Baxter peers over my shoulder. "Whoa, Astrid! What's up with that? Sending hot text messages to the boyfriend?"

I'm so shocked, I can barely process her words. "Oh my God! The sicko did it; he really, really did it!" I exclaim without thinking.

"Did what?" she presses, alarmed at my demeanor.

I slump down in my chair. "I'm being extorted by my past. I was a street kid who was essentially orphaned by my family after my brother died. I was sold to somebody to be his sex slave. I was there for almost four years before I was rescued. Now, someone is threatening to expose it all unless I pay them more money than I could ever hope to make in a lifetime. I don't even know how they got these pictures. They are more than fifteen years old," I blurt my whole story without thinking. It's a weird thing. There was a time when I told no one, and now the whole ugly truth seems to erupt from me without notice.

"It's dope that you escaped from that creep, I bet he's the one who's threatening you. You embarrassed him and now he has to pay you back," Kelsey suggests.

I feel the core of my being disappear into nothingness. I literally have to fight to breathe as everything that's muddled and confused suddenly makes perfect sense. My head spins and my teeth begin to chatter.

Vaguely I hear Kelsey ask, "Astrid, are you all right? Should I get help?"

Astrid? Who's Astrid? Oh … right, I'm Astrid. I should probably know that, it seems important.

Kelsey stands over me and mutters to herself "You know what? Screw it. I'm getting you some help anyway. This isn't like you."

I want to tell her what to do, but I can't seem to make my brain communicate with the rest of my body.

Somehow, she seems to understand my distress as she runs off in search of another adult. Moments later, Casey returns.

He rushes over to me and grabs my upper arms. "Sav—I mean—Ast—Astrid, what's going on? What's wrong? Did someone hurt you?"

Wordlessly, I hand him my phone. Mentally, I prepare for this to be the beginning of the end. It's one thing to know about someone's past, it's another thing to have it thrown in your face.

I watch as his jaw tightens as he flips through the sexually explicit, provocative pictures—most of which were taken completely without my knowledge or consent.

Casey turns to Kelsey. "I need you to do something for me, please. Can you check with Roberta and see if Bud Gerrick is still on the force?"

"I don't have to, River, he helps out with the youth offender program. We went bowling the other day. I have his number in my cell. Do you want it?" she responds, digging her phone from her backpack.

The room is stifling and more than a little terrifying. Of course, it's designed to be that way. We are in an interrogation room because the conference room is busy — or so the receptionist tells me. Casey tells me that the officer we are going to meet, Bud Gerrick, is one of the few people in law enforcement he actually trusts. I don't know who or what to believe at this point.

All of this is one big tangled nightmare for me.

Just as I'm about to get completely lost in the memories of the last time I was trapped in a police station, a big, burly man comes through the door. He is nothing like I expected. The detective looks like a relative of Santa Claus. He politely holds out his hand for me to shake. When I get a good look at him, I let out the breath that I have been unconsciously holding. He has the kindest eyes I've ever seen in my life. Yet, I sense a lingering pain.

"Ms. Lyons, my name is Detective Gerrick, but you may call me Bud or Buddy, whichever makes you feel most comfortable. I'm sorry we have to meet under these circumstances, it's very unfortunate." He turns to Casey and does a comical double take. "Man, is it ever good to see you. I have to tell you, there were times when you were growing up I had my doubts about whether you would actually make it all the way to full-grown maturity. You gave us some real heartburn, young man."

Casey flushes a deep shade of red. "I apologize. I am a little stubborn even when people are trying to help me."

"It's all good. Ms. Roberta tells me you're hot stuff out there in Florida."

"Well, I was doing pretty well, but I had to put all that stuff on the back burner to protect Savannah."

"A move which I appreciate, but strongly object to," I interject. "Casey shouldn't have to give up everything he has, simply because he loves me and wants to keep me safe. There has to be another way."

"I don't know how much I'll be able to help this time, Casey. I don't work the homicide unit anymore. I moved over to the sex crimes unit when they had a department reorganization a while back. So, I don't do much of the crime beat anymore. My stuff is mostly cold cases."

I'm a little stunned when I hear his answer. I thought when Casey called him into the case, he would know exactly what it was about. I guess I didn't realize that Casey was just calling him in because he is a friend. After a moment or two of awkward silence, I look at Bud Gerrick and decide if I'm going to ever trust anybody with the whole story of what happened to me, this man is probably one of the people who needs to know. I was honest with Shelby and Casey about the bare-bones facts of what happened to me both with the Brennan's and Ricard, but I barely scratched the surface about all the horrific things which happened.

Casey puts an arm around my shoulder and whispers in my ear, "I know you can do this. You are strong, and I love you."

I take a quick sip of water. "Which lowlifes do you want to hear about first?"

"You would think that working for the FAA, Mic would know about Geo-tracking features on photographs, wouldn't you?"

"I would think so, but I was surprised pictures that old would even have them," Casey responds.

"Gee thanks, you act like I'm a hundred years old," I

tease.

"No, I didn't mean it like that. Digital photography has come a long way in the last few years." Casey flips over the grilled cheese sandwich he's making for me.

"The lab technician said it was because he took a picture of a picture and sent it."

"So that's the way they caught him?"

Casey smirks. "Apparently, Mic is an aspiring amateur photographer who wants to set up a travel photography business. He programmed his website into the metadata of his photographs so they couldn't be stolen. Apparently, he was in such a rush to cyberbully you, he forgot to turn off the metadata feature on his phone when he sent you those pictures."

"That doesn't really surprise me; when Mic was upset, he became reckless and impulsive. That's what got him caught the first time. How will we know if they actually arrest him?"

"Gerrick is supposed to call us when he's in custody."

"That'll be a huge relief. Now, if we could just find the other two and toss them behind bars too — that would be like the perfect trip." I say wistfully.

"Bud and his department are good, but I don't know if even they are that good. In the meantime, we've got to celebrate the victories as we get them and be patient while we wait to see what happens with everything else."

"It's hard. I'm not very patient, and this guy should have never spent twenty minutes free, let alone years. I just feel so helpless," I comment as Casey gathers me into a hug.

"I am so proud of you. You kept it together, and now

this guy will finally face justice. Way to be tough, Savannah," he says as he kisses me and leads me by the hand to the deck. "You've done all you can do for now. Would you like me to help you forget the real world for a while?"

I nod and kiss his bicep as he walks us over to the oversize lounge chair in the screened in porch. He has laid out a pile of books and magazines with some beverages and massage oil. "This is your ejection kit from reality," he quips as he pulls off my shirt and offers me a swimsuit top.

Touched by his thoughtfulness, I toss the top away. If I can't be happy all the time, I can't let my past steal the moments of happiness I do find. I turn to face him and kiss him with slow deliberateness. "I'd rather disappear into us. What we've built together is better than any story I could ever read."

Chapter Twenty-Two

Casey

"LET ME GET THIS straight — we came all the way to California to keep Savannah safe and now you want to purposely put her in danger? What in the freak are you thinking, Gerrick?"

"I don't know? Maybe that I have highly trained cyber-crimes and sex crimes unit, who are backing her up or maybe it's because your friends, Isaac Roguen and Tristan Macklin, think it's the single most effective way to lure Esther and Reginald Brennan out of hiding."

"Great! Next you'll tell me that Ketki will be running the whole operation."

Bud shifts in his chair uneasily as he steeples his fingers under his chin.

"Well, actually that little computer whiz had a brilliant idea about including a keystroke logger program in an update to the P4K program. I'd keep an eye on that kid—I think she's going places. She really wants to be involved in catching these perverts. I've been talking to her dad. Ketki would like to go back to school. They would just as soon see this all wrapped up as quickly as possible. Mark is not opposed to having her help.

Although the captain is reluctant because she is a minor."

"As he should be," I argue, having a hard time keeping a lid on my temper. I can't believe they are even considering putting people I care about in danger. "Don't they have professionals to do this kind of thing?"

"Not that anyone actually asked my opinion," interjects Savannah softly, "but I think we should do it."

"What?" My mouth gapes open. "Savannah, you throw up when you think about these people. How are you going to do this without putting yourself in danger? I won't allow you to do this to yourself," I say crossing my arms in front of me. The moment those words pass my lips, I knew it was the completely wrong thing to say.

Savannah straightens in her chair. She turns to me with fire in her eyes. "The day I escaped from Ricard's mountaintop prison was the last day I ever allowed anyone to tell me what I could and could not do. If that's not okay with you, then you need to find someone else to love because I'm not the person you think I am. Is that clear?" She turns to Detective Gerrick. "What exactly do I have to do?"

"We would like to bring Ketki out to California and set you up with her and a bunch of our computer experts with a few folks from the FBI and Tristan's people to run some simulations of P4K."

"Is Reggie going to be able to see me?"

"That's the plan. We want you to look as young as possible. So, wear youthful clothes, please. We have evidence that Brennan still likes them young."

Savannah shudders. "That right there cinches it for me. Casey, don't you understand? I need to do this so he stops? I can't let more girls go through what I did. If I do, all the work I've done here at Uncommon Paths is just lip service and means nothing."

"I get that — but I don't like it," I say begrudgingly.

"Trust me, I don't like it either. I would rather be doing almost anything else. I ran from these cowards the first time just like I ran from Mic. The running stops here. For years, I let them rule every decision I made. I'm done. I want to move on with my life, I want to have a life with you without looking over my shoulder. I want to know that I stopped them. I'm taking my power back. They need to be off the streets and unable to hurt anyone else. This is important to me. I know it's risky, but it's less dangerous than having them out on the streets taking advantage of other little girls."

Garrick turns toward me and nails me with a serious look. "Will you be cool with this? I need Savannah's full attention on this case. I can't have her worrying about whether you'll have her back."

I reach under the table and squeeze Savannah's hand. "You know me. I'm a good team player. Whatever team you're on, that's my side. Always. Let's go get these creeps. Lucky for you guys, I know how to make excellent coffee. It sounds like you guys will need it."

I watch as Ketki nervously checks out each and every computer station. "It's weird, I thought everything would be much more high-tech. I don't mean to be rude or anything, but my stuff is better."

I have to stifle my grin. She's not wrong. "I guess the important thing is whether Tristan's games will run on this stuff, will they?"

"Yeah, I checked the video cards and everything should be good. The game is designed to be backwards-compatible. Tristan wanted everybody to be able to play the game regardless of the sophistication of their equipment — I think he calls it economic inclusion. Anyway, I think we're good."

"Are you nervous?"

"Only because everybody keeps asking me if I am. It's not like Reese hasn't been my bodyguard since this all started. I trust her to do her job."

"You have a bodyguard?" Surprise colors my voice.

"Of course. You've met my dad, right? He doesn't let me eat food coloring, you think he's gonna let me run around without protection if he thinks I'm in danger?"

"Come to think of it, that doesn't sound too much like Mark."

"It's not. I've been under the protection of the Cherokee where no one can get to me, but I can't go to school or have anything else normal in my life either, so I can't wait for this to all be over. I like my grandparents, but I don't like them quite that much."

"I hope this will all be over soon. Where's Savannah?"

"She's with a police officer getting ready. They're going over last-minute stuff and checking her wardrobe."

"I hope everybody's ready for this, it just seems like everything in the world could go wrong. I worry about all of you."

"I wouldn't worry about Aunt Savannah. I think she's ready to kick some butt," Ketki advises sagely.

"I'm more than ready to kick the bad guys' butt. Let's

get this over with." Savannah comes through the door to the computer war room and breezes past me to sit down.

This is a far different Savannah than I'm used to seeing. She is wearing a gold bustier, hoop earrings, dark red lipstick and tight jeans with stiletto boots. She catches me staring at her and shrugs helplessly.

"Remember — I'm playing a role. I'm not this person anymore. I'm embarrassed to think I ever was."

"Savannah, even when those were your circumstances, that wasn't who you were."

"Oh Gosh, Casey, I love you so much. My whole life I've needed someone to tell me that. This isn't the time or place for us to have this discussion, but what you just said means the entire world." Savannah gives me a tight hug.

"I'm sorry, Casey, I have to tell you to go, you're not officially part of this operation and your woman has to concentrate on what's going on." Tristan walks sideways to get past us in the doorway.

"I've got one question for you, man. Are you sure the Brennans won't be able to tell that anything is different from before?"

"Yes, I'm absolutely certain they will not perceive any difference in the interface," Tristan assures me. "I'll do everything I can to keep Savannah safe. I want to keep everyone alive and happy. They're like family to me."

"I hate that I don't get to watch this all go down. What if something awful happens? I can't even be there to help her. Did I mention she has a tendency to pass out when she's under stress?"

"You've only said that like ten times in the last two hours," Roberta tells me as she shakes her head. "However, you also told me Savannah single-handedly took down a monster of a guy in the middle of your restaurant without being asked to. It seems like the lady can handle it on her own. I have watched her here at the program, she is a little shy, but she's got great people skills and sharp instincts."

"Do you think so?" I desperately hang onto straws of hope.

Roberta gently cuffs my cheek. "You haven't changed much in all these years. You're all bluster and toughness on the outside, but a real tender heart inside. Don't ever change— it's one of my favorite things about you. I think you can take a deep breath and trust Savannah to do the right thing. She is tougher than she looks. Your lady is stronger and more resilient than even she believes. Sure, she is shy and reserved around people, but who in their right mind who's been through what she has been through wouldn't be? She has an incredibly strong will and bright mind. Whatever is thrown at her today, she'll be able to handle it with flying colors. I have absolutely no doubt."

"What if something goes wrong?"

"I have worked with Tristan Macklin and Isaac Rogan on their Elliott House projects. Those men are in the business of making sure things don't go wrong. You already know what Bud Garrick is capable of. I think they're an unstoppable team. I have no doubt the Brennan's days as parasitic pedophiles are numbered."

"I hope so, I really do. Because I don't know how much longer Savannah can live like this. She hates looking over her shoulder."

"Have you given any thought to what you guys are planning to do when this is all over?" Roberta removes a Styrofoam cup that I've demolished from my hand.

"Not really. I have been living day-to-day, trying not to think about my future. I've got too much on my plate trying to get through each and every day. I know it sounds stupid and shortsighted, but right now I can't focus on what I gave up to keep what I've got. It's not a fair comparison. Honestly, Savannah would win every time. I'll simply have to figure out another way to start over when the time comes. Until we resolve this situation, the time for new beginnings is not here yet."

Roberta smiles and pats my knee. "I understand, and after having met Savannah, I totally support your choice. I also want you to remember that Uncommon Paths is always open for you. I never rescinded your job offer I gave you years ago. In fact, I think you're even more qualified to do it now than you were then. Do me a favor and just think about it."

CHAPTER TWENTY-THREE

SAVANNAH

NINE HOURS. WHO IN right mind plays video games for nine hours straight? Well, I guess Ketki does it pretty routinely, but I've never played video games for that long.

Ever.

That's how long it took before Esther and Reggie finally signed off. I've never been so drained in my whole life. I don't care if I never pick up another game controller as long as I live, but Ketki and the cyber-crimes people were completely jazzed by whatever information they presumably got from the gaming session.

As we predicted they would, while we were in the private chat rooms, the Brennans pretended they had no idea who Ketki and I were and they simply started pumping us for what might seem to be innocuous details. Did we have any pets? When were our birthdays? What are our favorite foods? Do we like music? What's our favorite movie? In some ways, it was like a twisted, perverted job interview.

Throughout the course of the game, I noticed specifically that they were trying to determine which of us were the most pliable.

It was very disconcerting to see from the outside looking in having already experienced their tactics once. I've got teeth marks on my tongue from trying not to say anything contrary to blow my cover. Ketki handled things like a law enforcement professional. She was even able to get them to disclose a few things which might lead investigators to a location. The team says Ketki elicited valuable information which might confirm the identity of several of the other victims.

Everyone seems upbeat and hopeful — I pray they're not wrong.

Although it was nice of Detective Gerrick to offer me a ride home instead of simply giving me cab fare, I can't get out of the police cruiser fast enough. I pause outside on the porch to catch my breath before going inside.

Just sitting in the police car is enough to bring back an avalanche of horrible memories. I guess working with the counselors and the yoga teachers at Uncommon Paths has its limitations. Every time I think I'm making progress, something like this reminds me I still have so far to go. Even so, I guess I have made some progress because there was a time in my life I couldn't even walk on the same side of the street as a police car, let alone sit in one.

Taking a sip from the fancy water bottle Casey got me, I try to collect myself before I face him. I take a few focusing breaths as I spot a beautiful flower in the yard. I try to let go of all the pain and ugliness. Casey is going to be worried enough as it is, he doesn't need to see me in such an emotionally raw state.

At first, I don't even see Casey, but then I see him sprawled out on the couch. He is holding a book, and it is precariously dangling over the edge of the sofa. It looks as if at one point he was reading but, he looks exhausted. I carefully move the book and curl up on the edge of the couch in front of him. Instinctively, he drapes his arm across my torso and draws me closer.

"How was it?" he mumbles in my ear.

"I guess it's over for now," I answer softly. "It's kinda out of my hands. I don't know what else I could have done. Ketki did really well. My sister would be proud."

"Just so you know, I'm proud of you too," Casey drifts off to sleep.

When I wake up, I am drenched in sweat and tears are streaming down my face. I can't figure out where I am. I'm gasping for breath. I cannot seem to get enough air in my lungs. Glancing around, I try to focus on something familiar. I can't see much in the dark and nothing looks normal.

Suddenly, Casey appears in front of me with a damp washcloth.

"Savvy, wake up. It's me. I'm here. I wouldn't leave you. I'll keep you safe, I won't let them hurt you," he says, as he gently wipes my face with a cloth.

"Casey?" I mumble.

"Thank goodness!" he exclaims.

"What are you talking about?" I say as I lean into his hand.

"You've been screaming for the last twenty minutes.

I couldn't get you to stop. I tried everything I possibly could — but you seemed trapped in the past. Nothing I tried seemed to help."

"Shoot! I probably had a night terror. I haven't had one in a while. It was probably brought on by the stress of today. I'm not sleeping well."

Casey gathers up my hair and pulls it away from my face and eases me down next to him on the couch as he asks, "Can you tell me how it went today?"

I smile the ghost of a smile. "I can tell you one thing — I think Ketki may have found her career calling. They were quite impressed with her skills down at the station. The cyber-crimes unit was drooling all over her."

"I'm sure she thought it was cool to be respected as an expert, even though she has a few years to go until she graduates."

"Tristan wasn't kidding when he said nothing would seem out of the ordinary. It seemed as if we were playing in Ketki's gaming room. Everything looked exactly the same. Even the acoustics sounded much the same. It was so weird for me to be playing a part again because I left that girl behind so long ago. It was really helpful to have the other detectives in the cyber-crimes unit playing other potential victims to help steady my nerves."

"How were you able to control yourself when you saw them? I'd want to crawl through the computer screen and do some serious damage," Casey remarks.

"At first, I did. I was momentarily blinded by rage and I lost my focus for a bit. Then Esther started treating Ketki just like she groomed me in the beginning. That was enough to make the hair on the back of my neck stand on end. I knew I had to pull myself together and put my own anger issues aside so I could do my job and help get them off the street. The sex crimes unit and the cyber-crimes unit often work together and they have certain criteria an operation has to meet. There were a few things I couldn't say, even though I wanted to. In a weird way, knowing I was able to follow the rules while they were breaking them helped me take my power back from them."

Casey kisses my temple. "Way to be tough, Savvy. They may have hurt you in the past, but they don't own your future."

I shrug helplessly. "Don't get me wrong, there won't ever be a day I don't watch over my shoulder and question the motives of every person I meet."

"Understandable. I have scars on my psyche from my time on the streets as well," Casey rubs my tense shoulders.

I shrug away from him and pace. "No, I don't think you understand. Meeting the Brennans changed everything about who I am. Because of them, I don't sleep well at night. I don't accept food from strangers. Because of them, I don't have any friends, I didn't go to college or have a career, and I never had a typical relationship. Because of them, I can't ever have children. Do you understand? It's way more than just being a little gun-shy. I've been roaming around the country — isolated and alone — because I was young, dumb, and accepted food from people I don't know. The ironic thing is my childhood taught me I had to count on the generosity of strangers to survive. Talk about mixed messages," I say ruefully.

Casey comes over to where I'm standing and wraps me in a warm embrace.

"You've learned more harsh lessons in life than anyone has a right to, and I'm so sorry that no one was there to protect you. I'm sorry if this is wrong: but I hope when they arrest the Brennans, someone in prison treats them with the same disrespect with which they treated you. It's only fair. No one should have done that to you, ever."

Tears flow down my face. "I never stopped to think about what it would mean to the person I loved. To be honest, I never thought I would ever get this far. I figured no one would love all the mess which makes up me. Now that we're here, if you think about it, they robbed you of your future too."

"What do you mean? Savannah, my future is you. I can't imagine a future without you in it."

I want to stomp my foot in frustration. "Casey, what about kids? I know you love kids. I've seen you play basketball with the kids at Uncommon Paths. You deserve to have children. I can't give you that. How long would it be before you'd be totally frustrated with me?"

"How do you know you can't have kids? How many doctors have you seen? You know, there are many technologies to get around all that infertility stuff."

"All that infertility 'stuff' costs tons of money—"

"Yeah, so?" Casey counters with a raised eyebrow.

"It might be worth pointing out that neither one of us is gainfully employed at the moment," I answer. "By the way, I'm not completely over my guilt over that little development."

"No need to feel guilty. It might've been just the kick in the pants I needed to move my life in the direction I should have been going all along."

I'm completely baffled by the look of excitement on Casey's face.

"What are you talking about? I'm sitting here pouring my heart out to you, telling you all sorts of bad news and you're over there doing a little happy dance."

"I guess my level of happiness depends on how you feel about supporting me while I go back and get a college degree. Roberta says we stand a much better chance of getting grants for Uncommon Paths of Florida if the director has a college degree."

Of all the things I expected him to say, that wasn't it. Somehow, I remember to close my jaw and breathe.

"I want to back up for a moment. Can we be serious for a minute? You talk about this stuff like it's no big deal. Realistically, I'm not in my twenties and with my history, my likelihood of ever having children again after my miscarriage is pretty slim. I've looked into it, and infertility treatments are hellaciously expensive." I feel like I've unloaded a huge burden off my shoulders — but Casey seems remarkably unfazed.

"I'm comfortable with however you want to handle it. If you want to try fertility treatments, I'm cool with that. I got the means to cover it if you want us to try that option," Casey offers.

"Casey! This isn't like offering me prime rib or salmon. This is huge!"

"It's what we do when we're partners, right?" Casey says as he rakes his hand through his hair. "Look, my dad used money against my mom like a weapon. I won't do that. It's why I totally ignore the fact that I've got plenty of dough. I'd rather pretend that it's not there at all than have it affect my relationship with people. It's that big a deal to me — still, if it helps us be a stronger family, I'll use any means possible to make you happy."

Hearing Casey explain his feelings makes me realize that I am not the only person with ghosts in my past. We all have people in our past who leave marks on us good and bad. I know I haven't been grateful enough for the fact that Casey is willing to share the fact that he has his own struggles. I walk back over to Casey and capture his strong jaw between my hands.

After kissing him square on the lips, I say, "If there is anything I have learned through my long and twisted journey through life it's that there are many ways to form a family. How do you feel about adoption?" I ask after I pull away.

"Really excited. It sounds like a perfect solution. There are so many kids who need great parents." Casey replies with a huge smile on his face.

I can't help but respond with an enthusiastic hug. "Okay, it sounds like we've got a bit of planning to do. I think it would make sense for you to get your Bachelor's degree first, don't you? I think it would be easier to study without a little one running around."

Casey is like a kid at Christmas time as he starts to dance. "Now you're talking!"

"Casey, I hate to be a downer, but how in the world are we supposed to make plans if we don't know when or even if they'll be able to arrest the Brennans?"

"Well, today is not the day to worry about that. Today, we're celebrating our love and what it means to be happy. Do you swim?"

"Of course I swim," I answer, totally confused by his question.

Tough

"Okay, we are going to go visit my mom and Frederick. Prepare for the time of your life. Welcome to California, Savvy — it's time for a little fun in the sun …"

Chapter Twenty-Four

Casey

Just as I'm about to take Savannah's bikini top off, my cell phone rings. Although I'm tempted to ignore it, a voice in the back of my head tells me to pay attention. I reach under the lounge chair and dig my phone out of my jeans pocket.

It's Detective Gerrick.

I walk to the edge of the deck. "Hello?"

"Sorry to bother you, Casey, but I'm trying to get ahold of Ms. Lyons and I can't seem to reach her on her cell," he says.

"Oh, sorry about that. Savvy's phone got a little close to the ocean today and took an unplanned swim."

"Is she around? I need to speak with her, please."

"Bud, we've been friends a long time. Am I going to have to pick up the pieces after this conversation?" I ask as quietly as possible to shield my voice from Savannah.

"Moore, you know I can't discuss an ongoing investigation with you, even if it's good news. Sometimes, even happy is tough to digest, if you catch my meaning."

"I hear you," I respond. "Standing by. I'll get

Savannah for you." I walk back over to the lounge chair, sit down and hand my phone to her. "Savvy, Detective Gerrick needs to speak to you."

All the color washes from her face as she whispers, "Oh no."

"Don't worry, I'll be right here," I murmur as I sit on the lounge chair.

"This is Savannah." She crosses her arms across her body in an instinctual protective gesture.

I was hoping she might put the phone on the speaker setting so I could hear the others in the conversation, but she does not. Although Bud is a big, imposing man, he has one of the quietest voices I've ever heard. I think it comes from all the years he spent working undercover and on the homicide unit where he learned to speak in a quiet, respectful tone. It's probably great on the job, but it's lousy for eavesdropping.

Occasionally, I hear her say, "Yes, sir. I understand. No, sir. That won't be a problem. Really? No, you're right. I understand. We'll be in touch. I'll have Casey call you. Thank you."

Savannah lets the phone drop onto her belly as she cries silently. I move toward her to give her a hug. She waves me off, turning away.

"Give me a moment," she whispers hoarsely as she wipes away tears. She stands up and walks toward the beach. Blue follows her silently.

It takes every bit of willpower I've got to keep my butt in my lounge chair. Intellectually, I know she needs some space to deal with whatever Bud Gerrick told her. Reading between the lines, I have to believe it was positive news, although it probably still packed a punch. For now,

I'm going to give her time—but it goes against every instinct I've got to let her hurt alone.

After a couple minutes, she comes back to the patio and lays a chilled hand on my shoulder.

"I can't believe how much a few months has changed me. If you'd told me a few months ago, I would rather deal with this mess with you rather than alone, I would've told you that you were crazy. As I was walking down the beach, I realized that I not only want to tell you what's happened, I need to. It's like we are an artistic sculpture and we need each other to balance and survive," Savannah says and then adds self-consciously, "I know, it sounds really stupid, but that's how I feel."

"No, I think that's the perfect way to describe us: sometimes I push, and you pull, and sometimes you push, and I pull. I wasn't sure I believed in finding people who were the perfect match until I met you. I always thought the concept was something Hollywood or marketers made up to sell more greeting cards or movies."

"It's funny — I used to write stories about my future, but I guess I never truly believed my dreams could come true until now."

"So, the call from Gerrick — does that have anything to do with your newfound belief in the future?"

"I suppose it does. He called to let me know Esther and Reggie have been arrested. They were on their way to California. They were arrested in a Nevada casino. Apparently, Reggie got engrossed in online betting that he forgot to shield his IP address and location."

"Are they still in custody?" I ask, fearing the worst.

"I guess they had enough child porn in their possession to keep them locked up without bail. A few of the kids in the pictures were missing children whose parents actually gave a care."

"How do you feel about all this?" I gather her into a hug.

She walks right into my arms and clings to my chest. "I'm not sure what to do now. I have lived in fear for so long that I don't know what it's like not to hide."

"What does Gerrick say? Does he think the fight is over?" I've been through a fight with Bud Garrick, and it was anything but quick and painless.

Savannah trembles in my arms. "No, unfortunately not because I still have to face everyone in court. He says they could drag this out for years. Even worse, that stupid jerk-face from Tough Breaks could take advantage of the publicity from these cases to advance his own sick agenda against me. It could be one huge nightmare."

I wipe Savannah's tears away with my thumbs. "I think you forgot something critically important. Tristan's wizardry with surveillance caught that whole incident in living color from about a dozen different angles. There isn't a jury on the planet that wouldn't see you were acting in Natalie's defense. You saved her life. It's as simple as that. He's only making noise because he doesn't want anyone to pay attention to what he did wrong."

"What if somebody from Mark's firm ends up having to defend him or something? That would be awful!" Savannah cries.

I chuckle. "I'm pretty sure that Mark has appointed himself as your attorney. Any attorneys who may be left over will be helping Natalie. John Donelson doesn't stand a chance. He might as well line up and get ready for his prison tattoo."

Savannah gasps softly. "Really? Do you think he'll get serious prison time?"

I shrug. "I don't know. I know if Dylan Palmer has anything to say about it, they will file the most serious charges possible — despite the fact the creep is loaded."

Savannah nods. "Gerrick mentioned something about the DA pushing for hate crimes against Donelson because of some of the stuff he said to Natalie. I don't know exactly what he was talking about because Donelson said so much garbage during the whole nightmare. It's like he had diarrhea of the mouth, the guy never shut up. I know he said some super disgusting stuff. Some was probably racial. A lot of it was sexual and disgusting for sure."

I squeeze her hands. "Either way, I'm confident he won't get away with these bogus counter charges of tortious interference with his contractual relationships. Mark will simply call the older guy to testify that it was John Donelson's own behavior which cost him the contract, and it will all be over."

Savannah slumps in my arms. "Oh, I hope so. I can't take on three enemies alone. This is just too crazy."

"You know that you're not alone anymore, right?" I tease. "You've built yourself a whole support team without even realizing it. You've got an entire crew of people who totally adore you."

Savannah rests her head against my shoulder as she draws in a deep shuddering breath. "You're right, you know. Piece by piece, little by little, I've built a family around me where I once had none. Some of it's my real, genuine family who I once thought I'd lost forever, but the rest of it is made up of friends and colleagues I never thought I'd have."

I rest my chin on the top of her head as I smile. "I totally understand. We share the same group of friends, remember? Roberta became my mom at a time when I wasn't able to connect with my own and Bud was my dad when my own father epically failed. Even though Tristan is technically younger than me, he treats me like he's my big brother. Rogue's mom, Mama Rosa, treats me like one of her kids and feeds me on a pretty routine basis."

"Oh, I know! Every time I turn around the woman is trying to stuff food in my face. Not that it's bad food — it's really delicious. I always have to tell her I'm full or she tries to give me second and third helpings. That's why it's great to have Blue around. I can always plead that I need to take a doggie bag home for him."

"True. Let's not forget Mabel and Gretchen. Just face it — they think we are their grandkids, whether or not they pretend we are their customers."

Savannah lets loose with an unladylike snort. "Oh good! I thought maybe I was the only one who noticed. I figured I would have to break it to you at some point."

I continue to hold her in a loose embrace. "My family was so dysfunctional for such a long time. I miss having the influence of grandparents in my life. Those women are so loving toward me that it just feels like warm chocolate chip cookies every time I go to their house. Maybe it's wrong of me to take advantage of our relationship like that, but it doesn't seem to be hurting anything and I never short them any money. I always pay them what things are worth and I try to help out as much as I can."

Savannah strokes my cheek. "Casey, relax! I know

you're a good guy. They know you're a knight in shining armor too. I feel the same way when I hang out with them which is why I go out to tea with them once a week. They are like family to me too."

"I'm so glad you like my friends. They are the closest thing I have to grandparents — although I don't know how they feel about us calling them substitute grandmothers. I think they'd like to be considered hipper than that. I think they would like the notion of being part of our family."

Savannah frowns. "Speaking of family, I'm not exactly sure what's happening with mine. I keep getting cryptic text messages from my mom. The idea that she sends messages at all is a little strange. She got her own phone and her independence streak pissed off my dad."

"So, did she go back on the road with him?" I ask, concerned for Nancy's well-being. Personally, I think George is a punk.

"No!" Savannah says with a shocked laugh. "Apparently she's still at Diamond and Jett's place. She decided it was time for him to go if he couldn't accept that she had gotten current with normal technology. I guess she told my dad to shape up or hit the highway, and he decided to hit the highway."

"Oh wow! That must be a scary thing for your mom. Haven't they been married for like forty years or something?"

"Something close to that. Even when we were little, my dad didn't respect my mom's opinion about much. She probably feels a sense of freedom and validation."

"Do I need to send her some spending money?" I offer.

"No, that's sweet of you. I talked to Danica, the art student manning my business, and she hired my mom to watch the counter for me. I guess my mom is quite the talented tole painter. I feel a little bad I never even knew."

"I guess our only decision now is when we go home," I suggest.

"Detective Gerrick thought you might feel that way, so he said to tell you it would be a couple more weeks before he could let me go. I still need to talk to the investigators some more since they've arrested Esther and Reggie. He is certain their recollection of the past will differ slightly from mine."

"I wonder if that means they're still speaking with the police?"

"Knowing Reggie, he probably thinks he can talk his way out of it. Even if he has an attorney, he probably won't pay any attention to any advice they give him. He always thought he was smarter than every other person on the planet—that included Esther. I kinda wonder if they'll turn against each other."

"That would be a real bloodbath wouldn't it?" The corner of my mouth hitches up in a half smile.

"I can't say I'd be real sad to see them destroy each other. For me, it would be poetic justice. They put on such good fronts and pretended to be such good people when all they were really doing was luring innocent kids into sex slavery. I still struggle to accept the fact that they pretended to be like parents to me and, in the end, they sold me to be tortured," Savannah replies in a broken whisper.

"God may never forgive me for my thoughts, but I hope someone does to them in prison what they allowed to happen to you. The only thing which keeps me sane is the fact that I know Isaac and Tristan are the best at what they do and they'll find every little dirty secret Esther and Reginald Brennan ever had. Not only that, they will find every sexual predator they've ever dealt with — including Ricard. Countless pedophiles from coast to coast will be put out of business forever. You might not have been able to do anything about it years ago, but your bravery now will stop probably dozens and dozens of offenders."

"I wish I had your optimism, but I'm scared. I'm scared something will go wrong to cause them to walk, and I'll be victimized all over again. Or it'll be like all the stories I see in the news and I'll be made out to be some sort of hoochie-mama who asked for all of this and Esther and Reggie will be made out to be the victims."

"I think you've underestimated the heavyweights you now have in your corner. Remember when Roberta told you her own story? Sadly, it doesn't miss yours by much. Do you think she'll sit idly by if they try to destroy your reputation? If you do, you don't know her very well. She will have every top-notch expert from Alaska to Florida and California to Maine in your corner."

Savannah nods thoughtfully. "You're probably right. She's scary when somebody's been wrongly accused of something. The other day, I was working at Uncommon Paths and I saw her after they misidentified somebody on surveillance tape and inadvertently accused the wrong person of shoplifting. I thought the rafters would come down in our building. If that police officer thought he could pull a fast one in Roberta's neighborhood, he was sadly mistaken."

"She's not the only one you've got in your corner. Jade's father doesn't suffer fools lightly. He lost his son

Onyx to suicide because he was being bullied. If he gets even a hint that they are out to harm you, there will be hell to pay. Come to think of it, Jade's fiancé, Declan, is no lightweight in that area either. He has been the victim of people spreading false rumors about him before and he is quick to jump in and to help other people. You can pretty much figure you got a virtual army of friends and family behind you. Evil will not win this time."

"As great as all that is, I think maybe the biggest gift you have given me is the courage to believe I'm tough enough to stand on my own two feet in the face of my past because you love me anyway."

Running my fingers along her jaw, I tilt Savannah's face up toward mine and say, "You have done the same for me, Savannah. You have made me a better person than I ever could've hoped to be. Together we are tough enough to face whatever comes."

Chapter Twenty-Five

Savannah

A FUNNY THING HAPPENS when you build up monsters to be bigger than life in your head. When you face them down, they often turn out to be smaller than you expect. It's a lot like when you face down the monsters in your closet and they turn out to be dust bunnies. Of course, the Brennans were more than demons in my head. They were monsters in real-life. They were evil villains to dozens and dozens of children, both male and female. Some were as young as ten.

However, as soon as I exposed the house of cards they had built, the whole thing fell down. I was not the first victim, nor sadly, was I the last. I was just one of many. They counted on their victims being nameless, faceless, and forgotten. They peddled in fear, shame, and pain. As soon as they were exposed for the monsters they truly were, they were the ones who wanted to run and hide.

After several weeks of trial prep where I was a complete nervous wreck, it was finally time to go to trial. The adverse effects on me were so extreme, Casey resorted to making me special drinks out of half-and-half and heavy cream and homemade cookies every day just to keep me at a healthy weight. The day of trial, Mark and Shelby were right beside me as the judge called us back into chambers and announced there had been a last-minute offer of a plea deal.

The judge wanted to know if I would be upset if the DA accepted a plea deal.

I glanced at Mark and the prosecutor helplessly seeking guidance from their expressions. There was so much legalese being thrown around the room, I couldn't follow what was being said. I clutch the young law clerk's hand tightly as she attempts to decipher the rapidly flying words. Finally, the judge looked at the district attorney. "I'll give you until three o'clock tomorrow to evaluate the ramifications of this."

The judge studied me carefully. "Ms. Lyons, what are your feelings on this?"

"To be honest, Your Honor, I don't have a single, solitary clue."

"Fair enough," he answered with a laugh, "I don't think you're the only one in the room feeling that way — but I bet you're the only one honest enough to give me a straightforward answer."

In the end, we ended up accepting the plea deal and avoided a trial. There were enough charges that even with the plea, Reggie was sentenced to one hundred and thirty years in prison and Esther was sentenced to seventy-nine.

Facing down Esther and Reggie up close and personal during the victim impact statement taught me a lot about courage and how far I've come. They weren't so big and scary after I stared them down and tell them in graphic detail how their actions changed the course of my life.

Thanks to the efforts of Isaac and Tristan, it wasn't just me.

There were two dozen other men and women telling similar tales of destruction. It was like a club that no one wanted to belong to, yet tragically we all did. Until the trial, none of us knew of the other's existence. The whole experience has been strangely empowering for me. I have found my voice and it is powerful.

It's now several months later and we are in a new courtroom facing down a different monster and my newfound voice will come in handy today. The courtroom is church-mouse-quiet as my attorney leads me through my testimony. I can't help but think of how far I've come since the first time I told this story to Shelby and then to Casey.

Although it is still painful, I am not nearly as ashamed of my past as I once was. It is not my shame to bear. I did not ask to be raped. I did not ask to be kidnapped and held hostage.

Mic Ricard tries to intimidate me with a leering stare from across the courtroom. There was a time in my life when I would have cowered in my seat and dropped my gaze, but that time has long passed.

He may not realize that regardless of the outcome, I've already won because I have the strength to sit here and face him with my head held high. I've already beaten two out of four opponents who've sought to take me down by humiliating me with my past. If he wants to trot out his deeds and hold them up next to mine, more power to him.

When the judge summons me back to the stand after several hours of delay, I realize with horror that Mic has suddenly fired his attorneys and intends to represent himself. This means my personal tormentor will be cross-examining me. As the bailiff escorts me to the stand, I catch a glimpse of Casey in the gallery. I rarely ever see this side of him — serious, corporate, and formal. Casey decked out as an executive is formidable and is a welcome distraction. Ketki showed us the Cherokee hand movement for peace that they use in traditional dances. Casey flashes the sacred movement as he pretends to yawn.

For whatever reason, his tiny, unorthodox move settles me and I think back to my earlier conclusion that whatever the outcome, I've already won.

I try not to jump when Mic comes up to the witness stand and leans on the wooden railing next to where I'm seated. This draws an immediate objection from our side, which the judge grants.

Mic addresses the jury over his shoulder as he looks at me like the slimy slug he is. "Oh sorry, you didn't use to object to me being this close. In fact, as I recall it, you used to like it … a lot."

I look up at the states attorney, Tori Clarkson and try not to let my shock show. However, she's as wide-eyed as I am. Mark's partner is busy writing on the tablet. I can almost guess what she's writing. I watch as she rips the note off the pad and hands it to her law clerk. Mic just made a critical error. He doesn't realize it or can't remember what condition I was in all those years ago. I can't believe he didn't bother to look at the evidence as

Tori brought it up when she was questioning me. We ran through those questions only a few hours ago, yesterday afternoon at the most. Is he so narcissistic that he thinks the jury won't pay any attention to the pictures?

I take a shaky breath to calm myself. "You and I have dramatically different memories of that time."

He is visibly angry because he's unable to shake me. He resorts to mocking me. "If you hated it so much, why did you stay there for four years?"

"Because you had me chained to a bed which was bolted to the floor joists with railroad ties. I had eight feet and seven and a half inches of freedom during seventeen days of the month. I had a cuff around my ankle which was exactly the thickness of my middle three fingers and one on my wrist the thickness of my first two fingers."

"Geez, if you can remember that much, I should have kept you more blitzed," Mic mutters to himself. Unfortunately for him, he is right in front of the microphone on the witness stand when he said that.

The judge bangs his gavel and clears his throat as he addresses Mic, "Mr. Ricard, I'm beginning to question your ability to represent yourself. May I remind you what you say in this courtroom is on the record? See that excellent court reporter over there? His name is Eric. He's typing every single word you say — even the ones you mumble. You need to confine your questions and remarks to the ones asked on direct and you need to comport to the rules of the court—like we talked about in chambers. Do you need to consult with your co-counsel?"

Mic scowls up at the judge. "No, I got this."

"Mr. Ricard, this is fair warning: you need to keep

your question within the scope of direct," the judge advises sternly.

"Yeah, yeah, I heard you." Mic grouses. "Now back off, you're ruining my mojo here —"

The judge turns to the state's attorney and asks, "Do I hear an objection, Counsel?"

Tori shrugs. "Not yet — you know the saying, 'Give a man enough rope and all that …'"

The judge sighs as he instructs, "You may proceed Mr. Ricard."

Mic walks very close again and gets right in my face.

"So, Nanna-girl, why don't you tell the court here why were you so eager to see me that you made love to me almost every single day for four years? Did you cry when you couldn't have my baby? Tell me … does that sound like you hated me? No, to me, that sounds like you wanted me to be your sugar daddy. And, since you were into whips and chains and liked it a little rough, you don't want your new boyfriend knowing about your kinky past. Is that why you're making up all these stories? To make yourself sound better? That's it, isn't it?"

The judge raises an eyebrow at Tori and she pops up to her feet and declares, "Objection, outside the scope, badgering the witness, compound question — take your pick."

I raise my hand. The judge looks over at me with a startled expression as he asks, "Ms. Lyons? Do you have a question?"

"Your Honor, I don't want to avoid the questions because he's being a jerk. I don't have anything to hide."

"Ms. Lyons, I will give you the same caution I gave

Mr. Ricard, your answers will become part of the official trial evidence and if this goes up on appeal and it's not objected to, there are ramifications to that."

"I understand, Your Honor. I am willing to answer the questions, even though they are intrusive."

"You may proceed at your own risk Ms. Lyons. Do you want a word with your own counsel?"

I glance over at Mark, Tori, and Annette for guidance. Tori addresses the judge. "This is Savannah's story to tell — she's free to tell it however she feels comfortable. We ask the court to allow her to relate it in narrative form without interruption."

"The Court finds that, given the circumstances, this is a reasonable request." He looks down at me from the bench and says, "Ms. Lyons, you may answer his questions in whatever order feels comfortable to you. If you need a read back from the court reporter, simply ask."

I don't want to tell him that Mic's questions are forever burned in my brain and I will never forget it because that seems a tad dramatic—but it's true.

I try to remember all the things Mark's law firm taught me about presenting myself in front of a jury. How to stay calm and focused while appearing approachable, friendly, and believable. None of that matters right now. I'm just trying to calm the flock of hummingbirds in my stomach before I open my mouth to speak.

Finally, I organize my thoughts into some coherent order.

"February is my favorite month of the year," I declare softly. "A lot of people like February because of

Valentine's Day or because in some areas of the country it's still snowing, or maybe because of Groundhog's day — but that's not why I like February. I like February because it only has twenty-eight days. You see, Mic had an important job and a family somewhere. His job in the airline industry allowed him to travel … everywhere."

From where I'm sitting, I can see Mic grinding his teeth. The fact that I've rattled him gives me a boost of strength. In a louder, steady voice, I report, "There were seventeen days every month when I was not raped, sodomized, and beaten. The tricky part was trying to figure out when those days would be. Sometimes, I would have a few days to heal between, but often I would not. Mic purchased me from sex traffickers. He believed he was buying a virgin so, he didn't believe in practicing safe sex of any kind."

My gaze clashes with someone on the jury who reminds me of Isaac. He gives me a small nod as he winces in sympathy.

I struggle to take my mind back to the dark place I've walled off. I have been ignoring the pain for so long even when I want to think about it, my mind resists. "Eventually, I got pregnant. I'll admit that I was excited at the prospect of becoming a mother. My excitement had nothing to do with Mic. I'd just lost my little brother due to an illness he was born with and my little sister was taken away by the authorities. My parents had seemingly vanished from the face of the earth and I felt all alone. The prospect of having someone to love me unconditionally and without expectations was undeniably appealing. I was twenty-two years old and chained to a bed like a rabid animal. I had no friends, no family, and no future. If I could create a future, it was better than nothing — even if that future involved the offspring of my rapist."

I clear my throat as memories overwhelm me.

"I got really excited as my baby belly started to show. I remembered back to when my mom was pregnant with my sister and brother. She used to speak to her belly. My mom used to say it would make them smarter, so I did that every day for hours on end. I told my baby stories that I remembered from books I'd read and stories I made up. I swore I would make my baby smarter than I was. My baby would never be dumb enough to be caught in a trap like a wild animal."

I pause to blow my nose as I continue my story, "Then one day, she moved — I always thought she was a girl. I stayed up all night that night waiting to see if it would happen again. The next day I was so tired that I laid down to take a nap."

It kills me to even think about what's coming next, let alone talk about it. Still, I didn't come all this way to take the easy way out. I look directly at Mic as I continue to relay the awful truth.

"I was so exhausted I forgot to watch for you to come. You were furious that my hair was not fixed, and that I hadn't brushed my teeth."

Apparently, Mic forgot where he is because he bares his teeth at me in the same type of menacing move he used to do when I was his prisoner. His lawyer elbows him and he remembers to school his expression into something more neutral and socially acceptable.

"As soon as you saw me, you flew into a rage. You picked up one of the propane tanks from the kitchen and swung it around like it was a shot-put and struck me with it. You said nothing more that day except, 'You disgust me'."

"When you came back eight days later, you were drunk. You had another woman with you. You tossed me a roll of paper towels and said, 'Clean yourself up — we've got company. I might want some girl-on-girl action.'"

Mic gives his lawyer an eerie lascivious grin like he's won a major concession from me.

I narrow my gaze at him as I continue to explain, "What you were too stupid and self-absorbed to figure out was that I was chained to that bed and dying because you killed our child inside of me because I was too sleepy to brush my teeth. If it hadn't been for the fact that you were so horny that you brought another girl into the house to chain up, I would've died in your bed and no one would've ever found me."

I shudder at the memory and draw in a deep breath. I swallow hard before I can continue, "It's true. I have always dreamed of having a child. You took that dream away from me. Because of you, I can never have another child. You killed the only child I ever had the chance of having."

I hear a couple of sniffles from the jury box and I glance over to see two women crying. At this point, I'm too wrapped up in my own emotions to figure out whether this is a good or bad thing for me. I have one more thing to address with Mic and then I'm done. After this, I don't care what happens to him. Lose or draw, I'm finished. I am done giving him any control over my life.

I meet Casey's gaze and hold it for a few seconds. I calmly smile before I turn to Mic one last time.

"You were right about one more thing. I do have a boyfriend. He is amazing in so many ways, I can't even tell you. But you were also way off the mark."

"Mic, he knows all about you. He knows how you used me as a sex slave. And you know what? He loves me anyway. He is the reason I have enough courage to tell a bunch of strangers about the things you did to me. You took a lot of things from me, but I won't let you take my capacity to love and be loved. You will get nothing more from me."

The judge discreetly clears his throat and adjusts his microphone. "Thank you, Ms. Lyons." He turns and faces Mic. "Any further questions Mr. Ricard?"

Mic starts to stand and his co-counsel places a firm hand on his shoulder and pushes him back down into his chair. Mic looks entirely put out, but eventually comments, "No, I guess not."

"Any redirect?"

"No, Your Honor," the District Attorney replies somberly as she sits down.

"All right Ms. Lyons you are excused, subject to recall."

It's a good thing we are in one of the smaller courtrooms because if it had been much larger, I don't know if I would've been able to walk all the way down the aisle and out the door before the sheer enormity of what just happened hit me.

EPILOGUE

CASEY

I TRY TO STRETCH without moving noticeably as I wait for yet another legal sidebar to conclude. These witness chairs are notoriously uncomfortable. God knows, I've sat in enough of them recently—more than I ever dreamed possible just a couple of years ago. I let my gaze wander out to the audience, and I notice my girlfriend comforting a former employee. Natalie was once one of my favorite baristas. Now in an almost poetic twist of fate, she owns Tough Breaks together with her mom.

Finally, the judge dismisses the attorneys and resumes the hearing. He turns to me and instructs, "Mr. Moore, you may continue."

"The full statement?" I clarify, having overheard the topic of the sidebar.

The judge nods. "I overruled Mr. Donelson's objection."

"I'd like to preserve the issue for appeal," his attorney says.

"So you've stated. Several times. I'm sure the court reporter didn't miss that," the judge responds.

"I'd like to state for the record that I don't think it's

fair Mr. Moore gets to state his side without challenge," the attorney practically whines.

"Mr. Kellen, it's late in the day. Please don't make me remind you that your client lost the case. We are simply trying to get through victim impact statements here. Usually, this is an emotional, but straightforward, process. If you have any more objections to this portion of the proceeding, please reduce them to writing and submit them to the court by ten tomorrow, Thursday, morning and I will rule on them at that time."

"Your Honor —" the attorney protests.

"Counselor, are you as challenged at time management as you are at trial practice?" he reprimands sharply.

"No sir," he responds as he blushes.

"Very well, if the past is anything to go by, I trust I will see you in my chambers tomorrow morning." The judge turns and says, "I apologize for all the interruptions, Mr. Moore, please feel free to continue."

I rotate my shoulder and my neck as I try to get comfortable in my chair. As usual, I seek out Savannah in the room. It's corny to say, but she is my calm in the storm, but that's what she's become in my life. She is the reason I've got focus, drive, and passion—the reason everything makes sense in my world.

Things have not been easy for us. We've had to deal with one legal crisis after another. Surprisingly, the case which should have been the easiest to wrap up and put away has taken the longest. I think John Donelson thought he could buy his way out of this case. Yet, the main lesson I took from Ashlyn's death and the betrayal of my dad's descent into drug addiction is that I'm never again going to be intimidated into accepting things I know are wrong simply because it was easier or more convenient.

Donelson and his team of lawyers try to intimidate me by making a show of checking their very expensive watches and monogrammed leather planners. What they don't realize is that even though I dress like a local college coed, I came from that kind of money. Heck, I've got that kind of money sitting around in trust funds somewhere, or so my mom's new accountants tell me. I guess there's a college on the upper East Coast with an entire building named after my grandfather. As the song goes, "It don't impress me much.".

I adjust the microphone in front of me. "Mr. Donelson, you know, I wanted none of this. My only plan that day was to serve you a decent lunch and a darn fine cup of coffee."

"Well, you failed," he interjects.

The judge interrupts. "Mr. Donelson, you have been warned repeatedly in this courtroom to remain silent, I will remove you and hold you in contempt."

"It'd be better than listening to this crap. I want to go," he hisses as the bailiff cuffs his hands to his waist and then cuffs his leg shackles to those cuffs. As they escort him from the room, he is cussing at the top of his lungs. He's lucky he's not getting tased. When I lived on the streets, a lot of my friends were.

The judge looks at the jury. "Ladies and gentlemen, I apologize for the disruption. I can bring you the defendants, but I cannot always guarantee they know how to act like civilized human beings. I encourage you to listen to Mr. Moore's impact statement and take it for what it's worth. It's too bad Mr. Donelson won't be here to hear how his actions affect other people. However, you can take it into account when making your sentencing recommendations for the crimes which he has already been found guilty of."

I clear my throat. "Like I said, it was a normal day at my coffee shop, Tough Breaks. I was somewhat distracted serving a customer who had never been in before. I was explaining the menu to her when I heard my barista Natalie cry out in pain. The new customer was quicker to understand what had occurred. Mr. Donelson broke Natalie's wrist in two places, causing a compound fracture. That customer, Savannah, she was fearless. She actually jumped in the middle of the situation and deflected attention onto herself while I called 911 and held Natalie's wrist until the ambulance arrived."

One of Donelson's attorneys throws a smirk in Natalie's direction. Natalie does not cower. She straightens her spine and glares back.

I raise my eyebrow at him, challenging him to pick on someone his own size as I address him, "I offered your client nothing but hospitality in my restaurant, and he left complete chaos behind. I had to call Raffaella and tell her that her daughter was about to be wheeled into surgery. It's not something I ever want to have to do again."

I sneak a glance at Savannah. My heart squeezes as I watch a tear slide down her face.

"You know, it could've all pretty much been over between us at that point. All that was left by then was the very messy cleanup. Compound fractures bleed a lot, and it's difficult to clean up a facility which serves food. I had to close Tough Breaks for a couple of days to make sure my customers were safe and being served in the best possible environment. Unfortunately, your client couldn't leave it at that."

The snarky attorney raises his hands and makes a gesture of playing a tiny violin as he stares at me impassively. This does not go unnoticed by the judge as he glares at Donelson's attorney. Kellan quickly puts his hand over his colleague's and urges him to settle down.

At that moment, I notice Savannah is making the same supportive hand gesture Ketki taught me which means peace in Cherokee.

I smile at Savannah and take a deep breath before I continue, "My first reaction when your guy went after Savannah and Haley online to try to destroy their good names was the same as every respectable man's would be. I was furious. I wanted to rush to their defense. After that, I was sad. I hurt as I watched Donelson crumble their sense of security and well-being."

I pause to take a drink of water and collect my thoughts.

"Fortunately for all of us who were involved, I have top-notch security. The recordings from the cameras proved Mr. Donelson's creepy assertions that none of us who were present that day could remember what happened were simply not true. We could prove otherwise. If the cameras hadn't been there, his blatant lies and hostile racism could have been much more damaging. As it was, I watched three women who were nothing but heroic become more guarded, more fearful and less trusting as a result of John Donelson's behavior."

The courtroom is so quiet I swear I can hear every single person breathe. I take a deep breath as I look at the jurors before I add, "What I never saw from your client was any sort of acknowledgment that he was sorry for permanently damaging Natalie's wrist or going after Savannah and Haley on social media or to me for trying to destroy the reputation of Tough Breaks."

The obnoxious attorney is about three-quarters of the way to a standing position when he exclaims, "Your Honor, we did not enter a plea deal, we are not required to issue any such—"

The judge is clearly at the end of his patience as he points to the clock. "Mr. Newton, can you tell me what time it is?"

"It's 4:36 in the afternoon, Your Honor."

"What day is it, Counselor?"

"Wednesday, sir."

"What time did I say I would hear objections about this portion of the trial?"

"Thursday at ten in the morning,"

"Is it Thursday at ten o'clock in the morning?"

"No sir," Newton concedes.

"Can you please tell me why you're having such a hard time determining that it is Mr. Moore's turn to speak?" the judge asks pointedly. "Were my instructions unclear? I don't know if they were because Mr. Moore here can seem to understand them and as far as I know, he didn't go to law school."

I shake my head to confirm his hypothesis. "Nope, no law school here. Still working on my Associate's degree."

I take a deep breath and continue, "It's not about being perfect. It's a little late for that. He broke Natalie's wrist so severely that she had to have surgery. Can you wrap your brain around the fact that all she did was offer your client hot coffee as part of her job? If you can, you can begin to understand the horror of what happened. He demanded a lap dance and a blow job. Who does that, especially in a restaurant full of families and children? Yet, rather than apologize for being a jerk, he tried to destroy everyone who stood up to him. That's just wrong in my book."

I look up at the judge. "I have no special fancy presentations, a movie of my life or even any tragic B-roll footage from a news station, I can just tell you how my life has been changed by John Donelson's decisions that day."

The judge smiles at me. "Thank you, Mr. Moore, that's what the victim impact statement is supposed to be about. I'm sure the jurors will find your words instructive."

We are back at the scene of the crime celebrating John Donelan's guilty verdict — quite literally. We are gathered around the table where the incident happened. Tough Breaks looks quite different now that Raffaella and Natalie have taken over the reins from me. In many ways, much better. It's less cluttered and more sophisticated. There are tile mosaics on the walls and a slight Spanish flavor to the whole place. It's relaxing and homey.

When Savannah and I came back home, they offered to return my shop to me, but I declined. Savannah and I decided that we would focus on trying to get Roberta's dream of having an East Coast version of Uncommon Paths up and fully functional within ten years. To me, this sounds like forever. After all, I'm Mr. I-Want-It-Done-

Yesterday and patience is not one of my virtues. So, every time I get frustrated, Savannah has to remind me of the long game.

My 'Life Plan B', as Ketki calls it, involves attending college — mostly online. All while I make furniture in Savannah's studio at Paint Your Art Out. I've been teaching Nancy how to do what I do on a miniature scale so she can make little jewelry boxes she decorates with beautiful flowers to sell in Savannah's shop. It's been a fun partnership. She says when she has more experience under her belt she plans to teach shop classes for women. Gretchen and Mabel have already signed up.

As I help Natalie bring out a fresh round of appetizers, Mama Rosa and Raffaella are busy exchanging recipes. Everyone jumps when Isaac receives a phone call. The shrill ringtone immediately silences all the small talk in the coffee shop. The shocked, ashen expression on Isaac's face is downright terrifying. Usually, nothing rattles the man. This cannot be good. We are all holding our collective breath as he finishes his conversation.

Isaac clicks his phone off and places it face down on the table as he lets out a large heaving breath. He calls Savvy over to him as he asks, "*Guerrerita*, how are you feeling today?"

Savannah's voice is a little shaky as she responds, "Honestly, I was doin' great until you asked me that question. Now, I don't feel much like a warrior. It always baffles me when you call me that.

"I call you *Guerrerita* because you are incredibly strong and resilient. You never give up. Today will be no exception," Isaac answers with a tight smile as he pats her on the shoulder.

He points to an empty chair beside him and gestures for her to sit down.

"There's no way to cushion the blow, so I'm just going to come out and say this. You know I have friends across the nation in all agencies, correct? That was my friend who runs the Colorado Department of Corrections. It would seem that Mr. Ricard is not as tough as you were. Under much less severe circumstances, he lasted only fourteen months in custody before he decided to commit suicide. He was found hanging from a pipe in the shower this afternoon. Apparently, he used his own underwear. I'm so sorry he robbed you of your justice, *Guerrerita*."

I walk over and stand behind Savannah's chair as I ask Isaac, "With all due respect, how do they know it wasn't another prisoner who took him out because he killed a baby? They have their own internal justice system from what I understand."

"True. That might have played a role. Ricard was well known for complaining to anyone and everyone who would listen, including his ex-wife and children, about how much he was being picked on in jail."

"Oh, his poor wife and kids," Savannah exclaims.

"It certainly is sad, but I doubt that they'll be all that broken up about it. One of his children is a sex crimes prosecutor in the state of Hawaii. His wife remarried many, many years ago. I suspect they don't miss him all that much."

"I wondered why he was all by himself at his trial. I thought maybe it was to avoid media coverage. I didn't realize that he literally had blown up his entire world. Now that I know that his wife and children are okay, I can't bring myself to shed a single, solitary tear for Mic Ricard or the Brennans or John Donelson for that matter."

Savannah gets up and starts pacing back and forth in front of the table.

"I know Esther and Reggie will die in prison. I don't know what'll happen to John Donelson. It's entirely possible that his money will buy him some sort of fancy legal maneuver which will allow him to get out sooner rather than later. Even if he does, he'll still have to look himself in the mirror every day knowing deep down inside what he did and who he is. I know he says it doesn't matter, but I believe it does."

Natalie lets out a whoop of excitement. "Preach it, sister!"

Savannah grins at Natalie's remark, but I can tell she's on a roll. "Mic Ricard. Well, what can I really say? Mic liked to pretend that he was above it all and it didn't touch him, but he couldn't live with the person he saw in the mirror every day. But you know what? I didn't create that person, and I wasn't responsible for who he chose to be. If he couldn't live with the decisions he made when I was eighteen years old, he should have made better choices. If he finally had to come face-to-face with the fact that he killed our child and left me to die — it's about time. I live with the choices he made every single day. I'm done living in the past. I want to live for the future."

I make an exaggerated motion of wiping sweat from my forehead as I say, "Boy, I can't tell you how glad I am to hear you say that."

"Say what part, Casey? Your gal has been talking for a while now," Tristan teases.

"True—but it was important stuff. The part I mean though is the part where she was talking about the future."

Tristan winks. "Gotcha, I was just checking."

I kneel down in front of Savannah and hand her a heavy letter.

The color leaches from her face as she feels the weight of it. "Do I even want to open this? The last few of these we've had have not been good news. I'm a little afraid."

"Go ahead. This one is different, I promise. Open it carefully," I instruct.

With glacier slowness, she pulls the ivory colored letter from the envelope as I hold my breath.

I wait impatiently as she reads it. Awareness comes over her and her face lights up as she shrieks, "Oh my Gosh! You did it! You got into Berkeley. I am so proud of you! Congratulations!" Savannah reaches out and hugs my neck in a tight embrace. I pull away as I say, "Savannah, you missed a little something in the envelope."

She grabs the envelope off the table. "What? Did they give you a scholarship too?"

I chuckle as I respond, "No, I was too late to apply this year, maybe next year. Think smaller."

I breathe a sigh of relief when she finally digs the solid gold band from the corner of the envelope. She gasps and nearly throws it back in my hand. "You're supposed to put this on my finger. I've dreamed about this a million different ways, but this isn't how it's supposed to go."

I lean forward and kiss her on the lips as I tease, "Savvy, take a closer look. I almost got it right." I point to the fact I'm actually kneeling in front of her.

She holds out her trembling hand, and I slide the solid gold band on it.

"Savannah Georgina Lyons, we have certainly had our tough times, but they have strengthened us like this gold band that's unending. Those tough times have taught us that love is stronger than hate and can help heal pain. I don't know about you, but I'm tired of being tough. I'm ready to move on to a new phase of our life together. I love you. Will you marry me and move to California at least long enough for me to get my degree?"

Savannah smiles widely. "Yes, Casey I'll marry you. I'll follow you anywhere you need me to go."

She picks up the letter from Berkeley and reads it again before she comments, "You know, I actually liked California. It was nice not feeling like I was taking a shower every time I went outside in the afternoon. We can totally do the West coast for a few years. Your mom will be thrilled."

"Oh, I see, you're only agreeing to marry me for the perks," I quip.

"Some handsome guy I know once told me that some breaks are tough — and others not so much. I consider this a good break. Just so you know, Blue and I are a package deal," Savannah answers as she kisses me and smiles down at her large, furry companion.

"I wouldn't have it any other way." Eeveryone in the coffee shop breaks out in applause.

"I'm grateful that I decided to go get coffee on that horrible day when it seemed like my world fell apart.

Really great things happened when everything seemed like it was beyond tough. I love you, Casey Edward Moore."

Note from the Author

Dear Readers:

Thank you so much for going on Savannah and Casey's journey of healing, hope, and love. I hope you enjoyed Tough. This family's journey continues in Rectify.

Have you ever done the wrong thing for all the right reasons?

Years ago, Tayanita abandoned Ketki to save her daughter's life.

It was her only choice, but she's hated herself every single day since.

Can a guy who can't see her discover the beauty inside Tayanita she can't seem to find in herself?

How can John and Tayanita rectify their pasts with their dreams for the future?

If you love stories of second chances and redemption, Rectify is for you.

Get Rectify in paperback, e-book or through Kindle Unlimited now!

Thank you,

~Mary

Because love matters, differences don't.

RESOURCES

If you need help immediately, call 911.

**National Sexual Assault Hotline:
1-800-656-HOPE (4673)
National Human Trafficking Hotline 1-888-373-7888
National Domestic Violence Hotline:
800-799-SAFE (7233) or 800-787-3224 (TDD)**

RAINN (Rape, Abuse, Incest National Network) — The nation's largest anti-sexual assault organization. RAINN operates the National Sexual Assault Hotline at 1.800.656.HOPE and the National Sexual Assault Online Hotline at rainn.org, and publicizes the hotline's free, confidential services; educates the public about sexual assault; and leads national efforts to prevent sexual assault, improve services to victims and ensure that rapists are brought to justice.

Polaris An organization designed to disrupt and stop human sex trafficking. They run a national hotline to assist survivors as well as education and prevention programs. Their website is a comprehensive source of information and assistance. National Human Trafficking Hotline 1-888-373-7888 or Text "BeFree" (233733).
National Center for Missing and Exploited Children —

an organization dedicated to reuniting missing children with their families. It runs a national hotline designed to process tips on missing children and reporting child sexual exploitation 1-800 THE LOST. This organization has also been at the forefront of age progression technology and statistical analysis regarding the victimization of children. They have sought to publicize the dangers of teenage homelessness.

Domestic Shelters.org — A tool that enables you to find a domestic violence shelter in your area by ZIP Code or address. You can search by the specific service you need. There are also informative articles about how to help someone who may be a victim of domestic violence or sexual abuse.

American Foundation for Suicide Prevention — (http://afsp.org) A comprehensive program that includes educational materials for people at risk of suicide, family members and people affected by suicide. They have outreach offices in all fifty states and include legislative reform to improve the health resources for people at risk for suicide. The website is an incredible resource.

Volunteers of America — an organization which helps provide services to individuals who are homeless. These include providing basic toiletry needs to employment and housing assistance.

ACKNOWLEDGEMENTS

From the moment Savannah began to form my imagination, I knew her story would be important and difficult to tell. I was not wrong. I want to thank all the survivors who have taken the time to share their deeply personal stories with me. Although my words can never fully describe the pain and horror involved in your journeys, I hope Savannah's story touches all of my fans and readers everywhere and raises awareness.

As an author, I do not do this alone. I would like to thank Kathern Watts. She is my one-woman-cheerleading-beta reading-amazing-what-would-I-do-without-your-research-skills-team. Thank you for believing in this book from the first word to the very last.

I am so grateful for my beta reading team: Stacy Beduhn, Rosemary McKenna, Catherine Frye, and Tom di Giovanni. Thanks for having the courage to tell me when I don't get it right.

A huge shout out to my friends on the unofficial NaNoWriMo forum who have become like a very large functional/dysfunctional family — we are 29,000 strong independent-minded people who defend and promote each other fiercely. You all have helped me more than you can ever know. From helping me design a complicated cover to giving me character names and personality quirks, you helped this book come together. Thank you so much.

Leonard, Happy Wedding Anniversary. With you in my corner, I can conquer the world.

ABOUT THE AUTHOR

I have been lucky enough to live my own version of a romance novel. I married the guy who kissed me at summer camp. He told me on the night we met that he was going to marry me and be the father of my children.

Eventually, I stopped giggling when he said it, and we've been married for over thirty years. We have two children. The oldest is a Doctor of Osteopathy. He is across the United States completing his residency, but when he's done, he is going to come back to Oregon and practice Family Medicine. Our youngest son is now tackling high school and where he is an honor student. He is interested in becoming an EMT.

I write full time now. I have published more than thirty books and have several more underway. I volunteer my time to a variety of causes. I have worked as a Civil Rights Attorney and diversity advocate. I spent several years working for various social service agencies before becoming an attorney.

In my spare time, I love to cook, decorate cakes and of course, I obsessively, compulsively read.

I would be honored if you would take a few moments out of your busy day to check out my website,

MaryCrawfordAuthor.com. While you're there, you can sign up for my newsletter and get a free book. I will be announcing my upcoming books and giving sneak peeks as well as sponsoring giveaways and giving you information about other interesting events.

If you have questions or comments, please E-mail me at Mary@MaryCrawfordAuthor.com or find me on the following social networks:

Facebook: www.facebook.com/authormarycrawford

Website: MaryCrawfordAuthor.com

Twitter: www.twitter.com/MaryCrawfordAut